TEMPTING HER VISCOUNT

Scots and Scoundrels, Book 3

Allison B. Hanson

ARE YOU SIGNED UP FOR DRAGONBLADE'S BLOG?

You'll get the latest news and information on exclusive giveaways, exclusive excerpts, coming releases, sales, free books, cover reveals and more.

Check out our complete list of authors, too!

No spam, no junk. That's a promise!

Sign Up Here

www.dragonbladepublishing.com

Dearest Reader;

Thank you for your support of a small press. At Dragonblade Publishing, we strive to bring you the highest quality Historical Romance from some of the best authors in the business. Without your support, there is no 'us', so we sincerely hope you adore these stories and find some new favorite authors along the way.

Happy Reading!

CEO, Dragonblade Publishing

Additional Dragonblade books by Author Allison B. Hanson

Scots and Scoundrels Series
Winning Her Duke (Book 1)
Discovering Her Earl (Book 2)
Tempting Her Viscount (Book 3)

CHAPTER ONE

April 1809
London

BEING SUMMONED TO the Marquess of Penbrook's study was never a small matter. Would her father be in a drunken rage, a sobering depression, or giddy from a streak of luck at the gaming tables?

Lady Celia Dorsett could only hope her younger brother was in the house and could help her deal with whatever waited beyond the door. As the heir, Graham was better suited to manage their father. Though neither of them had managed the man much of late. For he was quite out of control.

With a steadying breath, Celia entered the sparsely furnished room. Her father didn't seem to care for casual comforts. Not when they could be sold for much needed funds. Forcing a smile on her lips, she felt her body tense when she found him sitting at his desk with a deep crease in his brow.

"Good afternoon, Father," she greeted him. It was nigh on two o'clock, but it was clear he'd only recently woken. His clothes looked like they'd been picked up from the floor where he'd discarded them the night before, and he'd yet to shave.

Having let his valet go recently had proved a poor decision.

"Sit, sit," he ordered as he straightened some documents on his desk.

Celia glanced around to find the room empty except for the

two of them.

"Will Graham be joining us?" she asked, her nerves making her voice shake slightly. Her father had never harmed her—at least not physically—but he frightened her all the same.

"What? Er… I'm not sure." He rubbed his forehead.

It appeared he was to be *muddled and distraught* today. She almost preferred the rage. When her father was muddled and distraught, he tended to make very bad decisions.

"I have a bit of news," he said and propped a smile on his face. Though ragged and bleary-eyed, the marquess was a handsome man for his age of four and forty. He looked like an older version of Graham who at two and twenty frequently attracted the attention of debutantes, with no plans whatsoever to settle down.

Despite his good looks, her father often appeared harried. As if something was after him. His demons, she suspected. Drink and gambling had taken hold of him years ago. Celia barely remembered the man he once was, back when she and Graham had been small, and their mother was still alive.

But that version of her father had died with her mother, leaving them with this broken shell of a man who appeared to be in constant search of something to ease the pain, and never finding it.

It was no secret the Penbrook finances were in a poor state. For whatever reason, the marquess still managed to earn credit at the tables. She knew her father's charm would run out eventually. At some point someone would want to collect.

She wasn't certain what would happen then.

At that moment, Graham came in looking a bit green and unhappy. She hadn't seen her brother in a few days. She'd warned him constantly of not falling into trouble like their father, but she couldn't blame him for wanting to have fun with his friends during the Season.

At three and twenty, Celia had never had a season. There hadn't been any funds. Her father might have left it at that for an excuse, but instead he'd added that he wasn't willing to spend money on something that was bound to be unsuccessful.

Celia hadn't minded since she preferred to stay at home with a book rather than attend social functions where she would be put on display and mocked. Still, it stung to be considered a lost cause.

"What is it, Father?" Graham asked as he slouched in the chair next to her. Like her, Gray had dark hair and eyes from their mother. She wondered if her eyes held the same wariness as her brother's. She imagined so.

"Wonderful news," her father said. "I've found someone to take Celia off my hands despite that deficiency." He waved his hand in her direction.

That deficiency being a birthmark that marred her temple, the corner of her eye and the edge of her cheek. She'd never gotten a full on look at it herself with where it was, but according to her father, it was enough to frighten off any potential suitors.

Celia had thought that perhaps a man who cared for *her* instead of her looks might be a better option anyway, but she'd never had the opportunity to find out. Outside of Graham's small group of friends, she'd not met many men.

Unfortunately, the birthmark was the least of her concerns at the moment.

"Take me off your hands?" she questioned, her voice barely a soft squeak.

"We already discussed this and have made other arrangements," Graham cut in with a lethal tone to his voice. "I said I would marry the heiress you chose for me, so Celia would be spared. We had an agreement." The last word sounded desperate.

They both knew an agreement with their father wasn't worth the air used to speak it. His honor had been called out numerous times, though to her knowledge he'd never attended a single dual. Perhaps he'd never bothered to show up.

She reached out to her brother, putting her shaking hand over his. She didn't know of the plan he'd mentioned, but she wasn't surprised that Gray would willingly make such a sacrifice for her. And a sacrifice it would be since her brother had vowed never to marry.

"Yes, well, your marriage to Miss Denton is off. There was a bit of a... misunderstanding, and it would seem her father has changed his mind." He cleared his throat and glanced at the floor—the only evidence he felt any guilt at all. But it was quickly brushed aside as he continued.

"This is better anyway. Celia needed to marry so I am no longer burdened with her expenses." Another wave of his hand as if she was the cause of their dire financial situation. Other than food, she barely cost him a thing. She hadn't had a new dress in years and her books came from the lending library.

To argue would be a waste of breath. Her father had moved on to another of his moods, *stubbornly obstinate.*

She felt a bit relieved that he did at least intend marriage. It would not have been beyond her father to trade her virtue for the right price. Anything to be able to continue on in his search for fortune at the gaming tables.

"We'll just find another heiress for me to marry. I said I would take care of this and I shall. Celia is not to be involved."

"There's no time." He became flustered which could only mean someone had called in his markers. He was now in the worst disposition of all... *recklessly desperate.* "Celia will marry the Earl of Hamlin at the end of the week. This is much better than finding an heiress anyway. Your sister will be a countess."

"The Earl of Hamlin?" Graham repeated, his eyes wide in surprise. "I wasn't aware the old earl had passed."

"He hasn't," her father said, looking everywhere around the room except at them.

Celia watched as her brother stood and slammed his hand on her father's desk. "He's got to be close to eighty!"

"He's only two and seventy," her father defended as if those eight years made such a huge difference to a man of that age.

"You cannot marry Celia to a man old enough to be her

grandsire." Graham threw his hand out as if making a point, but she knew her father was past hearing reason.

"I can, and I am," the marquess said firmly.

"Don't *I* have a say in the matter? As I am the bride?" Celia spoke up, already knowing the answer, but trying to grasp onto any possibility of freedom from this fate.

Her father looked up with a sneer. "No. You have no say. You are my daughter and you'll marry Hamlin or I'll put you out on the street to fend for yourself."

"You'll do no such thing," Graham said.

"And what will you do about it? I'm the marquess. You're but my heir. A word from me and you'll be cut off."

"Cut off?" Graham laughed. "From the pittance you offer?"

"That pittance is more than you deserve. If she won't marry Hamlin, I'll disown both of you and be done with it."

"There has to be another way," Celia said. She didn't want Graham to be disowned, regardless of how sullied their name was already. "Certainly, I could find someone more appropriate."

Her father scoffed. "You have no dowry. You're a spinster and with that revolting mark on your face, no one will have you. Besides, Hamlin is richer than Croesus and has agreed to clear all my debt." He frowned at her. "Now, go away. Both of you. I've things to do to prepare."

Graham helped her from the room. She was grateful for his assistance since her legs were unsteady. She was to marry a man she'd never met. The fact that the Earl of Hamlin would make a deal with her father, worried her all the more. What kind of gentleman could he be to agree to such a match with a much younger woman?

"I'll figure something out," Gray said. "I'll go see Miss Denton immediately and fix whatever Father has done. You won't be forced to do this."

She nodded and went to her room to wait, wishing neither of them were facing a fate of an unwanted marriage.

She had long given up any notion of romance or love, but

still, it would have been fortunate to marry based on common interests or mutual respect. To arrange a marriage based solely on financial gain seemed despicable, despite it being the reason for many unions among the *ton*. It was no surprise her father didn't even flinch at the idea.

Graham was only gone an hour and when he returned, clearly livid.

"Our father made advances on the man's *wife* in their home while he was arranging the marriage of their daughter to me. I've never known someone so capable of ruining everything he touches so thoroughly. Neither of us would even need to marry if it weren't for him and his gambling." Graham turned to her. "I'm so sorry, Celia. I don't know what else to do."

Celia shook off the shock and fear so she could concentrate on a solution to the problem at hand. The way she saw it, she just needed to marry someone else before she could be married to Hamlin. But she only knew a few men.

Her eyes went wide and she grabbed Graham's arm. "Perhaps one of your friends would agree to step up for me? Father would have to allow it."

"Hale and Julian are in Scotland. It would take too long to reach them." He scowled.

"Kit is in England. I could marry Kit instead. He's a viscount. Perhaps Father would accept his suit."

"Kit is a *penniless* viscount. Father needs Hamlin's coin."

Christopher Sinclair, Viscount Stormont, was only twenty—more than three years her junior—but he was a kind, young man who always had a smile for her when he visited. She'd found him attractive and funny. While they hadn't had many conversations alone, she'd sat with Gray and Kit for several meals.

Surely having a husband a few years younger than her had to be better than having a much, much older groom. One she'd never even met.

Graham paced while Celia went to the desk in the corner of her room and pulled out a piece of paper.

"Kit and I could elope. He's Scottish, he must have properties there where we can go. I'll write to him and you can deliver my letter. Tell him I'll be an excellent wife. I'll not nag or bother him in any way. I won't even mind if he has a mistress."

"Celia, you deserve better than that from a husband. And he'd never consider doing such a thing. He's much too respectable for that." Gray rolled his eyes as if this were a bad trait to have.

"Do I deserve a man who is willing to make an alliance with our father? How disreputable must he be to have a connection with such a disgraceful man as our sire?"

Gray swallowed and gave a small nod. "Give me the letter. I'll take it to Kit."

Celia poured her heart out onto the page, not even caring if it sounded like begging. She *was* begging. Desperately.

When she was done, she sealed the letter and handed it over to her brother.

Once again, Celia sat by her window waiting for Graham to return with an answer to her problems. She was certain Kit would agree if for no other reason than he would be inclined to save a desperate woman. That was the kind of man she knew the viscount to be.

She pictured him with his blond hair and piercing green eyes. He'd spent most of his youth in England with his mother, and only finished his education in Edinburgh. Unlike Gray's other Scottish friends, Kit had only an occasional Scottish lilt which she found appealing.

Her heart felt lighter as the minutes ticked by. Gray would return with the fortunate news, and she would leave that night. She packed a bag with her meager belongings in preparation, and set it by the door.

But like before, Graham returned with a frown. She realized she'd been wrong. Kit wasn't to be her savior. Her fear was confirmed when Gray cleared his throat and spoke.

"I'm sorry, Celia. He won't marry you."

CHAPTER TWO

Four years later

AFTER HER MAID helped Celia into a sage green morning gown, Celia left her room at Penbrook House to go down for breakfast. She paused briefly at the bottom of the stairs before stepping over the bodies to make her way to the breakfast room.

The exercise had become quite common in the three years since she'd moved back home with her brother. Graham and Kit were often found sprawled out on the floor somewhere in the house, victims of their nightly activities.

She knew neither of them spent a dime at the gaming tables. Gray refused to fall victim to the same vice that had claimed their father, and Kit didn't have the funds to lose.

Celia was grateful for whatever kept them from traveling down that road. However, they still managed to find other disreputable pursuits. Pursuits they rarely kept to themselves.

She frowned down at the men and wondered what absurd adventure had landed them here this time.

Graham's mouth was hanging open and a puddle of drool had collected on the floor under him. Kit was on his back with his hand resting on his stomach. His blond hair as disheveled as his clothing.

Turning, she continued to the breakfast room where the staff had set out the morning meal.

"Pardon, my lady," Guthrie said. "I was unable to move them."

"It's fine. It's not the first time my brother has mistaken himself for a rug. It is his home after all, he may sleep wherever he chooses." Celia brushed off the footman's concerns that she be scandalized over seeing her brother and his best friend asleep in the hall after a night of debauchery.

In truth, she should be grateful it was only the two of them she needed to traverse anymore. Hale, the Duke of Roxburghe, and Julian, Earl of Melville, were now married and lived in Scotland with their wives and growing families.

She'd only buttered her toast when the first of the two men staggered in and took a seat. She was surprised to see Kit was awake and able to function so early in the day. She would have guessed they'd only returned to Penbrook House a few hours ago.

"How are you this morning, my lord?" Celia greeted Kit louder than was necessary. She felt it was only right she get some amusement from the situation.

"Shh…" Kit winced. "Not so loud, please."

Celia took pity on him and gestured to one of the footmen to bring the viscount a cup of coffee. Even with his hair sticking up, Kit was impressive. Taller than her brother, he'd been rather lanky when they were younger. Now, however, he'd filled out. His shoulders had grown wider and balanced out his long frame quite well.

His green eyes were still filled with kindness and humor when they weren't squinted shut in self-inflicted agony.

"Thank you," he said to the room before drinking from his cup.

"I have to ask, never having been soused myself, is it so much fun while you're drunk to make it worth this level of discomfort in the morning?"

"No. Not even close," he answered while pulling a crumpled leaf from his tousled blond hair. She wondered if he would have the same answer later this evening as they prepared to go out again. She couldn't fathom.

"Then why…?"

He put a hand up to stop her. "It's much too early for logic, countess."

She chuckled quietly as she focused on her toast. In the three years since she'd moved back to live with her brother—now the Marquess of Penbrook—she'd forgiven Kit for rejecting her proposal of marriage.

The forgiveness was, of course, non-verbal since neither of them ever spoke of her desperate letter, or the ramifications of his refusal to help. Her brother had informed her that fateful night that Kit had refused because he didn't have the means to care for a wife. She'd wanted to argue and convince him she was well accustomed to living in poverty, and would not require much upkeep at all, but Gray shook his head. He'd told her Kit was beside himself with regret, and speaking more on the subject would just add more guilt to his shoulders.

Ceilia had given up with a simple nod, and had never spoken of it again.

She'd gone on to marry the Earl of Hamlin who, while being in his seventies and thus requiring a companion more so than a wife, had cleared her father's debts and put the estates back to rights a mere month before her father's slip into the Thames where he'd drowned—not that she'd actually believed it was an accident.

As plans went, her father's arrangement had worked out well indeed for her and Graham.

After all, her husband, Arthur, had been a sweet man who had doted on her, so the year she had with him had not been as miserable as it would have been at home with her father.

Now, as a widowed countess with an extravagant settlement from her late husband, she was set for life. Despite not having much of a life to speak of.

But that was about to change, because Celia was going to

take a lover.

She didn't quite know how to go about it. Yet. She wasn't sure how or where she would take said lover. All she knew was she was a young widow, and as such she was given liberties she had yet to take advantage of.

It was time.

CHAPTER THREE

KIT FINISHED HIS coffee and managed a piece of toast, all while casting glances at the smiling woman sitting across from him. She was much too chipper for this early in the day. Though he'd rarely seen her less than pleasant in all the years he'd known her.

The truth was, his sour mood had nothing to do with her. Kit had decided to give up late night debauchery and drinking. Over the last year, he had been working hard to get his affairs in order so he could move on with his life as the Viscount of Stormont.

Having inherited the title at the age of ten, he'd had little clue of how to dig himself and his estates out of the debt he'd been saddled with. But this year—with the help of a new steward—his properties had turned a profit. All of them. And last night his friends had taken him out to celebrate his success. A little bit too much celebration at that.

He smiled despite his roiling stomach. He'd done it. It hadn't been easy. Unlike Graham, Kit hadn't had a sister who could marry a rich earl and pay for everything in one fell swoop. But this was better. Kit had done it himself. He'd made sacrifices in order to make Stormont a name worthy of passing on to a son.

A son he would have only after finding a wife. Yet another reason for celebration and his relapse into debauchery and drinking. He'd informed Graham and their friend, Hayworth, of his plans to make a match this season. And despite their teasing,

Kit was sure it would be the best decision he would ever make.

Their responses were expected given they were both still bachelors. Had Hale or Julian been there, he thought he might find more encouragement. The fact his married friends were happily tucked away in Scotland with their wives was more proof he wanted off this path of debauchery. He wanted a family.

Again, he glanced over at the woman sitting across from him with the soft smile on her full lips. Lips he'd imagined kissing many times over the years. She'd been the reason he'd come to Penbrook House on holidays from school. He'd had quite the *tendre* for his friend's older sister at the time.

He'd thought one day they might find a happy life together. Up until she'd destroyed his tender heart all those years ago. He winced, at the phantom pain that her rejection still brought up. But, he had moved on… Or planned to anyway.

"Do you ever plan to remarry?" he asked before he'd actually thought to do so. Another downfall of drinking. His brain was always half a step behind his mouth.

"Me?" she asked and then looked around the room where only the two of them sat. "Heavens no. As you may recall, I never planned to marry in the first place."

His brow creased. "Why not find someone to your liking that you could care for and who would care for you?" He'd known she'd had no season, but he'd thought it had been an issue of funds. That was no longer the case.

She narrowed her eyes at him. "Are you mocking me?"

His own eyes went wide which caused another wince. "Of course not. Why would you think so?"

She gestured to the left side of her face and he waited for her to speak, when she didn't, he continued to stare at her, which was no hardship. She was beautiful. Dark hair and eyes that set off her creamy complexion. And those lips.

He was back to her lips again. *Bloody whiskey.*

"Must I say it?" she asked rather peevishly.

He tried really hard to make his brain function, but nothing happened. "Apparently you must. I'm sorry, I don't follow. There is quite a lot of whiskey sloshing about in my head."

Again, she gestured to her face, but this time she turned toward him so he could see the birthmark she was no doubt referring to. "This makes it difficult to find a husband."

"Really?" He frowned and leaned closer to get a good look. He'd known it was there, of course, but hadn't been concerned with it past his initial notice when they'd first met. It wasn't something he noticed now, not when the countess had so many other compelling features to claim his attentions. Like those lips... Blasted whiskey. He couldn't think such things of the countess.

That was how he thought of her. He always called her *countess* rather than Celia. Celia had been the woman he'd known before. The one he'd once hoped would wait for him to dig himself out of debt and be his.

Kit was interrupted from addressing the matter of the birthmark when Graham flopped into his seat at the end of the table and groaned.

"Good morning, brother. I'm surprised to see you awake so early. How are you feeling?" Again, Celia spoke much too loudly. Since Kit was already looking at her, he saw her luscious lips pull up in amusement.

She was toying with them. If he weren't wincing in pain from her boisterous greeting, he might have laughed as well.

"Shhh…" Gray hissed and rested his head on the table. "If you don't cease in speaking so loud, my head will likely explode."

She wrinkled her adorable nose. "I'd think that would surely ruin my breakfast."

Kit laughed and earned a glare from Gray before he dropped his head back to the table.

Clearing his throat, Kit revisited the earlier topic. Now that his brain seemed capable of continuing the conversation.

"Do you truly think that spot on your cheek would keep a man from wanting to marry you?" he asked her before taking a bite of toast.

Graham raised his head again. "What are you talking about?" He was glaring and Kit wasn't surprised. Gray was very protective of Celia. Nearly as protective as she was of Gray.

Kit often wondered what it must be like to have a sibling. Someone to stand beside you no matter what. To have your back when the world was too much, and to lift you up during triumphs.

"Your sister seems to think this spot on her face precludes her from being someone's wife."

"Ridiculous. You're lovely, CeCe. Whoever told you such a thing? I'll call him out this instant." He winced and rubbed his forehead. "Perhaps later today would be better."

"You'll be spared from dueling, since the man who said I was unfit is already moldering away in his grave and you now hold his title."

"Father? Why would you ever hold stock in anything that blighter has ever said?"

Celia blinked then looked back to Kit. He felt as if she needed his confirmation and offered a smile.

"I never knew your father to speak the truth often, and I can assure you—not being your brother—you are indeed lovely. The spot is irrelevant."

"Irrelevant?" she said too loudly, though he assumed this time was not intentional, but out of surprise.

"Truly," he confirmed since she seemed not to believe him. They spent a fair amount of time teasing one another, but in this case, he wanted her to know he was sincere.

Celia sat stunned for a moment. It did seem odd, given her father's propensity for exaggerating and skewing the truth, that she'd held this one thing as irrefutable fact.

Kit was well aware of how easy it was to believe such things and use them as an excuse to keep from moving forward. Still, he offered a wink to confirm his words.

Her brother might have offered up easy compliments to

make her happy, but Kit was not related to her and therefore had no reason to placate her. He wouldn't be offended that she'd call his honor into question. He'd just be sure to go out of his way to make it easier for her to believe the truth.

And the truth was he found her beautiful. Spot or no.

She sat a little straighter and smiled, the happiness radiating out from her warmed him from across the table.

The mail was brought in and Celia dealt with separating her invitations from her brother's. For the most part they were all invited to the same events, though they rarely ever attended *ton* events.

But Kit was ready to move into society in the hopes of finding a wife and starting a family. He knew as soon as it was known Viscount Stormont had entered the marriage mart, he would be the prime target of title hunters and matchmaking mamas. He would need to be on his toes, so he didn't find himself in a compromising situation.

Not everyone would consider him eligible. Those who considered his Scottish blood to be unfit, or those who still thought he lacked two farthings would likely avoid him. But he wouldn't let that stop him from finding the right woman to be his wife.

Now that he wasn't a worthless sot.

He only hoped he could persuade Graham to attend a few balls with him despite his disdain for such things. Kit surely wouldn't meet his future viscountess at the clubs and hells they frequented. A ball was the most likely place to meet a proper woman.

After Gray finished his coffee and ate more than Kit could manage, he began working through the pile of invitations.

"No. No. No. Oh!" He held one up toward Kit, a large smile pulling up on his face. "Look at this. An invitation to Lady Harrington's Exclusive Masquerade."

Celia flipped through her pile again and frowned. "I didn't get one."

Kit cleared his throat and looked away while Gray chuckled.

"I would hope not. You're a proper lady and as such would never attend an event with the *demi monde*."

"What is it, a night of gambling and drink? As if you would participate in the first or should do more of the latter."

Kit shared a look with Gray, but the other man must not have understood that Kit had meant for him to drop it. Instead, he needled his sister further.

"This, dear sister," he said dramatically while waving the invitation in front of her nose. "Will grant me access to the most notorious of parties. Where one's every desire is granted."

"Every desire?" she asked, her brows pinched together adorably. When Gray didn't answer, Celia turned to Kit for clarification.

Having no siblings, or any family at all anymore, Kit didn't understand the joy taken in tormenting one another. Rather than continue with the ruse, Kit had out with it. "Pleasure of a physical nature."

His clarification didn't remove the crease from Celia's forehead. He remained still, silently begging her to come up with the answer so he wouldn't have to utter the word *sex* in front of her and embarrass them both.

"Oh!" she finally said, and he relaxed with having that over. "I see."

"*Do* you see?" Gray taunted waving the invitation again. "No, you can't possibly see, because *you* weren't invited."

Kit frowned at his friend. Gray and Celia had been like this since he'd known them. He'd thought they'd grow out of it eventually. So far, there was no evidence of such a possibility.

"Perhaps I will attend anyway," she said.

Graham held out the card so she could read the words at the bottom.

"Admission granted upon presentation of this invitation only," she read with a pout. "I'm sure I'd not want to attend something so disreputable anyway." This last part she said exceedingly loud. Causing Kit to shudder and Gray to groan once more.

Celia smiled broadly as she spread jam on a piece of toast.

"I'm sure you received one as well," Gray said to Kit.

"I'm sure I did, but I don't intend to go." He glanced over at Celia hoping to see approval in her eyes, but she was looking dejectedly at her plate while tearing her toast to bits. Did she truly want to attend such a function?

"You have to go," Gray said, wincing at his own volume.

"I assure you; I do not *have* to go."

"You're planning to get leg-shackled this year. You must attend one last masquerade at Lady Harrington's."

He glanced to Celia as she tilted her head in interest.

"You plan to marry?" she asked.

He shrugged. "I'm of an age and I now have the means to support a family. I've been alone for long enough wouldn't you say?" His father, whom he barely remembered had died when Kit was ten. He'd stayed with his mother in England until she'd died when he was sixteen.

Kit's bachelor uncle was called on to raise him. He'd pulled Kit from Eton and sent him to Heriot's in Edinburgh to receive a proper Scots education while Uncle Robert spent most of his time at sea. And then he'd died the following year.

"And with you set to fall victim to the parson's noose, we need this one last romp of fun," Graham insisted.

Kit opened his mouth to decline or point out that once they got to the party, they always went their own ways and didn't see each other the rest of the evening anyway. But he didn't get the chance because Gray got that devious look on his face and leaned closer.

"If you go, I promise I'll be on my best behavior when you start courting your potential bride. If you refuse..." He smiled evilly. "I'll be forced to share all the stories of our previous forays at Lady Harrington's past masquerades."

"You are the devil," Kit said while Celia nodded solemnly in agreement.

As was her routine, Celia left Penbrook House that afternoon to visit the bookstore. As a woman of means, she no longer had to rely on the books at the lending library. Instead, she was happy to buy her own books and then donate them to the library for others to enjoy.

Preferring to walk, she only took the carriage on days when the weather was unfit. Today was not such a day. The sun had burned through the morning fog and warmed her face as she raised it to the sky.

She and her maid had only made it a short distance before a carriage stopped close by and a man called her name.

"Lady Hamlin."

She turned to see the current Earl of Hamlin coming closer. Edward was a thin man with the Hamlin nose. The fact that he was generally scowling did not help his appearance.

"Good afternoon, my lord."

"I saw you walking as I was driving by. Surely Lord Penbrook should not want his sister's virtue to be at risk. Allow me to give you a ride."

Having picked up on his verbal trap, she offered a cold smile.

"I assure you, my brother knows an *experienced* woman, such as myself is more than capable of strolling to the bookstore while accompanied by my maid."

"Experienced?" He picked up on the word she'd used to dissuade him from pursuing this unwanted conversation. "There is a maid at Archstone who will testify that there was no evidence of consummation in your marriage bed with my grandfather."

He stood straighter, an obvious attempt to intimidate her with his height, but he was not as tall as Gray or Kit and she was able to stand up to them quite well.

Narrowing her eyes, she stared at him steadily as she planned her retort, but it was Nettie who spoke.

"I'm sure a man such as you has not been with many women of virtue, but I can assure you, women of later years do not always provide such proof."

Edward looked at the woman as if she were too vulgar to address so Celia patted her maid in thanks for trying before attempting to explain in a more polite manner.

"I'm certain that same maid has also reported that your grandfather and I shared a bed. And as a mature woman can also confirm that it is common for women who marry later in life not to leave any evidence?"

She had brought color to his cheeks, either from embarrassment or anger. She didn't care which.

"They have the ability to confirm such things with a medical examination. Would you undergo such an examination to prove you were my grandfather's true wife?"

She gasped. "I certainly would not. I can't believe you would suggest such a thing." It was not unheard of for these matters to be called into question. Especially when large sums of money were involved. "Certainly, you do not intend to call my reputation into question?"

"I do if you have not earned the settlement you've been given."

"My husband, your grandfather, signed the agreement for the settlement himself. If you do not trust me, then perhaps you will trust that he would not have done so if our marriage was not legitimate."

"My grandfather was quite aged. It would not be the first time a young woman has taken advantage of an older man to secure her wealth."

"My settlement is nothing when compared to the gross fortune you have inherited. It's been three years since he passed. What reason do you have for calling this into question now?"

His face went splotchy with color and he glanced away. "There were some investments that didn't go the way they should have."

"You've lost the money?" The situation must have been dire indeed for him to resort to this tactic. Celia remembered how dangerous her father could be when he'd run out of options. There was nothing more frightening than a desperate man.

"It's none of your concern." He straightened, looking offended, even though it was she who should be offended. Or would be if his claims were untrue.

"You are despicable," she said because that was one thing that could not be debated. Whether or not she had slept with her husband or not, this man was an utter arse.

"You didn't consummate the marriage and I shall prove it." He smiled, a terrifying curve of his thin lips.

She looked around to see a number of bystanders staring at them, though not close enough to hear their conversation. Still, they were making a scene. Celia did not need other people questioning the validity of her marriage to Hamlin. Ignoring Edward was one thing, but if gossips of the *ton* got wind of this potential scandal, it would be too much.

"This conversation is over." She and Nettie turned away and continued down the street.

"For now. But I will plead my case to the House of Lords and they will require an examination," he threatened. "They do not take kindly to their peers being duped."

"If you'll excuse me. I have somewhere better to be."

"Don't worry about him," Nettie said. "No one will listen to him."

Celia wasn't so sure. It had happened previously.

She was still shaking a few blocks later when she reached the bookstore. Hiding behind one of the shelves, she allowed a few deep breaths to steady herself.

Edward's accusations were thin speculation at best. But if he could convince a few of the stodgy lords there was proof to his claim. An examination, if one was required, would prove she and Arthur had never consummated the marriage. She could be in danger of losing her independence.

Gray would never turn her out or force her into marriage. But she'd promised herself she'd never allow her choices to be taken from her ever again.

Her thoughts turned to one of those choices specifically. Her plan to take a lover had been an adventurous dream, but now it was like a necessity.

CHAPTER FOUR

A WEEK LATER, on the eve of the Harrington Masquerade, Celia carried a tray of broth into her brother's room and set it next to his bed. He'd fallen ill the day before, and now complained of a sore throat and stuffy nose.

She'd never seen such suffering as a man with a cold. Women managed to expel new humans from their bodies, but a man with a sniffle was to be celebrated for sitting up in bed to slurp broth.

She pressed her palm to his forehead and relaxed at the cool, dry skin. "You don't have a fever. I think you'll be fine in a few days."

He groaned. "A few days will be too late. Damn, Kit."

She was to understand Kit had fallen ill days earlier and sent his regrets for the last few dinners and breakfasts, as well as the masquerade to be held that night.

Celia hated the relief she felt knowing Kit wouldn't be attending the illicit affair. Not that she should care what he did, but she found she did nonetheless.

She remembered his smile the other morning during breakfast when he'd said she was lovely.

Unconsciously, she brushed her fingers over the mark on her face. He'd also said the spot was irrelevant. Gray had once told her that he hardly noticed it anymore because he'd grown accustomed to it being there. Had Kit merely grown accustomed to it as well?

"Get some rest," she ordered her brother. "I'm sure Lady Harrington will invite you next year."

"It will be too late," he grumbled. "This was going to be our last party together. We will very well get invited next year, but Kit will be married by then."

The relief she'd felt a moment ago was gone. Kit was going to start his search for a wife. His rejection still stung all these years later. She understood why he'd refused to marry her. Logically, he was trying to protect her. But her heart cared little for logic.

She swallowed and shook off her discomfort. She didn't care what Kit did. Especially since she was ready to enact her own plan to take a lover.

The problem being, she didn't know the mechanics of sex, never having had sexual relations herself. Her elderly husband had taken her to his bed on their wedding night to ensure no one would question the marriage was consummated and therefore contest her settlement upon his death. While she was grateful not to have been called on for such duties, her lack of experience added another challenge in her quest to find a lover.

What if the person she selected could tell she was inexperienced? Arthur's grandson, Edward, had already voiced his doubts that she had been Arthur's legitimate wife. If someone confirmed his suspicions, he would have more leverage of his claims in the House of Lords.

It didn't matter that it was Arthur who had been unable to perform his husbandly duties. If anyone knew she was still a virgin, it would leave the validity of her marriage in question.

His inability had been something she'd been grateful for at the time, given her discomfort with having a husband who was so much older than she. Now, however, she almost wished she'd been able to have a customary wedding night, just so she would know what to do and ensure Arthur's heir couldn't take away the settlement that provided freedom for a widow.

Graham stirred in his sleep. He'd taken her advice to heart and was resting. Most likely, he'd simply run out of energy.

She moved the tray out of the way and knocked something from the nightstand. She bent to pick it up, recognizing the invitation to Lady Harrington's Exclusive Masquerade to be held that night.

Graham couldn't attend, and neither could Kit, both being ill. *Admission granted upon presentation of this invitation only.*

It seemed she had access to a place where she might go to learn all she needed about what one does with a man in bed. And no one would even know it was her.

Was she ready to have her every desire granted? Yes. Yes, she was.

Clutching the invitation to her chest, she backed away silently from Graham's room and hurried off to prepare for the party.

Celia's maid, Lettie, was beside herself with excitement when Celia explained she would be going to a masquerade. Celia was sure to keep the specifics of the party to herself as Nettie selected a gown that had been stashed away in the back of the wardrobe because it had been too revealing.

The cobalt gown was perfect for what she was about to do now. It dipped much lower in front than her usual dresses and was stitched with intricate gold thread and glass beading. The back also dipped low enough that a man might touch her bare skin with his gloved hand as they danced.

Would there be dancing? Or was one expected to just get right to the desire?

Nettie fussed with Celia's hair until it was secured in a vine of braids on top of her head. A style she'd never worn before but was quite stunning.

Finally, the glittering blue mask she and Nettie had decorated with beading to match her gown was tied firmly in place and Celia gazed at herself in the mirror. She'd never felt so adventurous. Or beautiful. The mark on her face was completely obscured by the mask. She even had Nettie confirm that part of her face couldn't be seen.

"It's completely hidden," Nettie said with a frown. "Not that it's as bad as you make it to be."

Perhaps Kit had been right. Maybe she thought too much of her father's words. It was just easier to believe bad things about oneself than it was to trust the good.

While she'd believed Kit and Graham when they assured her the spot was of little import, she was still happy to cover the identifying feature so she could remain anonymous for the evening.

Nettie had given only a little fuss when Celia requested her to hire a hack to take her to the party rather than use the Penbrook carriage. The conveyance didn't boast a crest or any markings, but she wouldn't want the driver to report back to her brother regarding her adventure.

She was handed down from the carriage by two enormous footmen when she arrived. At the entrance, another strapping footman took the invitation she offered with shaking hands and opened the door.

Inside, it was like nothing she'd ever seen. The room was crowded with men and women, all wearing masks. Her dress was modest in comparison to most. Some were cut so low they barely covered the women's nipples.

Celia felt her cheeks heat as a bare-chested footman passed by with a tray of wine. When he paused, she quickly snatched a glass, being careful not to ogle him. Surely whatever she was about to do would be made easier with a drink to fortify her.

She edged her way around the room, noting the couples kissing and touching in the dark corners. She did her best not to stare but was rather captivated by their passionate exchanges. She wanted this. Or at least she thought she did.

Maybe not there in the crowded room where anyone could watch, but she wanted to be kissed and touched, and… whatever it was that came after that.

At the far side of the room, she stepped up a few stairs so she could better see her surroundings.

"Were you ready for a private chamber?" a woman asked

behind Celia, startling her.

Celia turned on the stairs to see a lady with hair so blonde it was nearly white. Her red dress plunged extremely low, exposing the valley between her breasts. *Oh, to be so comfortable in one's skin,* Celia thought.

Celia blinked and recalled the woman's question. *A private room?* That would surely be easier than trying to navigate on her own in front of the crowd.

"Yes, *merci,*" Celia said using a convincing French accent. "I'm Lady Selene." She hoped the woman didn't notice the way Celia stuttered on the lie. The blonde simply nodded and turned on the steps.

Celia followed her upstairs and was led to a room with walls covered in a heavy, burgundy brocade and dimly lit by just a few candles. The light scent of roses filled the air, making the room feel more intimate.

Then she spotted the bed. It was large and immensely sturdy. Clearly designed for the very act she'd come there to experience this evening.

Suddenly she felt faint, and the only sound was that of her blood rushing through her temples. Was she really doing this? It appeared so.

She shook the dizziness away so she could better focus on the woman speaking.

"Tell me Lady Selene, what is it you desire?" Her pale brow pulled up in question.

"Oh." Celia hadn't expected the question so directly but didn't need much time to answer. She knew exactly why she'd attended tonight. "The company of a man." Did she need to elaborate on the specifics? She waited and the woman nodded.

"Very well. Do you have any preferences as to his characteristics?"

Preferences? The woman made choosing a partner for this very special evening sound like selecting a gown from a wardrobe. She hadn't given personal characteristics a thought. She assumed she'd take whatever—or rather whomever—was offered.

To be honest, she wasn't sure what physical characteristics she even liked in a man. Her thoughts drifted to the only man she'd ever been attracted to.

"Perhaps tall? With light hair and kind eyes, maybe green?" Celia suggested as she described Kit. Her cheeks heated and she was grateful for the dim lighting and the mask. Keeping up her accent, she giggled. "But of course, I defer to you as I am rather inexperienced in these things."

Celia had meant relations with a man, but the woman smiled and said, "Oh, is it your first time attending one of my masquerades?"

This woman must be Lady Harrington.

Rather than risk any question of whether she'd been invited, Celia nodded and smiled. "Yes. And I thank you for including me in your festivities."

"I don't believe I invited you directly, but it's no matter. I trust my invitees. Whoever shared their invitation with you must have felt you needed the experience more than they."

Celia's thoughts went to Edward and the risk she was taking that he might find out she was inexperienced. Not to mention the risk to her reputation. Widows were granted certain freedoms, but to be found attending such a party would leave her vulnerable to scorn by the *ton*.

Not that she attended many events. But she planned to in the future. What better way to make connections with suitable men for her plan to take a lover?

The woman winked. "Please make yourself comfortable."

Lady Harrington nodded toward a dressing gown draped across the foot of a large bed. "I'll send in a maid to help you undress. And then *someone* will be with you shortly."

The woman's smile could only be called seductive despite Celia's limited experience with such a term. Some things didn't need explanation.

She slid elegantly from the room and Celia nearly fell over.

Soon a man would enter the room and later when he left, Celia would no longer be a virgin. It was the time in between that was unknown, but to her surprise it wasn't fear zipping through her veins, but anticipation.

An eager smile pulled up her lips. "Finally."

CHAPTER FIVE

K IT FROWNED AT the room full of masked guests and searched for Gray among them. There were many dark-haired gentlemen in attendance, but he didn't recognize any of them as his best friend.

Perhaps Kit should have sent a message letting Gray know he had improved and decided to attend the party after all. Had Gray not come because Kit couldn't? That didn't sound like Gray. He wouldn't have missed this party for anything.

Kit cleared his throat. While he was feeling his usual, hearty self, his voice had not returned to full strength. It still came out low and raspy. He might have used it as an excuse to avoid coming tonight. In fact, he didn't require an excuse since he'd already told Graham he wasn't coming.

He would have been free to remain at home as he'd planned.

But instead, he was here.

He'd thought over what Gray had said. That this could be Kit's final chance to attend Lady Harrington's Masquerade. Married men and women were not invited.

While Gray most likely assumed Kit would look back on tonight with longing, Kit cataloged every detail as something he'd never be forced to endure again.

The loud laughter and cloying perfumes served as motivation for him to find someone he could settle down with and be happy. Someone who would make such a party seem boring in comparison. Someone who would be his for all time.

His.

He saw this party as a passage from his old life to his future.

"My lord," Lady Harrington came down the stairs directly behind him. He turned and offered a bow. Despite his mask, the woman had recognized him as a regular to these parties. Just as he had recognized many of the people in attendance as well. The mask only offering the illusion of anonymity.

"Good evening, my lady. You are beautiful tonight, as expected."

She tilted her head and accepted his compliment with a smile. "Why thank you. You are as charming as ever." She lifted her brows. "I'm so glad you are here. You would be perfect for my needs. Can I persuade you to visit one of our guests in a private room?" she gestured over her shoulder.

"Actually, I only just arrived," he said as an excuse. While he was happy to attend and say his farewells to this life, he wasn't up for partaking in the activities.

"Lady Selene arrived only a few minutes ago as well. This is her first event and was a bit nervous to stay down here. I settled her upstairs and she's asked for someone tall, fair-haired with kind, green eyes. It was as if she described you exactly. Won't you be the woman's hero and provide her every desire?"

He looked out over the sea of people laughing and thought he'd prefer a bit of quiet. Perhaps one last evening spent in a woman's warm embrace would encourage him even more to find a wife.

"She's beautiful," Lady Harrington said.

He didn't doubt the woman waiting upstairs would be absolutely stunning. Lady Harrington didn't invite anyone to her parties who wasn't perfection.

Kit wouldn't set out to marry a perfect woman. He wanted a partner. A woman whose beauty came from within and radiated out in a witty sense of humor and kindness. He wanted a deeper connection than he'd find here tonight.

But Lady Harrington pressed on.

"I feel she is very shy. I hate to put one of these other stallions in with such an untried filly."

She'd managed to appeal to his sense of honor. If such a task could be seen as honorable in any way. But he knew he could be gentle and see to the woman's satisfaction, rather than rut upon her and move on like many men were known to do.

"Very well. Lead on. Let it not be said, I did not do my duty when called upon by a woman in need." He laughed it off as he followed her upstairs.

She tapped on the door and then pushed it open. "Right this way, *Lord Desire*," she announced mysteriously. He shook his head. He would not miss the drama of these parties. He wouldn't miss the emptiness of the liaisons. And he wouldn't miss the rush of anticipation as he stepped into a room with a warm, willing stranger waiting for him. Perhaps that last thing would remain a pleasant memory.

He blinked, giving his eyes a moment to adjust to the dim light. A movement caught his attention and he turned to his right as the door closed behind him.

A woman stepped closer into the stream of light from the nearest lamp. She was wearing a blue silk dressing gown. Her hair was black. In truth, it might have been brown, but in the low light it looked dark as pitch. Her eyes, what he could see of them with the distraction of a blue jeweled mask were also dark. But he didn't notice them very long for her lips entranced him. They were shaped for smiles, kisses, and speaking her mind, and he had an urge to revel in each.

He was spellbound when she stepped closer and smiled. She reminded him so much of Celia. He let out a breath and shook off the thought. Even if she'd had auburn hair and blue eyes, he would have been reminded of Celia. She'd claimed his interest long ago and he still had yet to let her go. He cast the thought of her aside. He'd promised himself he'd no longer think of the countess. It wasn't fair to this woman.

Nor was it fair to him. She was not an option. Even if he could get past the damage she'd done to his heart, she had said just days ago she had no intentions of remarrying. And he wanted a wife.

Tonight, would be for Selene. He'd see to her enjoyment.

"How fortunate for me to have the Lord of Desire attend me," she said with a heavy French accent in a low, rich voice that made his body stir. Perhaps he wasn't as altruistic as he'd first thought. This vision wouldn't be the only one enjoying themselves tonight.

"And who do I have the honor of spending the evening with?" he asked to confirm Lady Harrington had her name correct. It wouldn't do to address the woman by the wrong name.

"Selene," she said, looking away. Lady Harrington had been right, she was shy. She appealed to him. The way her hands trembled despite the cocky tilt of her head. She was nervous, but brave enough to continue. She wanted this. And for tonight he could pretend she wanted *him*.

He would do his best to ensure that her night was filled with pleasure, and when tomorrow came, he would begin his search for a wife in earnest.

CELIA WOULD SING Lady Harrington's praises until the day she died. The woman had truly outdone herself. It was as if the lady had looked into Celia's mind and plucked out the very man she had dreamed of.

He looked so much like Kit it was uncanny apart from his voice. His voice was all wrong. Much deeper than Kit's with a sexy rasp that was far from Kit's honey-smooth tones. Still, he was quite attractive from what she could make out of him with the mask and poor light obscuring his features.

She almost wished she'd asked for more candles and lamps so she could see him better, but if she could barely see him, it meant he couldn't see her either. Besides, being unable to observe the details made it easier to pretend.

She bit her bottom lip. It seemed rude to have this man offer his time only for her to use him while fantasizing about another man. She would do her best to focus on *Lord Desire*—or whatever his real name was—and what happened between them now.

"May I?" he asked with his hand at his cravat.

"*Oui*, of course. I was already encouraged to make myself comfortable. Lady Harrington provided a maid to help with my gown." She pressed her lips together tightly as if to hold in whatever else might have come out. She was babbling.

She'd never been much of a babbler, preferring to quietly stay out of the way, but she was so tense she was nearly erupting with nervous energy.

She needed to calm herself. This man didn't know who she was. And could never know. Whether this night was perfect or not was of no consequence. The only thing that truly mattered was that when she left here, she would understand the ways between a man and woman and would no longer be a virgin.

Even if Edward were awarded his way, and she was forced to succumb to a physical examination, no doctor would be able to question she'd lain with a man. The fact it wasn't her husband could never be proven.

Telling herself it had nothing to do with Edward's threats, she focused on the main reason she had come. Once she knew the ways of carnal relations, she would be free to take the experience she earned tonight to confidently take a lover of her choosing. Confidence being the key.

"How convenient for me not to have to battle through a gown and corset," Lord Desire said with a smile that once again reminded her of the man who had sat across from her at breakfast most mornings.

The man who had failed her when she'd needed him most.

She squeezed her eyes shut for a moment, trying to ward away the anger she'd thought was long gone. Everything had turned out for the best. And now she was free to do what she wanted.

Had she married Kit…well, she would have most likely spent each day laughing at his antics and enjoying each touch and kiss they shared. She shook her head.

"Is something the matter?" Lord Desire asked.

"Non. Nothing at all. Everything is wonderful." And she would make sure that was true, by not thinking of Christopher again tonight.

After Lord Desire removed his shirt, he stepped closer, resting his hands on her hips. His bare chest touched the fabric of the dressing gown she wore, causing her nipple to harden.

She felt the heat of his skin, somehow even warmer than her own flesh, which she'd thought might catch fire.

"Perhaps we can start with a kiss," he suggested and waited a breath as if giving her an opportunity to change her mind. She wouldn't, she knew that. She was set on her plan. And even if she'd wavered, seeing this man, ready to kiss her would have convinced her she was doing the right thing.

Not the proper thing, but definitely *right*.

When he made no move toward her, she leaned up on her tiptoes to meet his lips.

She'd been kissed before, so this joining of lips shouldn't have been anything new to her, but it was. This wasn't a rushed press of mouths and clinking of teeth in the stables. This was warm chocolate and her favorite book. It drew her in and heated her, melting her thoroughly into a luxurious puddle. All the more decadent for its subtlety.

Their masks collided and he pulled back with a smile. "Should we remove these?"

"*Non!*" she spoke louder than even she expected, startling them both. "That is, I prefer the anonymity they provide. We can say and do anything uninhibited. They are not just masks, but freedom, yes?" She made sure to keep up her fake accent.

"Very well. Freedom." One side of his mouth pulled up in a smirk as he ran a finger over the edge of her ear causing a shiver to run up her spine.

He kissed her again. This time he didn't seem distracted by the cumbersome masks as his lips trailed along the edge of her jaw and down her neck.

Giving into the freedom she'd just mentioned, she moaned in delight, finding the sound a pleasure in itself. She'd been so overwhelmed by the delight of his kiss she hadn't realized her dressing robe had been untied and opened until the cooler air touched her flaming skin.

Looking down she let out a squeal of surprise and pulled it shut again.

He smiled patiently and took her hands away from where they clenched the silk. "Freedom, remember?" he said.

She nodded slowly and allowed the gown to fall open. She closed her eyes as his fingers brushed up her arms to her shoulders where he pushed the fabric away so it slid down her back to the floor. Leaving her standing in front of a man. Naked. Except for a mask. His gaze raked over her and the smile faded into seriousness.

"Lady Selene, you are exquisite." His already raspy voice grew rougher, sending a shiver through her body.

She breathed in his words and allowed them to ignite into the confidence she had wished for.

Yes, she was vulnerable, standing bare before him while he still wore his breeches, but there was a power in her she had never felt before as his heated gaze lingered. He seemed utterly enraptured. The first stirrings of feminine pride swelled within her, she had him right where she wanted him.

CHAPTER SIX

K IT WAS SHOCKED by the need that ravished his body for the woman in front of him. This was supposed to be a mere dalliance. A way to spend his last night as a rogue. A proper send-off into the commitment and responsibility he so eagerly sought.

But all he could think about at the moment was throwing Lady Selene on the bed behind her and sinking deep inside her warm body.

He was certain he was ready for marriage, but this woman had reduced him to a rutting beast. He had to have her.

Grasping for what control he could summon, he maintained his slow explorations. She was inexperienced. He hadn't needed Lady Harrington's warning to know this. He felt it in the way her hands trembled when she caressed his bare skin. And the way she babbled nervously whenever he asked a lascivious question.

For whatever reason she'd come here tonight, she'd wanted this. He'd not allow this experience to be anything less than lovely.

He might not be the man who would take her to bed each night, but he would certainly set her up to know what she wanted from her husband.

The thought of her marrying another dimmed his enjoyment slightly but he brushed it off as instinctual male claiming. She was his. And while it would only be for the night, the thought of another man intruding and taking what was his, had him tense and prepared for battle.

"I believe you will be more comfortable lying on the bed," he said as his tongue traced the curve of her neck to her ear.

"The bed?" she said as if it was her first time hearing the word and she didn't understand the definition.

"Behind you." He nodded and stepped closer, pulling her with him.

"Yes. Of course." She swallowed and he lifted her and followed her down to the mattress, kissing her all the way.

In past encounters, he'd had a script he'd followed. One devised to pleasure a woman in the quickest fashion so he could complete the task and take himself off before the night was too far gone.

He knew he could employ that plan now, and she would walk away with no complaints. She would experience everything she'd need and more.

But for whatever reason, he didn't feel it would be good enough for him.

Strange, since it barely took him any time at all to be satisfied physically once he gave himself leave to do so. This was different. He wasn't just after physical satisfaction.

He didn't want to cut short his time with her. This divine creature who was giving herself to a stranger so she might have the experience she craved.

He would make their brief time together something they would both remember the rest of their days. And she would become the last woman he slept with that didn't bear his name.

LORD DESIRE PULLED away from their kiss and stared at her in what she could only describe as a mixture of confusion and awe. For a moment she worried she'd called out Kit's name when she'd moaned against this man's skin.

How rude that would be. She would need to keep her wits about her to make sure that didn't happen. But the way he kissed her, had her squirming and calling out nonsensical claims. Fortunately, some were in French.

"I must have you or I'll die." Had been a bit dramatic, though she couldn't be sure it wasn't true. Her heart felt as if it might explode either way—if she had him or didn't. It appeared she was done for no matter what happened next.

And when his lips pulled up on the corners in a devilish smile, she was even more certain she would not survive the night.

He pressed kisses lower on her jaw and then her neck. From there he dipped to her collarbone and when she expected him to return up to her lips he went lower still and sucked her left nipple into his hot mouth.

She gasped and nearly jumped off the bed from the surprise as much as the feel of it.

"No?" he asked, tilting his head as if waiting for her answer.

She blinked a few times and then relaxed. "Yes." The single word had been spoken with a hint of command she found she enjoyed. When he groaned his approval and continued his devouring of her breasts, she knew he had heard it and liked it as well.

If she'd had any ability to rationalize a thought, she might have been surprised to find a man—especially a large powerful man—enjoyed demands from a woman.

She smiled into the darkness as he continued, until she noticed he'd moved farther down her body. His tongue dipped into her navel and forced her back to come up from the bed in response.

His naughty laugh told her he'd scandalized her intentionally, but the shock was not over when he ducked his head between her thighs. How had her legs opened so widely to give him such access? She might have worried over it more, if his mouth hadn't done something so remarkable that she forgot everything. Even her own name. Or rather both of them.

All thoughts of stopping him from this unspeakable act were cut short when her mouth opened and the word *more* came out. "More," she repeated with that same demanding tone. She somehow knew exactly what she wanted and was unsure of it at the same time. She only knew she didn't want him to stop, especially not when she was so close.

Close to something she didn't quite understand. Or didn't until another few strokes of his tongue sent her spiraling over the edge. She couldn't get enough air and didn't think she required air any longer. She only needed this feeling. And him.

The intensity of the explosion subsided only slightly. Her breathing turned from gasping to merely panting. He propped himself up on his elbow and even in the dim light she could see the smugness in his grin.

She might have scolded him, though she felt he deserved to be smug for how well he'd made her feel.

"That was divine," she said instead. *"Magnifique."*

"And that was only the first course," he promised.

Her eyes went wide.

She knew what was involved in relations between a man and woman. Her brother's friends—mostly Julian when he'd been drunk—had taken great joy in telling her the details and making her cringe. She'd almost thought he made up such things, but no one had disputed what was said, only shook their heads as Gray called all of them out for mentioning such things in front of his sister.

Fortunately, the four men had made a pact to never dual with each other. No matter what the dishonor.

Celia would have to find some way to thank Julian for his bold description, for it gave her some reference of what was to come next. Celia felt Lord Desire's hardness through the breeches he still wore. It was true then that this part of his body would infiltrate her own.

Before she could begin to worry over it, he got up from the bed and unfastened his falls. He'd already pulled off his boots, so he bent to remove his pants and stockings and when he stood again, Celia saw every bit of him.

She gasped.

"Oh, dear. I don't think I could possibly accommodate… *that*."

His smile shifted from gloating to complete concern for her.

"I am surely not so much larger than your husband?"

"I have no husband."

"But in the past?"

"*Non*. I—I have never been married," she lied.

"You are a maid?" he asked, pulling away from her. His blond brows pulled together. He was going to stop. She couldn't allow it. Not when she was so close to getting what she wanted.

But she thought it would be easier to tell the truth at least in one aspect.

"*Oui*. But I do not wish to be any longer." She spoke with the confidence that could only be feigned when using a fake French accent. "I am not some young miss. I am a woman and wish to know the things a woman should. If you think to dissuade me, you will not. And if you leave, I will only seek out another man to fulfill my needs."

He pressed his lips together as if considering her words. Then he nodded.

"Very well. As long as you are sure, I am no one to contradict a woman who knows her own mind." His smile was back as he looked down between them. "As for my size, I'm certain every untried woman feels the same at some point, yet it has been working fine for humans since the beginning of time. Shall we give it a go?"

This was the last step to becoming a worldly widow who would command her wishes upon the men of the *ton*.

"Yes," she said. "Tell me what you wish me to do."

SHE WAS A virgin.

He assumed she'd been a widow, knowing Lady Harrington generally invited widowed women to her parties. He'd expected this woman was newly widowed if this was her first visit, and the reason Lady Harrington claimed she was shy.

But a virgin?

Still, who was he to try to convince her she was making a mistake? It wasn't as if the woman had mistakenly wandered in from the street and up to this room unknowing of what was to happen here.

She'd come here with a purpose. A plan. And he would help her see it through.

Having never laid with a virgin before, Kit was concerned for Selene. He, of course, had heard stories of virgins experiencing some bit of pain during the act the first time, but hearing such a thing and causing it were two very different things.

Had the lady said no or even so much as shied away, he might have gladly ended the evening and taken his discomfort elsewhere, but Selene was looking him over eagerly and was now reaching out to touch him.

She was not a young girl. She was a woman. He would trust her to know what she wanted. If she had the courage to come to this party tonight and claim a private room to meet with a man, he felt sure she had considered everything and still wanted to go through with her plan.

He would respect her choice.

As if on instinct, she wrapped her fingers around him, causing him to lose his breath. Her hand, so much smaller and softer than his, sent his blood rushing to fill her grip.

"How?"

"Lie back and I'll take care of everything. There might be a bit of pain, but I understand it's better after a short while."

She nodded, no doubt she'd heard the same from her mother or a sister or friend. She laid back on the bed and watched him as he reached for his coat and extracted the folded vellum.

Her brows creased and he offered an explanation before she even asked.

"It's a sheath. It protects us both from future responsibilities." He meant a pregnancy. But it also protected against disease. He would not allow memories of his sea-faring uncle to intrude on this moment. But those recollections had served to keep him safe through his days of debauchery. Watching someone waste away from syphilis was an enlightening and terrifying experience for a young man.

He shivered as he covered himself. He had nothing to worry over tonight in that regard. Virgins didn't spread such suffering.

He smiled as he positioned himself between her legs. After testing her readiness, he pressed forward just a little and waited.

She nodded and he moved a little more and more still, until finally he had breached her completely and she was lifting her body in time with his, welcoming him deeper with each thrust.

"More," she said as she had before. The command in her voice set his blood on fire.

Despite her inexperience, she was brave enough to voice her desires. There was nothing more stimulating than a woman uninhibited enough to declare what she wanted.

"You are incredible. Perfect," he praised her with the simple truth. Never had he had such a responsive lover. One that seemed to know exactly what to do to fit them together as closely as possible.

The way she seemed to reach into his very soul and stir his desires had him kissing her again. Offering her everything. Their fingers intertwined and he couldn't help but feel their lives were connecting as well.

This would never be enough. This one night.

The tingling in his spine alerted him to the threat of his release. He either needed to slow down to make the moment last or speed on to his peak. There would be no in between.

Before he could react, Selene threw back her head and cried out as her inner walls clamped around him.

The choice was taken from him when her legs tightened around his waist, fixing him to her. A few more thrusts and he spent into the sheath while buried deep in her body.

He managed to shift off of her so not to crush the poor woman with his weight but could go no farther. He rested his head over her heart listening to the rapid beat. It was maybe the most wonderous sound he'd ever heard.

Her fingers played through his hair and he felt... cherished. Her other hand stroked his back. It had been so long since another person had held him and offered comfort.

He couldn't get enough.

"That was amazing," she said, her voice still breathy. "I can't even... I never imagined... It was so very... amazing."

He couldn't argue. "It was."

"*Merci*," she whispered.

He couldn't help but chuckle. "It is I who should be thanking you for this very great honor."

"Is it always like that? I mean with other people?"

He sat up to look at her wishing again he could see the features of her face without the mask. "I can't say what it would be like for you with other men, but for me. No. Never so consuming as that was."

She nodded. "*Oui*. That is an apt description. *Consommant*," she repeated in French.

"And amazing," he reminded her playfully.

She laughed and the sound reminded him of Celia. Not that Celia was one to laugh overly much, but he had made it his life's work and had earned some mirth from her on occasion.

Perhaps it wasn't the laugh so much as the way he felt when hearing it. Like when he was with Celia, he felt comfortable with Selene. He wanted to know more about her. But instead, she said, "We should get dressed."

And his heart lurched in his chest.

CHAPTER SEVEN

CELIA WASN'T CERTAIN she was capable of dressing, or even standing for that matter. Her bones had taken a jelly-like quality and it was questionable if they'd be up to the task of supporting her. But she had accomplished what she'd come there to do.

No, that was too simplistic. It was not a mere accomplishment, it was—what was the word he'd used? Consuming.

Yes. The person she once was had been consumed and what was left behind was somehow more than she'd been previously.

"Do you need to leave so soon?" he asked. "The room is ours for as long as we'd like it."

"But we have finished. What more would we do?"

He smiled patiently. "We could start again." He pressed his lips together and shook his head. "I'm sorry. I just remembered, you are probably too sore and wish to stop now."

"We could do it again? Right now?" she asked, hope clear in her voice.

He chuckled. "Not *right* this second, but if you give me just a few moments to recover, yes. Unless you're uncomfortable from the first time."

She felt a dull ache, but it was not enough to discourage her from taking advantage of his offer. The throbbing bliss overshadowed any discomfort.

"I am not so uncomfortable that I would not wish to do it

again."

He smiled, his rogue grin, and kissed her.

She expected him to go about it in the same way he had the first time, but he did not. Instead, he rolled her onto her stomach and placed kisses along her back while he caressed her bottom, his fingers teasing between her thighs from a different yet enticing direction.

His manhood rested against her hip, soft and heavy at first, but soon it grew hard and demanding.

She rolled over, wanting him—needing him—to enter her, but instead of coming over her, he rolled on his back and affixed a new sheath before pulling her astride him.

"What...?"

"Like this," he encouraged, holding his cock out from his body with one hand as he guided her closer with the other. When he entered her, she let her body slide closer.

She closed her eyes and let her head fall back as the fullness of him set her on fire once more.

"You move this time. As I did when I was above you. Set the pace in the way that brings you the most enjoyment."

She would be in control of it?

"I don't know the way to do it correctly." She'd only just learned how to do it the regular way. "I didn't realize there were different ways."

He laughed, but not in a way she felt he was mocking her. As if he was sharing a secret, he pulled her down to whisper in her ear. "There are many ways to join. And there is nothing you could do that would be wrong. Take what you want."

Encouraged by his words, and enflamed by the way he nipped her ear between his teeth after he'd spoken, she sat back and looked down at the luscious man beneath her.

His hands resting lightly on her hips gave the slightest tug of suggestion. His hint spurred her into action. She rocked against him, taking him deeper and drawing a moan of pleasure from both of them. They shared a smile and she increased her rhythm.

"Be careful. If you go fast, our fun will be over too quickly. Best to build the fire slower."

"Yes," she agreed. As he'd said, they had use of the room for as long as they needed. There was no reason to hurry. But as her need grew, she was unable to go slow. Soon enough she was slamming into him as he pushed up to meet her thrusts.

"Yes!" he shouted. She might have been the one above him, but at that time, she was no longer in control as he reached between them and rubbed his thumb in a place that sparked her release.

As she broke around him, he continued to direct their activities and she was grateful for it because she could no longer move. He grasped her hips and drove up into her a few more times before throwing his head back in what looked like pain. But she knew it was not.

Collapsing on top of him, she felt a few more jerks of his member inside of her as she continued to throb around him. Eventually their bodies stilled and their breathing slowed.

The room was peaceful as her mind drifted. She focused on the soft stroke of his fingertips over her spine and floated further.

Her bliss was disrupted a little while later when he kissed her awake.

"I'm afraid our night is at an end. The party is breaking up. You'll most likely want to return home before anyone notices you're away." His voice held a question and she nodded in answer.

He rose and went to the washstand to get them something with which to clean up. He helped her into her dress and they exchanged warm smiles as they put themselves back to rights.

She felt she should say something, but the silence was comfortable and their glances were enough for the moment.

"I don't want to leave you without some expectation to see each other again. Perhaps we can remove the masks now that freedom is no longer required?" he suggested.

She shook her head. "*Non*. I don't think that is a good idea. I think it better for us to remember this night as strangers. With no expectations to weigh it down."

If things were different, she might have wished for the same thing, but as it was, she couldn't risk it. This man knew she'd come to this room a virgin. Gentlemen knew one another. Whether it be the loose ties of acquaintance, or the stronger bonds of friendship, it was likely her Lord Desire knew Edward or her brother.

She shook her head and placed her hands over his as he lifted them to his own mask.

She wanted the opposite of him. It seemed to be the first time that night they were not aligned. But this was her night. She had orchestrated this meeting and she would not allow him to push her into changing what she wanted from it.

"I know you're not familiar with how things are, but know I enjoyed our time together immensely. What happened here was a deeper connection than just sex. I would like to see you again."

She might have wanted that as well, but she couldn't. She needed him to go.

"I cannot. But I will never forget this night."

She could give him that small truth at least. The smiles they'd shared. The freedom she'd felt was more than could be attributed to the wearing of a mask.

"Neither of us would need to worry about forgetting any-thing if we could be ourselves."

He wanted to prolong their arrangement.

She was tempted, but it couldn't work. Even now she was having difficulty keeping up her ruse as Selene. She wanted to come clean and tell him who she really was. But this night was all she could have.

She couldn't dare risk it. Not even for a chance at a future with this lovely man.

"As much as the idea intrigues me, I must pass on your offer. You see, this is but the first step for me into a new life. I must continue to take each step forward, even if it ends in disaster.

Because not moving forward is a disaster of its own. Life doesn't wait for one to be ready."

And one couldn't go back and mend a moment once shattered by truth. Which meant she needed to move on.

"Perhaps fate will intercede and we shall meet at a ball in the future. Maybe we might even manage another of your steps together."

"Perhaps we shall." She stroked a finger lightly across his chin. "Thank you for making this step so wonderful. I'll never forget it as long as I live."

"Nor will I." He laughed. "I won't pretend it's the first step for me. But I tell you honestly it was the most wonderful. Thank you again for the great honor." He kissed her lips and then her fingers. "Until we meet again."

"*Au revoir*, Lord Desire."

He paused for a moment at the door and she thought he might say something, but he simply turned and left. The room felt cold for his absence and she shivered.

Perhaps she should have asked his name. Or given him hers. Maybe he would have agreed to be her first lover and they could have continued what they had started here.

She shook the idea away. Not only was it too late—as he was gone—but she could not. She cursed Edward silently for stealing this opportunity from her and tainting it with his crude threats.

She let out a breath. Even if she weren't faced with the risk of Edward finding out, this ending was for the best. It was better to hold this memory apart from anything else. Protecting it so it could never be ruined. She would treasure it as one would cherish a precious artifact or a priceless heirloom. Locked away from any threat of damage.

The soft knock at the door made her heart race. Had he returned?

"Did you need my services, my lady?" the maid asked through the door.

Celia cleared the disappointment from her throat and forced a smile. *"Oui,* please come in."

The woman helped with her hair and Celia refrained from begging the poor girl to help her find the man who'd just left. Where had he gone? Who was he?

No. That wasn't what she truly needed to know. The most important thing was, would she ever see him again?

As she left Lady Harrington's house out the back and returned home, Celia could only hope Fate had heard his earlier challenge and would bring them together again.

CHAPTER EIGHT

THE NEXT EVENING Kit found Gray at White's nursing a glass of brandy.

"How many have you had? You're looking rather rough, friend."

Gray sniffed. "This is the first one," he answered in a raw voice that made Kit cringe. Kit had sounded the same way for the last week, but was finally better this morning when he'd woke. His thoughts caught on what had happened the night before.

When he'd been with Selene.

Memories of her skittered through his mind randomly. He'd even dreamed of her. Though in his dreams she'd started out as Selene and had transformed into Celia.

He shook thoughts of both women away to focus on his ill friend.

"I take it you didn't attend the masquerade last night?"

"No. And I would have stayed to my bed tonight as well, if not for my need to get away from Celia and her hovering."

Kit stifled a laugh knowing Gray was the worst kind of patient when he was ill. Kit doubted very much Celia was hovering as much as trying to get away from Gray's insidious requests.

It was yet another thing about siblings that baffled Kit. The desire to help the other person while also acting as if it was a huge burden. He didn't understand the bond of family, having gone so long without his. He'd been too young to pay attention to the way his parents had looked at one another. But he wanted that kind of happiness. He wanted someone to care for, and someone to care for him.

"I've already heard from a few chaps who were at Harrington's last night. It appears we both missed a lively evening. However, for you, it was your final chance to attend one of Lady Harrington's parties. You'll have to be satisfied with my accounts going forward." Gray laughed but it turned into a hacking cough.

For a brief moment, Kit considered not telling Gray he'd attended, and an even longer moment to decide if he wanted to mention Selene. In the end, he decided his friend might be able to help him.

If not to find the woman, then at least to help him forget her. For it was clear he regretted having no way to find her and he already missed her. He shook his head at his fanciful thoughts. How could he miss someone he barely even knew?

"Actually, I did attend," he found himself saying before actually deciding to do so.

Gray's watery eyes widened. "You did? Without me?"

"I thought I'd meet you there. I didn't realize you were ill until I arrived here and saw what a mess you are." He frowned as Gray blew his nose loudly. "I thought, perhaps, you'd already been pulled away to one of the private rooms yourself."

Gray cocked his head and Kit could feel the other man studying him.

"Christopher Ethan Anthony Sinclair! Were you pulled away to a private room last night?" The man's smirk might have been more intimidating if it weren't followed up by a sneeze.

Only Gray and Celia knew all his names. Most days, he wished it were only Celia.

"Yes. As a matter of fact, I was."

"And who, pray, were you enlisted to serve?" If anyone ever needed the definition of a roguish grin, they need only look at Graham Percival Alexander Dorsett at that moment.

"I'm not certain. She gave only her first name. She was lovely and we had an engaging evening. I asked her full name so I might find her again, but she refused. I thought I was content with her decision, but I find myself wishing I could see her again."

Gray nodded. "Then we shall find her. There are not so many ladies in London."

"She is French."

"Even better. It narrows it down immensely. I daresay you'll be calling on her with a handful of posies by tomorrow at visiting hours. What is her name?"

"Lady Selene."

Gray blinked. "Selene?"

"Yes. Do you know her?"

"I must know ten Selenes at least that are French or pretending to be French. None of them ladies, however. Most of them—"

"My Selene was a lady. In fact, she was a—" He lowered his voice and looked around the room, not wanting to air the woman's personal information in a room full of men. "She was a virgin until last night," he whispered.

Gray snorted. "Oh, I'm certain she was. She'll no doubt be a virgin at the next party and the one after that."

"No. One knows such things."

A cloud came over Gray's face, one Kit had seen only a few times. When Gray was forced to discuss things like love. And now as they discussed taking a lady's virtue.

Kit often wondered what memories haunted him, but Gray refused to discuss it, even at times when he was drunk when most men opened up and allowed their worries to pour out of them.

But something had happened. If Kit was a betting man, he would have wagered his friend had been in love at one point. Perhaps with a lady who'd given him her virtue.

Gray's face cleared and he gave an abrupt nod.

"Very well. But why would a virgin take a stranger to her bed at Lady Harrington's masquerade? How did she even get invited?"

"I'm not sure. Perhaps we can ask her when we find her."

Gray frowned. "Let me ponder how best to do that. For now, I must get back to my bed before Celia realizes I've snuck out."

Kit laughed at the idea of a grown man sneaking out of his house to get away from his sister. Their antics made him grateful he was an only child and long for a sibling at the same time.

CELIA HAD WAITED for Gray to sneak off to his club before calling Nettie in to help her dress for the Compton Ball. It wasn't that Gray would forbid her to attend. How could he when she was a grown woman?

It wasn't his approval she was concerned with as much as the teasing he would inflict if he found out she was attending a ball. He rarely attended *ton* functions himself, calling them frivolous. If he found out, he would be relentless.

She smiled at the thought of telling him the truth of why she was attending. To find a lover. Wouldn't that bit of news shut him up quickly?

Nettie selected one of the new gowns Celia had purchased recently to assist in fulfilling her plans. Like the sapphire gown from the night before, this one was cut lower in the bosom than the pastel gowns she usually wore. The deep emerald told everyone in attendance that she was not a blushing debutante, but an experienced woman.

She found the situation to be paradoxical. She wanted the world to know she was available for a liaison while also appearing respectable and guarding her reputation. But she couldn't guard it so stingily, observers might think her a virgin and agree with Edward's claims.

A smile pulled up on her lips. She was no longer a virgin. Even if the Lords came to the vulgar decision to request an examination, it would only prove her rights to her settlement.

She didn't feel the least bit guilty for knowing the truth of the matter. Arthur had set up her funds months after they'd wed when he'd had no plans to consummate their vows. He assured her he didn't care about the lack in their marriage for he enjoyed her company. He'd told her numerous times that he wanted to provide for her after he was gone because she'd brought happiness into his life for his final days. Therefore, in his eyes, the settlement was not contingent on sex or fulfilling her wifely duties. The funds were proof of a generous man who wanted to show his appreciation for a kindness.

She knew if he was here, he would have something to say to his ruthless grandson.

As she had the night before, Celia had Nettie secure a hackney so she wouldn't need to use her brother's carriage. She arrived at the Compton home at the appropriate time and was announced as she entered the ballroom.

"The Countess of Hamlin," the majordomo said in a bold voice.

The title still sounded odd to her. She was a countess. And a woman who had taken a complete stranger to her bed. She was alluring and powerful. She was unstoppable.

"What is that upon her face?" a woman whispered to another as Celia passed by the group, causing Celia's resolve to waver.

Perhaps it would have been better to see if someone else she knew was in attendance so she wouldn't be alone.

Had she truly thought she would walk into the ballroom and choose a gentleman to be her lover straightaway without having to interact with the other people present?

The Comptons would be fortunate to have Lady Harrington assist with their balls. While scandalous, at least the woman knew how to get to the point of things in a timely manner without all the frivolity.

Celia found she much preferred guests who were engaged in lewd acts to the people in attendance tonight who gawked at her rudely.

Feeling the weight of their scrutiny, her heartrate picked up and she felt the air thin under the weight of perfumes and people. Would she faint? She'd never done so before, so she wasn't able to tell what it felt like when it came on, but surely the way her chest had tightened was not a good sign.

She needed to leave.

She turned to escape and nearly ran into a woman who had come up behind her.

"Lady Hamlin, I'm sorry to startle you. I'm Lady Winthrop."

Celia didn't recognize the name and stepped back in case the meek-looking woman turned out to be a viper.

"Before I married, I had been Miss Denton. There was discussion of my marrying your brother for a short time, but that didn't come to fruition."

"Ah, yes. Because my father…" How did one explain in polite company that one's father was a scoundrel? Miss Denton had been the heiress her father had planned to force Gray into marrying for her money.

"Quite," Lady Winthrop said and shook her head. "At any rate, I married another and was quite happy until he died last year. This is my first ball since coming out of mourning. I must admit, I am thinking of running from the room."

Celia smiled. "I was just about to do that myself."

"Perhaps we can shore each other up and get through it together," the lady suggested.

"Yes. That would be lovely."

Celia was relieved beyond belief to have someone to stroll the ballroom with. Lady Winthrop, Katherine, confided the reason she'd attended when they'd reached the other side of the room.

"I wish to marry again. I found it to be a pleasant thing to have a husband. While ours was not blessed with children, I enjoyed the stability and safety of having a man take care of me."

Celia wondered if she might have felt the same if her marriage had been different. As it were, Celia's plans for the future were so far from Katherine's as to be the direct opposite.

But she did know a man who wished to marry and would benefit from his wife having a fortune as well.

Celia opened her mouth to suggest an introduction between Katherine and Kit, but found herself unable to force the words from her mouth.

Celia had no intention of marrying. In fact, she was at the ball solely to find a lover, yet the idea of Kit marrying another did not sit well. She was clearly the worst of friends to not want two people who wanted the same things to meet.

Perhaps, she assured herself, she would feel differently once she knew Katherine better and could be certain she was a proper match for Kit. Yes. That was surely the cause of her hesitation.

Before she could think on her behavior too deeply, a man stepped up offering a smile.

"Dear sister, might you introduce me to your friend?" the man inquired. He gave her a devilish smile and Celia felt her heartbeat pick up for a different reason than earlier.

"Of course. Lord Timmons, may I introduce Lady Hamlin?"

"Lady Hamlin?" His smile went wider. "Might I request the honor of a dance this evening?"

"Yes," Celia answered and held out her otherwise empty dance card. If things went well, she may get something other than a mere dance from the man. Celia watched as he strode off, taking in his powerful physique. He was no Lord Desire, but he had broad shoulders and dark hair she found appealing.

"You should know, he's not my brother. Rather he was my husband's brother. He now holds the title and is looking for a wife to fill his nursery. Though he's a rogue through and through." Katherine tutted and shook her head. "He needs to marry a strong woman who will make a good husband of him."

Or perhaps a merry widow who would allow him to continue in his roguish ways…

While pleased she had stayed and had even met a man who could possibly become a lover, she spent the rest of the evening looking for a tall, blond man with a husky voice that had made her melt.

Chapter Nine

"No. That's not her," Kit said in disappointment from his seat in Gray's coach. "And why must we skulk about watching women come and go? I feel the worst kind of lurker."

"The moment someone finds out we're looking for someone named Selene they will be thrusting them upon us. We'll be up to our ears in Selenes."

"Since we've spent the last two mornings hunting for my Selene with no luck, I'd much prefer a pile of them to sort through as this is taking much too long," Kit complained. Why he thought Graham, of all people, would be able to help he didn't know.

"Perhaps the longer it takes, the more likely you will be to see the woman is not to be your bride," Gray said, his face pulled up in distaste.

"Are you purposely delaying my finding my Selene so I won't marry? You are the very worst kind of friend." They'd been at this ruse since early that morning. He'd missed breakfast and was dearly longing for luncheon. His hunger was now fueling his irritation with his friend.

"Or the best friend ever. Time will tell." Gray winked. "But no. We've not been delaying. The sooner we find your French seductress the sooner you will see the truth of her and can put the search aside for more entertaining pursuits." He wiggled his brows.

"Quite." Kit rolled his eyes. As if Selene was his only hope for finding a wife and he'd give up if she wasn't found.

"I have an idea." Gray stepped out of the conveyance to have a word with the driver and soon they were on their way again.

"Whatever are we doing here?" Kit asked when they pulled up in front of a familiar house on Berkley Street. Familiar because he'd been here just three nights before. The night he'd met Selene.

"Lady Harrington no doubt knows the woman if she invited her to the masquerade."

Kit's mouth fell open. It wasn't like Graham to be so intuitive, but this idea was bloody brilliant. He slapped Gray on the back in approval.

Kit practically pushed Graham out of the carriage in a hurry to get to the woman and learn the truth. Though it was late in the afternoon by the time they arrived, Lady Harrington greeted them in her dressing gown looking as if she'd just tumbled from bed. From the smile on her face, it was clear she'd not been alone in that bed.

"Gentleman. What brings you here at such an ungodly early hour?" she asked while pouring them a brandy.

Gray looked at Kit expectantly. Right. It was Kit's search. He should be the one to explain.

"As you may recall the night of the masquerade, you called on me to be of service to a woman by the name of Selene."

The woman leaned forward from her lounging position and Kit could see down the gaping gown to her rosy nipples. He looked away recalling the darker shade of Selene's. "Did she steal something of yours?" the lady inquired.

"No," Kit said at the same time Gray muttered, "His peace of mind."

"No," Kit went on. "But I feel the lady and I made a connection. When we parted, we agreed to leave things in Fate's hands as to if we would see each other again."

"But now you find yourself impatient with Fate's schedule?"

The woman said before taking a sip of her drink and licking her painted lips.

Kit smiled, glad she understood. "Yes. Very much so. If you know her direction so I might find her, I would be most grateful."

The woman nodded. "I'd like nothing more but to assist you in finding true love, but alas, I do not know who she is."

Gray moved to the edge of his seat and leaned in. "But you invited her to your masquerade. Even if she didn't remove her mask, you must be able to consult your guest list to determine who the woman is. How many Selenes could there be?"

"I'm afraid I didn't invite her. It's not uncommon for my guests to pass their invitation off to another. I've even heard of my invitations being used as payment for gambling debts, so coveted as they are. I've had to turn people away even if they held an invitation if they were not of the... proper standards as my other guests."

Kit understood that to mean if the person were not titled or beautiful.

"But Lady Selene was of those standards so you allowed her to stay even though you didn't know who she was?"

"Yes. And because I saw her innocence and her wish to have away with it. I would never hinder a woman from exploring her desires and learning what she needs in order to find her way in the world. It is quite silly that a woman is to be married off as a virgin to a man who may or may not see to her pleasure. How does one truly know what one is getting in a husband unless they've had the opportunity to try them out first?" She trailed her fingers along Graham's leg and he leaned closer to the woman.

Kit coughed and tugged at his cravat. He couldn't say he didn't agree with the woman's suggestion, but to speak it aloud was another matter.

He also knew many married couples did try things out first. That's what he supposed had happened with Hale and his duchess as well as Julian and Elaina.

Gray let out a breath and hung his head for a moment. "I

suppose we're back to combing the streets to find the woman."

Kit nodded and smiled at Lady Harrington. "Thank you for your time. We're sorry to have bothered you."

"I assure you it is never a bother to me to have such fine-looking gentleman visit," she said.

Kit and Gray stood and offered a bow. They were nearly to the door when she stopped them.

"I just realized, while I might not be able to tell you who the woman was, I might be able to determine whose invitation she used to gain entry."

"Really?" Kit came closer.

"It will take a few days for me to puzzle it out, but you see I mark each invitation with a symbol for my own knowledge. As I said some of my patrons give their invitations to those they should not. I'm able to determine who I extended the invitation to originally and make sure they do not receive one in the future."

"Very clever, my lady." Gray winked at the woman who preened at his compliment.

"I'll send word once I work out whose invitation she might have used. I know everyone else who was in attendance."

"I appreciate your help," Kit offered.

"I'll surely think of some way you can repay my kindness." Her gaze lowered over his body, stopping at a very specific body part.

"Come. There's nothing else to be done until we hear back from Lady Harrington. Let's seek other entertainments this evening."

"I would rather stay at home."

"You'll have the rest of your life to stay at home. I only have a limited time before my final friend falls into wedded bliss and I'm left alone."

"Very well… carry on."

Kit could only hope their nights of debauchery would come to an end once he found Selene.

WHILE HER BROTHER and Kit missed breakfast and had stayed out all day doing God knew what, Celia had her first caller.

Lord Timmons arrived with a modest bouquet of blush roses and a dashing smile. Celia invited him into the drawing room and noticed the man looked a bit confused. Where else would she take him?

"I wished to thank you again for the honor of dancing with you last night. It was the highlight of the ball for me," he said.

"As it was for me," she answered honestly. No other men had asked her to dance. That was fine with her. She had been much too busy comparing every man to the likeness she kept in her mind of Lord Desire.

She'd dreamed of him again last night. If she didn't find a distraction soon, she might have to visit Lady Harrington to see if the woman could tell her who he truly was.

But for now, a distraction had landed in her drawing room. And they had already fallen into an awkward silence.

"I shall ring for tea," she offered, remembering her manners.

"That won't be necessary," he said.

She nodded in agreement, though she would have rather liked to break up the uncomfortable visit. Drinking tea would give her something to do with her hands.

"Might I be so bold as to make a suggestion?" he asked.

"Of course." She relaxed slightly glad it wasn't just her who had noticed the tension.

"Perhaps if you told your footman we were not to be disturbed and then locked the door we could make use of the settee?" He raised his brows.

Celia had seen her brother and Kit do something similar when they were talking about disreputable things and wanted a rise out of her. But this was no jest. Lord Simmons was propositioning her for…

She'd wanted to take a lover, and had even considered this man, but now…

"No. I'm sorry. That won't do. I think it best that you leave."

"But I got the impression—"

"I'm sure it is my fault for giving you such an impression, but as I said, this won't do. Good day." With that she went to the door and held it open.

"Is it because you are unfamiliar with such relations?" he asked while staring at her as if looking for something. What could he…?

She was so shocked by the situation, it took her a moment to figure it out. And a longer moment to collect herself so she might respond appropriately.

"Lord Hamlin sent you here to determine if I am yet a virgin?"

He at least had the good sense to look embarrassed. She shook her head. "I assure you, I'm an experienced woman. That is not the reason I am rejecting your offer. It is that I can already tell you will not suit." With that she looked down at the unimpressive bulge in his breeches and shook her head again.

He glared as he took his leave but said nothing.

When he was gone, Celia flopped down on the settee that might have been the place she completed her second affair and let out a breath in disappointment.

She'd thought she'd wanted Lord Timmons as a lover, but when the time came to make it happen all she could think of were all the ways in which the man was not Lord Desire. Timmons had somehow disappointed her before he'd even begun. At least she was no longer in danger of anyone reporting back to Hamlin that she'd been a virgin.

And, in some way, she'd managed to lure a man to her… settee, at least. It was a step in the right direction to getting what she wanted.

She squealed in delight and called for tea.

THE NEXT MORNING, Kit entered the breakfast room at Penbrook House for the first time since he'd been ill. He couldn't spend his days thinking of Selene and the way she'd felt in his arms. That was apparently what his dreams were for.

He was hopeful Lady Harrington would have a clue for him to follow that would lead to Selene.

What an interesting story they would have to tell their children one day. He laughed when he realized they couldn't tell anyone the story of their indecent beginnings.

How he'd made love to her without knowing anything about her and utilized the most scandalous woman in the *ton* to locate her after they'd left each other without any plan to connect again.

No. Certainly not. It would be a story for them only. That is *if* he could find her. He shook away the doubt. He wouldn't stop until he located her. And then he would convince her they belonged together. He knew exactly how he wanted to convince her…

Kit was still smiling as he entered the breakfast room. His smile grew wider when he was greeted by the second most enchanting woman he'd ever known.

"Good morning to you, countess," he said to Celia. "May I say, you look even more lovely than usual this morning?"

He wasn't certain what it was that was so alluring about her today. Her dress didn't appear to be new, but the coral satin served her coloring well. Her hair was done a bit differently. A few small braids twined through the rest of her hair. This must be the newest style, for Selene's hair had been done similarly. Celia seemed to glow with some inner light. She was happy. Truly happy, not merely trying to convince everyone she was happy.

He couldn't help but wonder why.

"You may," she returned with a smile that was barely restrained. "And thank you."

Kit laughed at Celia's mischievous response and earned a bigger smile from her. Those full lips reminded him of Selene as well. Would he forever see traces of his lover in other women he knew? What torment that would be if he never found her.

"Is Gray unwell?" he asked while gesturing to the empty seat at the end of the table.

"If he is, it is because he was out last night and did not return until the wee hours of morning. I'm sure he'll be down momentarily to groan into his coffee." She laughed.

"Your brother's plight amuses you?" Kit had to admit he was relieved to have woken up at a normal hour without a pounding head and riotous stomach for once. This new life was better in so many ways and he hadn't even found a wife yet.

"Perhaps," Celia answered with the grin of a minx. "But I'm not that mercenary. I'm happy for other reasons as well." She cleared her throat as if she wished she hadn't shared so much.

Had she met someone? A tremor of jealousy wracked his body before he cast it away. He was instantly shamed by his hypocrisy. He'd come to her table thinking of another woman and yet he wanted Celia to remain alone indefinitely? Or at least until he'd married.

Forcing himself to be happy for her no matter what she said next, he asked the question he feared the answer to. "Did you meet someone?"

Her cheeks instantly colored with a blush as his fingers clenched into a fist on his thigh. The smile faded slightly and the sparkle in her eyes dimmed.

"Not exactly."

Ah. Her interest was unrequited. What a fool this man was to not see how fortunate he was to have her attentions.

"What does that mean?" he pressed. If she confided the man's name, Kit would do what he could to make sure the man deserved her. Kit would see her happy, even if it wouldn't be with him.

"It doesn't matter. He's not the source of my happiness. Well, he was a piece of it, I suppose, but I've made some decisions. I've taken the first step in my new life, and I plan to take the next this evening at the Haverstrom's ball. Even if it ends in disaster, I need to take the next step."

The room seemed to tilt. Kit reached out to grasp the edge of the table, just to be sure he didn't fall from his chair. He looked at Celia, studying her chin, her eyes, and of course her lips. He'd seen them nearly every day for years, but he was looking now for something else.

Her words... about taking another step despite the chance of disaster. It couldn't be a coincidence that Selene had used that same phrase a few nights ago after he'd made love to her. After she'd shattered his world.

Celia's lips pulled up in a soft smile, and he saw the proof he'd been searching for. Celia was Selene. He was certain of it.

He cleared his throat unsure if he should address it. What if he was wrong, or worse searching for a similarity that didn't exist because he was still drawn to Celia?

He took a steadying sip of his coffee and set it down before speaking. "I hope your next step is found with success. After all, life doesn't wait for one to be ready." He tilted his head to the side, waiting for some sign of recognition.

As risks went, this was not a large one. If she didn't respond, his words were still relevant to the topic at hand. But his suspicions were confirmed when she reacted with a soft gasp and wide brown eyes.

His lips curved up into a smile once more. Life certainly didn't wait for one to be ready. It came charging in when one least expected.

"It's a pleasure to see you again... *Selene.*"

Chapter Ten

K IT KNEW. No. He didn't just know, *he* was Lord Desire. They had… He'd… She'd… with *Kit*. Celia opened her mouth, but no words came out. Which was a good thing because at that moment Graham shuffled into the room.

"Good morning," he said, taking his seat with a groan. "Fair warning, if anyone speaks too loudly, I will graciously stab them with a fork."

Taunting her brother and risking a stabbing were the least of her concerns this morning.

She'd made love with Kit. *Kit!* The man who had abandoned her when she'd needed him most.

She'd told herself she'd forgiven him long ago after everything had turned out for the best in the end, but deep down she must have still held some animosity for his rejection because it was resurfacing now.

She swallowed loudly and a sound similar to a whimper slipped free.

"Sister? Are you well? You look quite pale."

"What?" she said, looking away from the man she'd seen naked a few nights ago to blink at her brother.

"What's wrong? Are you ill?" Gray reached out and placed a hand on her wrist. "I hope you haven't contracted what Kit and I had. It was terribly inconvenient."

"I—I'm…" She cleared her throat. She couldn't exactly speak

the truth, that she was in shock. That she'd taken her brother's best friend to her bed and done all manners of things with him there.

But Gray had given her the perfect opportunity for escape, and she grasped onto it.

"I think it would be best if I went to rest. My stomach is a bit off this morning. Please excuse me," she said and practically jumped from her seat.

"Should I summon a doctor?" Gray called after her, stopping her at the door.

"No. I'm sure I'll be fine. I just need to lie down." She met Kit's eyes briefly on her way out. He'd stood when she had as was gentlemanly and now offered a bow and winked at her.

Winked.

Memories crowded in as she rushed up the stairs so fast, she was breathless when she arrived in her room. Or perhaps it was from those memories rather than the running that caused her shortness of breath.

How had this happened?

If she hadn't stolen her brother's invitation and gone to that bloody masquerade she wouldn't be in this situation.

Except that up until a few moments ago, her time at Lady Harrington's had been the most exciting and memorable of her life. She couldn't even now force herself to regret what had happened. Even knowing it was Kit, didn't ruin the experience. In fact, it seemed to make the moment sweeter in some way.

Lord Desire was no longer a stranger. He was the man she'd made love to, wrapped up with the man she'd respected and called a friend for years.

Hadn't she asked for someone who looked like Kit? She'd described the man exactly when asked her preference. There had to be a reason for that.

But what would happen now? Now that they both knew what had transpired between them.

Would he tell Gray? Worse, would he tell Edward?

No. She was sure he wouldn't. Kit would be more at risk if Gray learned of their night together than she. And she wasn't aware of an association between Kit and Edward. She should be safe.

Perhaps Kit would agree that they would just continue on as friends and pretend the night at Lady Harrington's had never happened.

She let out a breath and hung her head. How was she supposed to pretend the night had never happened when it was the single most amazing night of her life? She couldn't.

"Are you well?" Nettie asked as she came into Celia's bedchamber. "I thought you'd gone down for breakfast already. Did you need something adjusted?" Her maid looked her up and down, no doubt witnessing the blush Celia felt creeping up her neck. "Are you ill? You're pale, but also seem flush at the same time."

"I assure you, I'm quite well. I just decided to lie down. Perhaps I woke too early."

"That doesn't sound like you? And you seemed fine when I dressed your hair this morning."

"Yes, well. Things have a tendency to change when you least expect it. But just to be safe, would you mind going to get a draught in case I'm coming down with the same head cold Gray experienced last week?"

"Oh, of course. You should get some rest."

"Yes. I'll rest. Alone." Why had she added that? Of course, she would be alone. "Thank you."

As soon as her maid left, Celia flopped on her bed and squeezed her eyes closed. She wasn't sure what to do.

But she did wonder what good would come of speaking about it. Kit had made his feelings clear many years ago when she'd begged him to marry her and he'd refused. Besides, she had her own plans for a happy future. One that involved many nights like the one she'd had with Kit, but with other adventurous men.

Yes. She would move forward with her original plan, and she

and Kit would simply go back to being friends.

She'd make sure of it.

"You don't think she could be with child, do you?" Graham said, taking his seat again. Kit's response was to spit his coffee, catching the table and part of his sleeve.

"W-What?" he sputtered.

"Celia. She's been acting strange the past few days. I even caught her humming a jaunty tune yesterday. Why is she so happy all of a sudden? Unless she has been carrying on with a man." He frowned. "This sudden illness in the *morning*... You know what kind of illness women experience in the mornings."

In truth, he hadn't been up on such matters. Not being around any other women regularly other than Celia who was most definitely not *enceinte*.

She'd been a virgin just a few days ago and he'd worn a sheath. Even if his protection had failed, they wouldn't know of any complications as of yet.

Kit glanced over his shoulder at the door where Celia had fled, but Gray thumped his fist on the table.

"If some blighter has compromised my sister, I'll have him in Hyde Park at dawn. You'll be my second," Gray continued.

Kit coughed. It would be difficult to be Gray's second while at the same time being his opponent. Not that it would ever come to that. At least he didn't think so.

He had no plans to tell Gray what had happened between Celia and himself. Surely Celia wouldn't speak of the matter with her brother. Still...

"I would remind you of our vow never to dual," Kit pointed out.

"We vowed never to dual with each other."

"Right. But, why would you automatically jump to the conclusion that a pregnancy would be a bad thing?"

"I guess you're right. So long as the man stands up and offers for her quickly."

Now Kit's stomach was unsettled as well. The thought of having to marry her because he'd…

Warmth washed over him as he realized the position he was in. All his youth was spent hoping he'd not get caught in a compromising position and forced into marriage. But now getting married was his goal. And if he could have Celia…

If she was carrying his child? His heart pounded at the thought and he knew well it wasn't from fear but rather excitement. Except, he wouldn't want her to accept him because she was trapped. She hadn't wanted him years ago. What had changed just because they'd spent the night together? The most incredible night of his life. He'd thought as much before he knew Selene was Celia. Now he understood why he'd felt such a strong connection to her that night.

If she married him…

"She could get married and have a happy life with the right man." Was he the right man? "I'm sure everything will be fine," he added though he didn't know how she felt about this. He needed to speak to her.

"Oh, God." Gray dropped his fork. "What if it's something else? Something serious? She's all the family I have left. While I wasn't sorry to see my father go, I'd miss Celia immensely."

"As would I. I remember what it was like when she was married. Breakfasts weren't the same without her." Nothing had been the same without her. He'd wanted her and she'd rejected him. She'd chosen money over him. Gray had nearly killed him when he'd returned to explain that Celia had refused his offer of marriage in order to go forward with her marriage to Hamlin. There was only one reason a woman would choose a man of that age as her husband. Money.

Hamlin's wealth had won out over Kit's heart.

In the past four years, he'd come to realize she'd made the

only choice that offered security at the time. But it still stung when he remembered how hurt he'd been.

Now, however, things were different.

"You know I would marry her," Kit said.

Gray frowned at his plate and Kit didn't think his friend was upset with his rasher of bacon. They way his shoulders hunched, Kit would almost think him guilty of something.

"You would make her a fine husband. I'm sorry things didn't…work out before." He cleared his throat before changing the subject. "Celia doesn't think I know, but she's been out in society. She's attended a *ball*," he said solemnly. As if she were headed to the gallows instead.

"She mentioned she was going to do so. She seemed very excited about it actually." She certainly didn't seem very excited after realizing what had happened between them. Rather unsettled, actually.

Could it be she was repulsed to find out her *Lord Desire* was actually him? She was always pleasant. They even flirted. While she'd rejected his offer years ago and chosen Lord Hamlin over him, Kit had always gotten the impression she'd liked him. At least as a friend.

He definitely needed to speak to her.

Now was preferable. He excused himself when breakfast was over saying he had things he needed to see to at home. He knew Gray would leave shortly for his daily ride in the park.

Once Kit was out of the house, he turned toward the mews and sneaked back into the house through the servant's entrance as he and Gray had done many times while the old marquess was still alive.

Being a friend of the family had its benefits. Specifically, in knowing which bedchamber belonged to Celia. He couldn't linger in the hall for very long. He didn't want to have to explain himself to Graham before he'd managed to understand the situation himself.

At her door, he paused, debating whether to knock. To do so

would grant her the opportunity to send him away, and he had too many questions to let them go unanswered.

Instead of knocking, he listened for a moment and then entered.

CHAPTER ELEVEN

CELIA STOOD STARING out her window as she had for the last quarter hour.

It hadn't taken long for her to realize that not speaking of it would never do. Of course, she and Kit would have to settle things between them. They'd just need to make sure no one else found out. Especially Graham.

She'd wanted an adventure and now her night of recklessness had led her to this place where she'd had sex with her brother's best friend. Of all the men in all the world, how had he ended up in that room—in that bed—with her?

She'd requested someone tall, blond and green-eyed and Lady Harrington had delivered Celia's every desire.

It just happened that Celia's every desire had been Kit.

A few more minutes had passed by, but Celia was no closer to figuring out what to do now. How would she get Kit alone to speak to him without alerting her brother?

Her door swung open. She assumed it would be Gray coming to check on her—though he normally knocked first. She turned to remind him what happened when he forgot to knock and how the last time he'd wished to have his eyes burned out. But it wasn't her brother who'd barged in.

"What are you doing in here?" she asked looking about the room as if someone was going to jump out from behind the drapes and force them into marriage.

He didn't answer, instead he strode to the door connecting her maid's chambers to hers and locked the door. Nettie was still out on an errand and wouldn't disturb Celia since she thought she was resting.

"I think we should talk about what happened," he said in a steady voice that unnerved her. How could he sound so casual when just days ago they'd seen each other naked?

Not just naked but crying out in passion.

Perhaps this was how it was when one had numerous partners. She would have to learn how to face her lovers if ever she wanted to have more of them.

She closed her eyes briefly wishing away her blush and faced him.

"Talk?" She held in a groan. She agreed that was what needed to happen to clear the air, but at the same time it was the very thing she didn't want to do.

It wouldn't help preserve her most perfect memory to drudge it up and view it through the filter of Kit's commentary.

"Please no. I'm sure from your perspective our time together was quickly forgotten as any other liaison, while for me—in my limited experience—it was perfect. I'd beg you not ruin it or make jokes." She didn't mind begging. This was too important.

He smiled and rested his hand on her shoulder. It soothed and excited her.

"No doubt you think I have vast knowledge of such things. Gray and our friends have shared more than we ought over the years in your presence. But while my carnal wisdom far exceeds yours, it is not as substantial as everyone has assumed. Even still, whether my experiences boast hundreds of women or the mere twelve that would actually be true, I can promise you this; our night together was just as perfect for me."

She looked at him, her gaze narrowed as she searched for proof he was appeasing her. She knew him well enough to know when he was teasing.

"Do you mean it?" she pushed and watched again.

"I do. If you recall, it was I who suggested we continue our acquaintance at the masquerade. Why would I do such a thing with a poor lover?"

This was reasonable, but still she doubted his words.

"I'm to believe a bumbling virgin somehow appealed to a man who's slept with eleven other more experienced women?"

"I hope you will believe it, for it's the truth. I know our relationship to date has been mostly jokes and flirting, but please know I have never had a more amazing night than the one I spent with you."

He was being sincere. He would have given up by now if not. Kit wasn't patient enough to keep going with a ruse once he was had.

She swallowed and stepped closer. "Please don't think I'm looking for compliments if I ask, but why? What made me different from any of the others?"

He smiled and also took a step closer. "Mostly it was the way you touched me. The comfort between us to be free with one another. I had thought it was the masks, as you said they gave us the freedom to be uninhibited, but now I think on some level, I must have felt connected to you so deeply because it was *you*."

As explanations went, that was possibly the worst. She would have preferred being alluring or mysterious. But *comfortable*?

"Very well, it's good I wasn't pressing for compliments. To think I remind you of your favorite chair. Comfortable." She rolled her eyes. "Thank you for your visit and explanation. Please go now."

He laughed but didn't turn to leave. "It's possible I didn't explain it very well if this is your reaction."

"More than possible. Likely."

"Yes. Likely. May I try again before you kick me out?" He crossed his arms and she was sure she'd not be able to remove him. Still, she had no doubt if she asked him to leave, he would oblige her wishes. He'd always been respectful.

Her precious memories of their night together were already

in jeopardy, there was no saving them now. She gestured that he should continue.

"While I won't downplay my sexual cravings, I also have deeper needs that I hope to satisfy when I'm with a woman. I long to be held and touched. To connect with someone in more than just a sexual way. However, many of my other encounters lacked simple touch. Including one such coupling where the only parts that touched were…" He held up his hand to stop himself and shook his head.

"Never mind, that's not relevant except to say that the other night with you it fed *all* of my needs completely. Both the carnal, sexual beast within, as well as the man who just wants some form of contact with another person."

She reached out and took his hand, to offer support. He was sharing something very personal and she could see he was nervous to do so. She wasn't prepared for him to take her hand and pull her a step closer. She definitely wasn't expecting him to put her fingers to his lips where he placed a hot kiss that sent a shiver of anticipation down her spine.

"I can't let it go without saying it was also special because of the gift you gave me." He tilted his head. "You were a virgin?"

It was a question, though he must have known by her lack of experience it was true.

"You lied when you said you'd never been married," he said.

She nodded. "Yes." Could she trust this man with her secret? Her very livelihood was at stake. She need only consider the question for a second before she determined she could trust him.

"Hamlin was unable to consummate our marriage."

"I still can't believe you chose him over—"

"*Chose* him?" she screeched and then lowered her voice. Was he mad? "I had no *choice* at all." Thanks to this man who'd let her down when she'd needed him most.

"I'm sure it seemed that way."

She held up her hand. This argument served no purpose. What was done was done. They needed to figure out what to do now. She cleared her throat and tried again to explain. "While I sought out the adventure that led to us sleeping together, I did have another motive for hiding my identity. You see the new Lord Hamlin, Arthur's grandson has threatened to take the matter to the House of Lords. He expected the marriage was not legitimate and therefore I should not retain my settlements. If the lords determine there is merit to his case, I could be forced into an examination that would have proven his claim. So, you see…"

"You needed to expend with your virtue as quickly as possible."

She nodded sadly while he cursed Edward's name quite inventively. Eventually he settled and came back to stand before her.

"Do you regret what happened between us, Celia?" It was the first time he'd spoken her name in a long time. Usually, he addressed her only as *Countess*. She found she missed hearing her name on his lips and disliked the distance between them when he used the cold title.

"No. It was the most wonderful night of my life. I could never regret it. It was everything I could have hoped for. Lady Harrington did me a great service when she selected you as my first lover. And I am glad it was you I chose to give my virginity to."

He tilted his head to the side. "She mentioned you had requested someone tall and blond with kind eyes—green eyes. Why did you ask for those specifications?"

She felt frozen as he looked at her expectantly. Could he see the answer in her eyes? That she'd thought of him when she'd been asked her preference in a man.

"I see." His smile turned knowing. *Damn and blast.*

She covered her face and turned away. "Please leave now. Spare me whatever dignity I may have left."

Of course, he didn't leave. Instead, he stepped close behind her and wound his arms around her waist. His large body pressed against hers and she felt the hardness of him everywhere, especially in the one place where his hardness was most arousing.

"Please don't be embarrassed. I am humbled and honored that it was me who was able to give you the most wonderful evening. We are aligned in that. And I thank you for your precious gift despite the lewd reason you felt you needed to dispense with it." He placed a kiss against the back of her neck and her breath caught at the memory. "If I'd been given a choice in selecting a partner, I would have chosen you."

He would have chosen her?

Another kiss made her blood heat and her body came alive at the memory of what this man's lips could do to her. But they shouldn't.

His admission gave her the courage to turn and face him.

"Kit?" she whispered.

"Yes?"

"What happens now?" She had wanted to take a lover. At the time she'd enacted this plan she hadn't been sure what it entailed, but now she hoped Kit might be interested in taking up that position.

"We should marry," he said.

Marry? The word tumbled through her mind absently. Almost as if she'd never heard it before. When it finally settled, she pulled away.

"Marry? *Why?*"

"I deflowered you."

"I'm a widow. I planned to take a lover, not settle with another husband. I want to experience… things."

"I assure you we will experience many things if you become my wife." He brushed his fingers along her temple causing another shiver.

"But that would be it. Just you. Forever. Until I die."

"Yes. They specifically state that in the vows." He gave a quick nod.

"No. I had that already."

He cleared his throat. "Forgive me for pointing out that you did *not* have that. You were married for a year and were still a virgin until two nights ago. I'm glad for it, don't get me wrong, but you did not experience the joys of a real marriage with Hamlin."

"And you know these joys? You, the bachelor who goes out nightly with my brother to experience all sorts of debauchery?"

"We also have married friends, so I know there is something to be said in having a partner who knows you better than anyone. There's freedom in knowing they want to please you as much as you wish to please them. To know they are yours and you are theirs. No, I haven't experienced it, but I long for it. As I told you before, I plan to take a wife this season. You and I obviously suit. Please be my wife."

"No," she said rather abruptly and shook her head. "I want adventure. I want lovers and to be open to do whatever I wish. With whomever I want. I want freedom."

She tried not to focus on the fact that as of right now, Kit was the man she wanted most. How he made her heart pound and heat pool in her most intimate places, made her consider for a moment the thought of being in his bed each night.

But surely, she would feel the same with another man as soon as she found one.

And she would find one, because she would not marry Kit now that *he* wanted to marry. Not when he'd rejected her when she'd needed him.

CHAPTER TWELVE

KIT GLARED AT the woman in front of him. If she thought he was going to walk away and let her carry on with every man in the *ton,* she was mistaken.

Except, what could he do? Tell her brother? That option would not only make him lose Celia but possibly his life as well if their vow against dueling was reconsidered.

She stepped closer and looked up at him through those long, dark lashes and his body responded despite having heard her plan to take other lovers. Not to mention the way she'd rejected his proposal yet again, without even a moment's consideration. *Would his heart survive this woman?*

"Would you be interested in being my lover?" she asked, her voice came out steady but the way her gaze flickered away from his spoke of her insecurity. He'd given her an education on making love, and she'd wrapped the power of that knowledge around her like a cloak, yet she still wasn't sure.

His eyes went wide. "You want me to be your *lover?*" Once his mind managed to focus on her actual words, he was both flattered and frustrated.

She nodded and leaned up on her tiptoes to kiss his chin. With his height and his unpreparedness, that was all she could reach.

She pulled away and looked at him, her brows pulled down. "I see. I'm only good enough to be a wife or a fake French woman at a party, you don't truly want *me*."

He swallowed and shook his head. "That's not it at all. I'm just having a hard time following. I've compromised you and offered marriage, but you turned that down and instead suggested I treat you as a mistress. Is that correct?"

Her eyes narrowed in a glare. "There's no need to mock me, Kit. Do I want something so different than what men search the city for each night?"

He put his hand up in surrender. He was making a complete hash of the situation. Partly because he expected he'd wake up at any moment and realize it was all a dream.

She only wanted him as a lover. Not a husband. And damn it if he wouldn't take what he could get because he wanted her however he could have her, and even more, wanted to make sure she didn't go out and find a legion of men to take to her bed.

"Yes." There, he'd finally said it. Except it was the incorrect response for what she'd just asked. He winced and tried again. "I mean, no, it's not different. Though I'll remind you I don't find someone new every night. Not that it's relevant to the topic, but *yes*, I want to be your—for Christ's sake."

He gave up on talking and bent down to take her lips with his. His attack was a bit aggressive but Celia responded in kind, crushing her mouth to his and opening so he could sweep his tongue in and tangle with hers.

The taste of her paired with chocolate and bacon drew a groan from his chest. He was kissing Celia. He was kissing Selene. The two combined were nearly too much to bear.

Of course, he now knew he'd already kissed and done more with Celia at the masquerade, but this was different. It was Celia. He pulled away to look at her. A large smile pulling up his lips that were wet from her mouth.

"I know I haven't done well with words recently, but I just need to say how happy I am that you picked me."

"It wasn't as if there is a long line of other men for me to choose from."

"I'm going to kiss you again and pretend I wasn't your only option."

He stole the laugh from her lips when their mouths crushed together again. He was still grappling with the possibility he'd wake up soon when he felt her hands move to his coat and push it over his shoulders.

She'd wanted a lover. Apparently, they were starting immediately. He caught up quickly, helping her with his waistcoat and shirt. Then he spun her around so he could unbutton her gown while she laughed.

"I was beginning to worry you were too shocked you'd be useless for my needs." She pulled the pins from her hair, letting it fall over her skin like dark silk.

"I'm still surprised, but not so much so that I'm willing to miss a minute of this." He kissed her neck as he pushed her gown down to her hips. Another shove and it dropped to her feet. Her chemise had slipped off one shoulder and he trailed his kisses along the bared flesh while his arms wrapped around her from behind, fondling her breasts through the thin fabric.

"I should have worn something more alluring, but how was I to know I'd be doing this? With you? Right after breakfast?" she said.

"I surely didn't."

She turned to face him and he stared as she slid the chemise over the other shoulder and let it slide to the floor.

"God, Celia. You're so beautiful. Seeing you in the light of day... You don't need to wear anything to be more perfect than anyone I've ever seen."

Her cheeks turned an enticing shade of pink and her shoulders straightened slightly. She seemed to be settling into her confidence and was all the more beautiful for it. But then she glanced at the windows where the morning sun was streaming in through the gauzy curtains.

"It is very bright," she said, her earlier confidence receding.

"It certainly helps me to see you more clearly. I feel as though

I was cheated the other night in the dim room. I missed out on seeing the dusting of freckles on your shoulders. And the lovely color of your nipples that only sunshine could reveal so perfectly." He bent to take said nipple into his mouth and moaned in pleasure. "You are divine."

"And you are still wearing boots and trousers." She wiggled her fingers at his breeches and pouted adorably.

"Gracious, you must think me the worst lover you've ever had," he teased.

She laughed as he tugged off his boots and went to work on his falls.

"You are my worst, but…" she placed a finger absently on her lips—swollen from his kisses and said, "You are also my most magnificent."

"Ah. Then I'll do my best to hold my place."

She smiled and sat on the edge of the bed as he stalked closer. Then froze. And cursed.

"What is it? What's wrong?"

"I came here for breakfast, so of course I didn't bring any protection with me. I only take a sheath when there's a chance I might meet a woman. Not when I'm having toast and coffee with my friend and his sister."

"Oh." She frowned and then bit her bottom lip. "Is there something else we can do? To make sure we don't have to worry about… anything."

He smiled at her eagerness. She'd been a shy virgin the night of the party and while she'd explored that night with him, it was clear she was now more comfortable with her body—and his—by the way her fingers trailed over his side.

He wanted her. He'd always wanted her. Back when he'd been barely a man, before she'd wed Hamlin, he'd hoped to claim her as his wife one day.

Even now he didn't know if being her lover would be enough for his tattered heart. But like always, he was willing to take whatever she offered.

And now she was offering her body and he wouldn't miss the opportunity to win her heart.

"We have hands," he answered her question while sliding his hands across her breasts, smiling when her nipples hardened in response to his touch. "We also have mouths." He kissed her on the lips before placing other kisses along her neck to that place by her ear that made her sigh with desire.

Both his hands and his mouth could bring her great pleasure, but he wanted to be inside her. To claim her as his for whatever period of time she'd allow. Perhaps if he left her before his release… Except that method didn't always work. If only he'd thought to bring—

"Gray."

Celia winced as one would expect when the man kissing her breasts called out her brother's name.

"Gray would most likely have letters," he explained. "I could sneak into his room and get one."

"Yes." She practically shoved him out of bed. "Of course. That's brilliant. And he's surely left for his ride by now."

"What if one of the servants sees me?"

She touched him then curved her fingers around his length to stroke. "Make sure they don't."

After putting himself to rights, Kit peeked out the door in both directions before hurrying down the hall. He'd never realized how much noise a man of his size could make just by walking quickly. Fortunately, no one saw him.

He pushed open the door and went to the stand beside Graham's bed, where such things were kept. Nothing. Around to the stand on the other side of the bed, he found what he was after. He tucked it in his jacket and was halfway to the door when the inner door opened and James, Gray's valet, stepped in, being the attentive servant he was. Damn.

"My lord. Is there something you needed? I believe Lord Penbrook is already out for his ride."

"Ah, yes. He is. He asked me to stop and pick something up

for him. Something of a delicate nature." Kit patted his coat pocket.

James frowned. "Very well. I'll replenish his necessaries immediately."

"You're a good man." Kit paused at the door. Should he say something to ensure the valet's silence or would requesting silence force James to mention it to Gray when otherwise he would just chalk the matter up to their normal roguish behavior?

Deciding not to say anything else, Kit left the room and once he felt sure the door wasn't going to reopen, he turned in the opposite direction to go back to the willing woman waiting for him.

He entered and held up the vellum. "Now, where were we?"

He gazed upon the naked woman stretched across the bed and nearly came undone. The sun touched her body in places he wanted to press his lips.

All thought of that was pushed aside when she spread her legs and nodded. "I believe you were right here."

For being new to the act of sex, she certainly knew what to say to make his blood run hot. His fingers fumbled with the sheath and he cursed once until it was secured in place and he knelt between her thighs.

"Celia?" he whispered, quietly confirming her approval. The damage had already been done a few nights ago, but he would still make sure this was what she wanted. He couldn't bear regret from either of them when it was over.

"Please," she said in a begging tone. Her hips came up from the mattress and her heat brushed against him where he already burned.

It was an easy thing for him to push inside her fully. Without the need for care that he'd hurt her, he pulled out and thrust home again, harder.

"Oh!" she said and he stopped instantly, his back quivering from the effort of waiting.

"What? Have I hurt you?"

"No. That's just it. There is no pain at all this time. I thought it was good the other night, but now…"

He smiled and kissed her. "It's exquisite."

"Yes." She pulled him closer, her fingernails biting into his flesh. "More," she demanded and he was quick to follow her command. After all, he was completely hers.

And for the moment, at least, she was his as well.

Kit was perfect and patient. He gave her what she asked for while also exploring other things. Always asking if she liked what he was doing. To which the answer was always undeniably yes.

He was a wonderful lover. Not that she had anyone to compare him to. But he'd brought her to completion more than once before taking his own release. And then teasing another orgasm from her with his talented fingers.

In addition to his unselfishness and skill, she was comfortable with him and he definitely suited her needs. She also cared for him. He was fun to be with and made her laugh during those times of quiet bliss after he'd thoroughly wrecked her with passion.

She pressed her lips together and shook her head. No. She would do well not to think about him for anything but physical pleasure. She'd once hoped he'd be her hero and her husband. But he'd let her down.

Back then she hadn't had much time to think things through, but she'd known she didn't want anyone else but him. She knew she could find happiness as his wife, but he hadn't wanted her.

It wasn't a surprise that a then twenty-year-old young man wouldn't want a wife. Not when he had wild oats to sow. Still, she'd thought he would be willing to put that aside to save her from a marriage she thought would be horrible.

Fortunately, it hadn't been as bad as she'd expected, but at the time she'd reached out to Kit for help and he'd refused.

She'd forgiven him for his abandonment. She'd welcomed his friendship, but this was beyond friendship. Could she take him to her bed but keep him from her heart?

He shifted and kissed her shoulder. His warm body next to her was almost as pleasurable as the orgasm. She smiled and kissed him, earning a soft moan from him. He moved closer and she felt his growing hardness against her hip.

Unable to resist, she locked down her heart and pulled him near.

"Now. Show me how to use my hands and mouth to pleasure a man," she said in her most seductive voice.

"Oh, the demands you put upon your lovers, my lady. But alas, I shall do my best to fulfill my duty."

They laughed easily at his jest, but quickly their mirth faded once more to desire.

CHAPTER THIRTEEN

ONE OF THE things Kit most looked forward to in having a wife were those lazy moments after sex. The binds of marriage would grant him the freedom to spend as long as he wanted with his wife in their bedroom without the threat of scandal.

Generally, women were quick to send a man on his way after they had received their pleasure so they wouldn't be caught together. And when they weren't, he was the one who was eager to go.

But no one had ever been Celia. Being friends, they could lie next to each other and talk and laugh in the same manner they did at the breakfast table each morning. Though unlike their breakfasts he was able to feast on her nakedness instead of a rasher of bacon.

Unfortunately, the concern of being caught together eventually slithered in. Made worse by who exactly might catch them. He had a friendship at stake if they were found together.

There was an unspoken rule among men that one didn't dally with a friend's sister. For the most part that generally pertained to younger sisters, not older widows, but still, the rule was clear.

He didn't want to leave her, but he couldn't stay. With a sigh, he kissed her quickly. "I must go. Gray will return soon. If he catches me with you, I don't think he'd even bother with meeting me in the park, he'd just shoot me dead where I stand."

"Ridiculous. Shouldn't I have a say in what I do in my bed?" She stood and tugged up her chemise.

He was momentarily distracted by the sight but forced himself to continue. "Yes. Except your bed, I might point out, is in his home."

"I suppose reminding him he'd never have afforded to keep his home if not for my marrying Hamlin wouldn't serve to aid my case?"

"Probably not. He's a brother after all. While I don't know what that is like myself, I know the man takes the job quite seriously."

She had stopped moving and was standing there holding her dress.

"What is it?"

"I must ask for your discretion and not just with Gray."

"Of course. I would never tell any of my friends, they would just use the information as leverage and threaten to tell Gray if I didn't do their bidding."

She shook her head. "No. Not just that we were together, but that I was... a virgin."

He tilted his head, not understanding why that would be a dishonorable thing in comparison to sleeping with a complete stranger.

"As I said earlier, Edward—Lord Hamlin—has made threats to my settlement. He's certain my marriage to Arthur was not consummated, making the contract void. As you are well aware, he is correct, but Arthur wanted me to have that money regardless of what happened or rather didn't happen on our wedding night."

"What happens between a man and his wife is private. How does he plan to prove such a thing?" He frowned when he remembered her mention of an examination.

Kit felt his face heat with fury as his hands tightened into fists. "He thinks to bring such a thing before the Lords and have you forced into such an indignity? I'll not have it. I'll tell him you were knowledgeable about such things when I took you to my bed."

"You can't do that either, not just because it is a lie, but because my reputation would be ruined if the entire House of Lords knew I slept with you at Lady Harrington's party."

"Celia, you cannot have it both ways. You can't plan to take random lovers and keep a pristine reputation."

"Most of society will happily look the other way so long as it's not spoken of. Widows are expected to have a bit of fun, they must keep the details private."

"Then what do you plan to do?"

"Nothing. I doubt anything will come of it. Edward will realize it is dishonorable to call a lady's honor to question and give up."

"Your brother once mentioned the size of your settlement. Depending on Edward's situation, I doubt he will be eager to give up as easily as you hope."

Celia let out a breath and shook her head. "If it comes to it and an examination is required, I'll not be found a virgin."

"The man should rot. You need to tell Gray."

"No. You know how he will react. As you just said, he takes his job of protector much too seriously."

"It is his duty."

Celia nodded. "I shouldn't be so put out with him. As brothers go, he's not so bad. He doesn't run up large tabs at the gambling tables and leave them for me to cover. He hasn't sent me off to some cottage in the far reaches of the wilderness to get away from me."

"He loves you, even if he enjoys taunting you entirely too much. He will want to protect you."

"Is it so bad that I wish to protect him as well?" Celia let out a breath. "I know he loves me. Even though he teases me mercilessly."

"You give as much as you get. That's why you'll get no defense of me." He winked to let her know he was joking. They were quiet as he helped her dress and finished buttoning his waistcoat. "You need to tell him what Lord Hamlin has said to you so he's prepared."

Celia nodded and offered a strained smile.

"Will you attend the Addingshire Ball tonight?" she asked as she pinned up her hair. Seeing her neck exposed, he couldn't help but to place a kiss there and watch her smile in the mirror.

"I was planning to, but now I'm not sure. I mean, things have changed in my situation." He had no desire to search for a wife so soon after leaving Celia's bed.

She turned to look at him. "Not permanently though. This arrangement between us is temporary."

He knew her plans for having a lover only, but hearing her confirm them now caused a painful twisting in his stomach. She didn't want to marry. He could take relief in knowing it wasn't him specifically, but that she didn't want to marry anyone. But the rejection felt oddly the same as it had the last time he'd experienced it. He had to wonder if at least part of the reason was because she thought him unable to keep her in the luxury she had from Hamlin's settlement. She'd chosen wealth once, it served it would still be a factor today.

He would be wise to remember Celia would never be his wife. Which made his situation more dire. If he could find a woman he cared for, it might not hurt so much when Celia cast him aside.

"You're right." He pushed a brittle smile to his lips. He'd wanted to find a wife. Now it was as if he *needed* to find one. "Yes, I will attend."

"Then I shall see you there." She nodded once.

"You're going?"

"Yes. My situation is not permanent either. I planned to go to the ball to find a lover and while I have one currently, you might snatch up a bride tonight and then I'll be on the hunt for someone else. I might as well see who interests me so I'm prepared when the time comes. Besides, this is my first step. Remember?"

"Then, yes, I'll see you there. Will you save a waltz for me?"

"If you haven't already promised them away to the beautiful young ladies in attendance."

"I already know no one will entice me as much as you, Celia."

"Then the first waltz is yours."

CELIA ENTERED THE home on Bolton Street on Kit's arm. He looked incredibly handsome in his formal attire, with a sash of tartan across his wide chest. She'd rarely seen his clothing while still crisp and clean. Generally, she saw Kit in the mornings after a rough night of drink and whatever else they'd gotten up to.

But this Kit was a welcome sight.

When he'd suggested they attend together, she'd considered refusing so not to give anyone the wrong impression. However now, she welcomed having a friend by her side.

He assured her it wasn't uncommon for a friend to escort a sister of another friend. Whether that was true or not, it was too late as they had arrived.

Once they were announced, they picked up a glass of refreshment from a passing footman and stood out of the way to observe and formulate a plan. Except he was looking at her instead of the room full of guests.

"What is it?" she asked.

"You're absolutely lovely."

"As you've said four times already. Not that I mind hearing it a fifth time, mind you, but you're supposed to be looking for your future viscountess."

"Seems a waste when there's a perfectly good countess right here not being utilized."

"You utilized me so well this morning, it's a wonder I was able to make it down the stairs."

They laughed at her lewd joke and turned to the crowd. Kit waved and a couple headed in their direction with bright smiles on their faces.

The Duke of Roxburghe bowed at the same time Celia curtsied.

"Celia, it's a treat to see you here this evening. You remember my wife, Gia," the duke said. It was still strange to think of Hale as a married man. She'd once seen him naked as the day he was born after he'd lost his clothing at one of Graham's games.

"Of course, it's so good to see you again, Your Grace," Celia addressed his wife.

"Please, Gia is fine."

"What brings you all the way from Scotland? I didn't think you cared much for the Season any longer," Kit said.

Celia knew the duke had hated the country, at least until he had someone to enjoy it with.

"My father is to be wed, so we decided to attend a few events while we were in town."

"Is Julian here as well?" Celia looked around the room.

"Nay. He and Elaina are expected to arrive back from Egypt in a few weeks with their little one," Hale said.

She knew her brother's friends well. Oddly enough, she'd always thought of Hale and Julian in a similar way as her brother. It was only Kit who had tempted her.

"I still can't see Julian digging about in the desert. He was always so tidy," Kit said earning a smile from everyone. Celia liked his easy charm. It would do him well in finding a wife.

The thought caused a slight twinge in her stomach. When he married, she would lose him. While she knew he would not be unfaithful to a wife and would therefore no longer be her lover, she now realized that because of their current relationship, she would most likely lose his friendship as well.

What wife would allow her husband to be friends with a previous lover?

The orchestra began playing the beginning notes of a waltz.

"I believe this is my dance," Kit said, holding out his elbow for Celia.

She took his arm with a smile. For now, he was hers. Despite what she'd said, he was unlikely to find a bride tonight. While she didn't want to waylay his plans to marry, she did hope she had a little more time with him first.

A hush of whispers seemed to follow them as they moved, but Celia didn't hear any specific comments. She grew nervous being in front of everyone. What if they were staring at her? She fought the urge to touch the spot on her face. Was everyone wondering why someone as dashing as Christopher Sinclair, Viscount Stormont, was dancing with a woman with a large mark on her face?

Her hand brushed over her temple. She had asked Nettie to do her hair in a way to help hide the spot, but now she felt exposed.

"Celia, I swear to you upon pain of death, if you touch that birthmark again, I'll carry you from the room and take you somewhere to give you a good spanking," Kit said sternly.

"Hmm…" She tilted her head to the side thinking over why that threat didn't seem much like a threat at all.

Kit's eyes darkened with lust. "Now you've made me want to carry you from the room regardless to explore what put that look on your face."

She smiled and glanced about her. No one was looking at Celia at all, and she was happy for it. It was easy enough to ignore the people surrounding the dance floor as Kit whirled her around the room.

She didn't know those people nor did she much care what they thought of her.

As Arthur had told her once, life was much too short to spend it in fear of doing what one wanted to do.

"The things one most regrets at the end of their life are the things one didn't have the courage to do."

"What was that?" Kit asked, causing her to realize she'd said it out loud.

"I'm glad you're here for the first step of my journey."

He smiled and twirled her once again.

Chapter Fourteen

T HE NEXT MORNING, when Kit returned to his home after having breakfast with Gray and Celia, he received a letter from Lady Harrington.

Dear Friend,

I've deduced that your Lady Selene most likely used Lord Penbrook's invitation as he was not in attendance, yet his invitation was produced for entry.

Might I suggest you ask him who he might have given it to?

I wish you luck in your quest of finding the lady.

Your faithful servant,
Lady H

Kit chuckled at the woman's use of the word *faithful* and put the note aside to peruse the other invitations he'd received. More than he usually received. Perhaps his attendance with Celia had improved his standing with the ladies of the *ton*.

The more balls he attended, the more likely he was to meet someone who might entice him. Hopefully someone who enticed him more than Celia. Or at least as much.

What if he ended up with a woman who paled in comparison to Celia and he forever compared his poor wife to the woman who wouldn't have him?

He shook that thought away and smiled at the knowledge that if he hadn't figured out who Lady Selene was by now, he surely would have known after receiving the news from Lady Harrington.

He probably wouldn't even have needed to petition Gray on who he'd given his invitation to. Just knowing it originated from Penbrook House would have been the clue Kit would've needed to bring him to Celia.

He would have found her after all. Fate had interceded and brought them together as he'd hoped. He just had to hope Fate had other plans in store for them.

Rather than confuse people as to if they were courting, Celia had suggested they meet at the ball instead of arriving together as they had the night before. From his place in the ballroom, he was able to see the interest in the other men's eyes as she descended the stairs. An angel coming down to visit Earth in a gown of scarlet.

He was not the first to procure a dance, but he was able to secure the most coveted position of dancing with her and taking her into dinner. It meant, however, he had to wait for his turn and he found himself impatient to put his hands on her.

To distract himself, he danced with a few other women. Women he'd known already. He couldn't help but notice the mamas on the edges of the room with their young daughters who attempted to catch his attention.

He didn't know what exactly he wanted in a wife, but he was quite sure a young girl wouldn't do. He couldn't spend his days with his home filled with giggling and inane chatter.

Of course, he knew a young wife would not stay young and would mature, but surely, he wasn't the one cut out to assist with that. He'd rather have someone already matured.

His gaze caught Celia's and the way she licked her lips had him wanting to take her into the nearest room and make love to her.

He patted his jacket where he kept a sheath—not to be found without one ever again—and smiled.

"I WONDER IF I might take you outside for some air, countess. You seem rather heated," Kit whispered from behind Celia. She could feel the heat of his body as he stood so close.

She may not have been overheated previously, but she was becoming so now. Which she knew was the rake's intention.

"That would be lovely. Thank you." He stepped to her side and offered his arm. She took it and allowed him to lead her out onto the balcony.

After a quick glance around to make sure no one would notice, he spirited her down the stone stairs and into the darkness of the gardens.

"Wherever are you taking me?" she asked, feigning innocence.

He smiled. "As if you care so long as it ends with your skirts around your waist and me buried deep inside you."

She laughed, unable to offer the charade of offence at his lewd suggestion. She was already damp for him and his plans sounded like heaven. She'd had him after breakfast that morning, but she needed him again.

"I find the more I'm with you the more I want. Is that how it is with everyone?"

"No. I can't help but think of you throughout the day. And when I might be able to taste you again."

"I squirm in my bed at night longing for you. I have—" No, she surely couldn't tell him that.

"Have you touched yourself down there while thinking of me?" He asked as if he'd heard her thoughts.

She nodded hoping the shadows hid her blush.

"I have as well," he confided without the least bit of shame. "Tell me what you thought of."

"I couldn't possibly."

"You can and if you do, I very well may do it." He placed a

kiss below and slightly behind her ear where she'd thought of him kissing her last night.

"That," she admitted. "You kissing me there in that spot. But moving lower and lower until… Until…"

"I was kissing you between your legs like I did yesterday morning."

"Oh yes. Tell me what you thought of when you pleasured yourself. I may even do it."

He growled into her neck. "I'm going to have to start carrying French letters in all my available pockets. Perhaps I'll have my valet sew extra pockets for just such a thing so I'll have plenty of sheaths with me."

He set her on a low wall and tossed her skirts up before kneeling to lick her in the place that made her cry out. His fingers tightened on her thighs, a silent reminder she wasn't in her bedchamber but a garden where others might be near and could hear them.

Staying quiet was almost too much effort, but she managed to crest in her pleasure without screaming or making so much as a whimper. There was nothing, however, to be done for her harsh breathing except to press her face into Kit's jacket and wait until it slowed.

But instead of giving her a moment to recover, he was standing and pressing inside her. Taking her orgasm higher still instead of allowing it to fade into the mist of the garden around them.

"You didn't tell me what you thought of," she reminded him. His face was caught in a bit of light coming from the house and she saw him falter and then shake his head. "Please."

He paused and let his head fall back. "Very well. Can you stand?"

She wasn't certain. "I may manage to stand, but walking is beyond me," she answered.

He lifted her down from the wall and spun her to face it. "You can support yourself by leaning on the wall."

She did as he said, unsure of his plan until she felt the night air on her backside when he raised her skirts again. Then he was there in that place but from a completely different angle that filled her in a completely different but exquisite way.

From this position he was far better suited to thrust into her, deeper than he'd ever been. His large hands spanned her waist pulling her back to meet each thrust. She quickly caught onto the rhythm and was able to keep up with his tempo. They were quickly swept away by their pursuit to desire. It didn't take long at all for both of them to find it.

"I daresay, you were louder than me," she said when they were able to pull apart and breathe easier again. "And after you scolded me to be quiet."

He helped brush out her skirts while laughing. "I should apologize."

She tilted her head and narrowed her gaze. "You said you should apologize, yet you didn't actually apologize. I'm beginning to think you are more of a Scottish brute than you sound."

"I might be. But I can't bring myself to be sorry for anything that just transpired. And now you'll return to the dance floor with a beautiful flush to your cheeks and my scent hovering around you while I on the other hand will stand smugly in a corner with a knowing smile on my face."

"You are the devil."

"Yes. You are right again. I fear you've known me for too long."

And yet, not long enough.

She shook her head indulgently and fixed a few pins that had come loose from her hair.

"I'll return first. You wait a few minutes and come in later so it doesn't appear we were together."

He nodded. "The oldest trick of a rendezvous. I'm sure it still works." He winked and gave her bottom a pat as she passed him. "See you soon."

Once inside she glanced around expecting people to point at some issue with her gown or the mess of her hair or as he had pointed out, not falling for the ruse of her not being with the man who was currently sneaking in through another door to the ballroom. But no one seemed to notice anything amiss. No one stared or pointed or laughed.

It seemed strange after what had happened just outside. She was still rattled when it was time to dance with Kit. Having his hands on her soothed her nerves.

"I was sure someone would see through our façade."

"Oh, have no doubt anyone who noticed our return would instantly have known what happened. But they'll not comment on it because they, themselves are either planning to do or have done the same thing."

"So, you're saying all of polite society makes a habit of meeting for trysts with their lovers in the garden during a ball?" Of course, it made sense. It was dark and away from everyone.

"Oh, yes. It's quite done," Kit said. "Or the library, or the study, or any other vacant room."

Celia couldn't help but see some other ladies in attendance with the same blush on their cheeks that she felt on her own.

"Hale and his duchess?" The Duke and Duchess of Roxburghe looked slightly ruffled.

"Definitely. I'm surprised they are still here. Normally Hale would have spirited home with Gia so they could be alone."

Celia laughed. "It does make these events much more fun to speculate on such things."

"It does. Though I would say it is you who has made the ball so much more fun for me."

This wasn't said in jest, but sincerity. She could see it glittering in his green eyes. He was paying her a compliment and telling her how he felt in the same comment.

She decided to play it off rather than to allow the moment to become too serious.

"I was thinking… Perhaps we can assist one another with our endeavors," she said, effectively changing the subject.

"Endeavors?" He cocked his head as he led her through the

dance.

"Yes. You want to find a wife and while debutantes generally all seem very alluring when in the presence of a potential suitor, I would be able to see what they are really like and find one that suits you."

"And what could I offer in exchange?"

"You know these men. You know which would be suitable for my needs."

His eyes went wide. "I assure you all will most likely have the necessary equipment. As to how well they would perform their duties—"

"I don't mean their actual performances. I meant whether or not they are honorable."

"You want a man honorable enough to be a lover but not a husband."

"Yes. Exactly." She realized she was asking for two characteristics in direct contrast to one another. But she'd already found a man who had both. How difficult could it be to find others?

CHAPTER FIFTEEN

KIT GLANCED AROUND the room and nodded. For the most part he did know which of the men attending the ball might serve Celia's needs as a lover. Even if the thought of setting up such an introduction curdled his blood.

"Very well." They spun at the corner of the dance floor and he looked down at her again. "May I ask a question?"

"Of course."

"Why don't you want to marry? It wouldn't have to be like the last time." Married for money to an older man who couldn't perform his husbandly duties. She could marry for any number of reasons. Common interests, respect, lust… love. Or all of them. He cleared his throat.

She shrugged. "I told you. I have a fairly large settlement from Hamlin. I've no need for a man to take care of me. And no desire to turn my fortune over to a grasping husband."

"I see. What if he had his own fortune? Or if not a fortune, if he was settled enough not to need your money?"

"It might make it easier to see his true intentions, but again, why? I had no choice when my father forced me to marry Hamlin. Now I can make my own choices and do what I wish. I'd be a fool to give that up."

He nodded, understanding the allure of freedom and independence when she'd been without.

"May I ask you a similar question?" She tilted her head. "Why do you want to marry?"

She'd already asked him this question before they'd become lovers. Perhaps, she expected a different answer now.

"I'm a viscount. I'll need an heir at some point. But it's more than just the duties of my title. I'm alone. And have been for some time. My friends are finding love and starting families. It would be nice to have someone. Someone to share my life with. Being someone's lover is just about pleasure. But I also want the everyday things. I want to laugh and talk about mundane bits of the day. To spend the winter months in our home, just sitting and reading by the fire. I'm sure it sounds boring. But most of all I want someone to whom I can belong. To be part of a family again. I've almost forgotten what that feels like."

"I hope you've felt part of our family as small as it may be."

"In a way, Gray has been something of a brother to me, but I've never thought of you in a sisterly way. Not since I returned to London at nineteen and made it my life's work to sneak a look down your dress." He laughed.

"I thought you gave that up after I caught you that one time."

He shook his head. "No. I've just become better at it."

"You're doing it right now, aren't you?"

"Of course."

"Scoundrel," she accused.

"I never claimed to be anything else."

THE NEXT MORNING, Celia called for her maid to help her dress as was usual even if the time of morning wasn't.

"I expected you to be abed late this morning since you only returned from the ball in the early hours," Nettie said with a knowing lift to her brows.

When her comment incited no response, the woman added, "I'll have to have someone look after your clock as it must not be keeping correct time. You are going to breakfast earlier and earlier each morning."

Celia had sent Nettie away the first morning Kit appeared in her room. The other mornings she'd locked the door between her rooms and Nettie's chamber and hoped for the best. There was a sitting room between Celia's bedroom and Nettie's door. Surely, that was enough to keep her older maid from hearing anything.

But from the smug smile on her maid's lips, it was apparent she knew something was going on.

"You know?" Celia confirmed.

Nettie shrugged. "I wouldn't say I *know*, but I suspect. After getting you ready for the Harrington Masquerade, I expected you to have many invitations to a fine fellow's bed. I never expected you'd claim the one that came each morning to have breakfast with your brother, but a fine specimen he is, so I don't blame you for grabbing hold of him with both hands."

Celia swatted at the woman with the edge of her shawl. "Such insolence from a servant," she joked, causing Nettie to laugh.

"Do you wish to talk of it?"

"No, thank you."

Nettie let out a disappointed sigh. "'Tis been a long time since this old body has known the touch of a man. I had hoped you'd spare a detail at least."

Celia wasn't swayed by Nettie's act, though she did relent because she found she wanted to share her joy with someone.

"Fine. I will say this; it is going quite nicely so far. And yes, I'm eager to catch him in the mornings for a kiss or two before my brother arrives. So, you're correct that I seem to wake earlier and earlier. There is time for a nap later. After…" Celia felt her lips pull up into a mischievous grin.

Nettie smiled. "Has he offered for you?"

"Yes." Celia couldn't hide her frown.

"But you set him right?"

"I did. But I didn't realize he would truly want to marry. Who would suspect the naughty Scottish rake to be the one who wants to settle down in marriage while the prim widow wants to have many adventurous liaisons with multiple lovers?"

"An adventure is a fine thing, so long as you know when it's time to settle down yourself. Men tend to want the young ones. You'll need to marry before you come of an age that you don't get the offers of adventures any longer."

Celia hadn't considered such a thing. Mainly because she saw other things standing in her way. "To be honest, I'm not so sure I'll be able to claim any man as it is."

"Why not? You're in your prime."

Celia pointed to the side of her face where the birthmark marred her otherwise clear skin.

"Don't you dare think that silly mark makes you any less alluring to men. Stand tall and know that any of them would feel lucky to be chosen to share your desires."

Celia nodded but looked away from her reflection until Nettie took her chin and pulled her round again. "Look at you, love. You're perfect. Now go down and steal a few kisses from your gentleman. I'll be certain to visit the kitchens when breakfast is over. I'll only enter your rooms when called until you tell me otherwise."

"You are wonderful, Nettie."

"So are you. Don't forget it."

As planned, Celia was waiting outside the breakfast room when Kit entered. She grabbed him and kissed him hard, pulling away just enough to see his smile.

That smile had lifted her spirits each morning since she'd moved in with her brother. But now it held a hint of promise as well.

"I need to go riding with Gray after breakfast today," he told her.

"Why?" She did her best not to pout, but only just succeeded.

"Because he's bound to get suspicious if I don't. I've missed our rides every morning since we've been ill. I can't keep using a sore throat as an excuse when he's completely improved."

Celia crossed her arms. "What about tomorrow morning?"

"What about his afternoon? You could come to my home. Tell him you were invited for tea." He kissed her. "I'll be sure to have some so we won't be lying."

"Will we drink it in bed?"

He kissed her neck. "My naughty minx. That is a splendid idea."

They managed to make their plans for the afternoon and get in their seats at the table by the time Gray came in. He still had a rough look about him, as he did in the mornings, but he didn't smell of drink and didn't wince when she greeted him enthusiastically.

"Good morning to you, sister. I hope you slept well?"

"Yes. Very well."

"Kit. How was the ball? Any plans to get leg shackled yet?"

"No. I'm just reacquainting myself with society. I haven't started the hunt in earnest."

She coughed and focused on the roll on her plate. Was he not starting his hunt for a bride because of her? She didn't want to keep him from finding what he wanted. Kit deserved every happiness and she'd not be so selfish as to keep him with her just because he made her heart pound.

She needed to do better by him.

Tonight, she would assist him with his search so he would be closer to finding the life he wanted. He deserved as much. He'd waited long enough for a family of his own.

She didn't say much through the rest of the meal and didn't dare look in Kit's direction. He didn't speak to her directly either.

It seemed it was hours later when Kit suggested he and Gray go for a ride. Gray looked a bit skeptical but was quick to agree.

Finally, she could flee to her room and start planning for their afternoon assignation.

CHAPTER SIXTEEN

"I DON'T KNOW what is going on between you and my sister, but I don't like it," Gray said as soon as they left the stables.

Kit nearly fell from his horse as he stared at his friend. How had he found out? He'd been so careful.

"Whatever do you mean?" Kit's voice was so weak, he worried the man wouldn't hear him.

"She wouldn't look at you and you wouldn't look at her. She barely said anything to you. Did you have a disagreement?" Gray winced. "I love you like a brother, but she's blood so I have no choice but to take her side. Unless…"

He tilted his head. "She didn't scold you at the ball for bad behavior, did she?"

Kit blinked. It wasn't a surprise where Gray's loyalties would lie, but the fact he cared for Kit like a brother came as some surprise. It made him even more leery of putting their friendship at risk by dallying with his sister, but he shook away the guilt.

"Whyever, would *I* require a scolding for bad behavior? I'm not the one who misbehaves, I'll remind you."

"True, but she's cross with you about something. You'd do well to figure out what it is and have it dealt with. Or, you could take a page from my book and just apologize straight out."

"Even if I don't know what I'm apologizing for?"

"Yes. I'm sure you're the cause if Celia is mad about something. Best just to apologize and have it over with."

"And how will you know to avoid such a thing in the future if you don't even know what has made her unhappy with you?"

Gray shrugged. "It doesn't matter, does it? If I do it again, I simply apologize again and everything is set to rights."

Kit wanted to press the logic, but that way was bedlam. Instead, he pushed on. "I have no doubt that's the way for you, but I assure you, Celia is not angry with me because I'm not a selfish blighter of an older brother."

"Still, she spoke to the selfish blighter and didn't speak to you."

"I'm sure she was just thinking of other things. She mentioned she had been invited for tea this afternoon. Perhaps she's just nervous about the invitation."

Gray nodded. "That could be it." He bit his lip and whispered. "How is she doing? Have many men offered to dance with her? I hope you have. She needs a friend as she navigates the shark-infested waters of the ton."

"I stood up with her at every ball so far. But she doesn't need me to fill her card. She has plenty of eager gentlemen addressing her."

"Truly?"

"Why do you act so surprised? She's a young, attractive woman with a clever wit and a kind heart. What man wouldn't want to be near her? And keep in mind if you mention the mark on her face, I'll unhorse you and trample you."

"Of course not. It's only I know how shallow men can be about such things. While it isn't so noticeable to us because we see her every day, other men might be put off by it."

"Other men can go to the devil."

"Agreed." Gray nodded. "I'll need to rely on you to frighten off any that come too close."

"And why would I do that?"

"Because she has said many times she doesn't plan to marry again, so I only want to respect her wishes."

"You only want to make sure you're not faced with a man

taking her away? Then you would be alone. Even for you that is low."

"I don't want a man to hurt my sister and men inevitably hurt the people they are supposed to love."

They spent the rest of their ride not speaking of women at all, including Celia. To which Kit was entirely grateful. He didn't want to be forced to lie to his best friend and the truth…

Promise not to duel or no, Kit was sure to find himself on the business end of a weapon if Gray ever found out what he'd done with the man's sister.

It was all Kit could manage to keep a normal speed as he returned to his home, eager for Celia to arrive.

WITH THE ASSISTANCE of Nettie, Celia arrived through the back entrance of Kit's home without anyone seeing her. Seeing his dashing smile when she arrived, sent a shiver of something pleasant through her body.

She called it lust but wasn't sure that was the correct term.

Yes, she was pleased to be in his arms again with his lips pressing against her skin. Yes, she was impatient as he slowly undid the laces of her gown and freed her breasts to caress and tease them with his mouth.

Yes, her breath quickened and her body readied for his invasion as it had before.

But that smile? That crooked grin that spoke of humor and friendship brought on more than simple lust. Which was why she made quick work of shutting that thought away.

She could not feel anything for Kit other than the physical and their normal friendship. To do so would put her at risk of getting trapped into more with him.

That couldn't be. She had other plans for her life. Freedom, being the most important. Never again would her life be upended by a man. Be that a father, a brother or a husband. She was in control of what she wanted to do and who she wanted to see.

Right now, she wanted to see more of Kit.

"Take off your clothes," she ordered.

He growled and nipped the skin over her rib. "I love it when you're bossy."

"Then I shall assume you want me to be as bossy as I like?"

"Yes. Tell me everything you desire, and I'll make sure you get it."

His eager agreement spurred a thought that came on quick and unsolicited.

Kit would never force you to do anything you did not wish.

Rather than face this truth she gripped him and smiled. "Teach me how to pleasure you in the way you do me. With my mouth."

"Lord help me," he whispered. She heard a rip and a pop of a button as Kit removed his clothing in a frenzy.

SOMETIME LATER, CELIA lay across his bed with her head resting on his stomach as he lay in the opposite direction from her. She wasn't quite certain how they'd ended up that way, but she knew it had been great fun getting there.

Stretching to reach the tea tray on his night table he held out a biscuit to her.

She accepted his offering with a smile and didn't care that a few crumbs fell on her chest when she took a bite.

"I must say, the tea tray does more than just keep us from lying to Gray but provides needed substance after you depleted my energy from breakfast."

"Are you complaining?" she asked while handing back the rest of the biscuit for him.

"Of course not. But I do think I will instruct my cook to include some meat and cheese on the tea tray going forward."

"You are a very clever man."

"A clever man who can't remember a time when he's ever been happier than he is at this very moment."

She couldn't argue. She couldn't think of a time of greater happiness either. Which came as a surprise as she remembered how elated and empowered she'd felt when she'd left Lady Harrington's party, no longer a virgin, but a woman with carnal knowledge.

This—lying with Kit in lazy conversation and playful comfort—was so much better.

She couldn't help but wonder again what it might be like to be married to Kit. After all, it wouldn't be a casual contract between two strangers, but a promise of companionship and understanding.

Except she'd wanted those very things from him years ago and he'd rejected her offer. She'd thought he would always be there for her, until he wasn't. She would be wise to remember how quickly he had changed his mind on matters of friendship.

She took the last bite of biscuit and savored the sweetness on her tongue, even while feeling the familiar bitterness of betrayal in her heart. Men weren't to be trusted. Even dashing men with smiles filled with kindness who shared their biscuits.

Her resolve was tested over the next month as she and Kit met regularly—sometimes after breakfast in her rooms and other times at his home for tea. They spent most evenings at some society entertainment sharing looks and smiles from across the room.

"If you keep looking at me like that, I will sweep you from the room and take you to some dark corner of the gardens," he threatened during a waltz.

"Oh, please do," she whispered.

They'd missed their normal meeting that day and it felt like it had been weeks since she'd last felt him inside her instead of just the day before.

"Minx. Meet me on the terrace after the next dance."

When their dance was over, she obliged Mr. Daniels with a dance. He was a kind older man who put her in mind of Arthur.

She let a sad smile pull up her lips at the memory of her husband. She'd thought being forced to marry him would be the worst thing to ever happen to her. But he'd allowed her the freedom she cherished and wanted only a companion in return.

Had he known what a kindness he was doing when he offered for her? Had he intentionally saved her from a worse fate with another man?

He'd paid off her father's debts and helped get the properties set right without an unkind word. He had saved her life.

When Kit had not.

Blinking away the unhappy thought, she curtsied to her dance partner before skirting around the edge of the room to sneak out through the doors to the terrace.

But she was stopped by a most unpleasant distraction.

"Lord Hamlin," Celia greeted the slimy cretin who stood in her way.

"I was hoping to speak to you," he said, though he looked less than sincere. "Neither of us want to go through with bringing our family matters before the House of Lords. I know I would rather save you the embarrassment as my grandfather would have preferred."

Celia said nothing. This man was a serpent. His willingness to be decent could only mean he couldn't wait that long for the money and planned to go about it another way. Knowing she was safe from his plans to prove her a virgin, Celia simply tilted her head to the side and waited for him to reveal his new strategy.

"We both know the truth. There's no chance the man was able to consummate the marriage. That being said, if you would simply surrender but half of your settlement, we could both go forward as family. I think that is more than fair."

Fair? How could he think that fair?

"I must refuse your offer. As you've said, I don't wish to go through such a ridiculous ordeal as an examination forced upon me by the lords, but I assure you, sir, your grandfather wanted me to have that settlement as his wife."

"You have dispatched with your maidenhead," he spat. "Know this. Whomever has touched the likes of you will surely speak of it. This isn't over."

She glanced around to see only a few people staring in her direction. She didn't know if they could have heard the words as he'd all but hissed his threats at her. But she couldn't be worried over it. Not when she had somewhere else to be.

On the terrace there were a few people caught up in their own conversations, so it was easy for Celia to skip down the steps and rush toward the gardens.

A warm hand touched her upper arm and, even in the darkness, she knew it was Kit.

She relaxed into his hold and let him lead her into the privacy of a high hedge.

"What took you so long?" he asked.

"Nothing important," she said, wanting to forget about Edward.

"We must be quiet," she said as he pulled up her skirts.

"Me? I'm not the one we should be worried about. I can be subdued when the occasion calls for it. It's you who cannot help but shout my name when you reach your pleasure."

She wanted to argue, but he was right.

"Very well, then let's at least be quick about it so our absence is not noticed."

"Quick." She heard the frown in his voice rather than saw it. "What if I smother your shouting with kisses? If we're forced into one of those two options, I would sooner choose quiet over quick."

"I'll do my best," she promised.

"That's all I can ask."

She immediately broke her oath when he slid into her. A moan of happiness escaped but it was matched with his own. They smiled against each other's lips.

"So much for that," he said, laughing.

They managed to find their pleasure in a timely and somewhat quiet manner.

As she smoothed down her skirts and tidied her hair, she couldn't help but notice how after a month, neither of them were any closer to finding the people they were looking for.

She had yet to find a man she wanted to invite to her bed, and Kit hadn't mentioned anyone filling the role as wife.

Yet, when he kissed her softly before they parted, she couldn't be bothered to worry about that now.

Soon enough, they would have reasons to move on.

For now, he was hers.

CHAPTER SEVENTEEN

"CELIA, WILL YOU marry me?" Kit asked his reflection. It had been well over a month of them spending time together, both in and out of bed. Despite their plans to assist each other in finding other people, they hadn't and he could only hope that meant she was content with being with him.

For his purposes, he was more than content. He was happier than he'd ever thought to be. Celia was everything he wanted in a wife. She was funny and beautiful, but more than those things he could converse with her about nearly any topic, big or small.

He'd been practicing his proposal every morning before leaving for Penbrook House to enjoy breakfast, but though he'd mastered the five words days ago, he'd yet to speak them to her.

Today would be different. He left early so he could speak to her before Gray joined them. How wonderful would it be to announce their betrothal the second the man arrived at the table?

Kit frowned. Depending on the state of Gray's head, it might do better to wait until he's had his coffee.

Shaking his head, he left the house knowing the first thing he needed to do was earn Celia's hand. Worrying about what he might say to Gray would come after she's said yes.

And if she didn't?

She'd refused him years ago. As a young man of twenty, he'd been laid low by her rejection. Gray had told him she chose Hamlin over Kit because the older man could care for a wife easier than a man strapped with debt. Kit understood, and a very small part of him had wondered how he might afford to take care of Celia as she deserved. But his heart…that wound had yet to heal fully.

He took a deep breath before entering the house with a nod to Alfred, the Penbrook butler, who was clearly waiting for Kit to arrive as always.

Sneaking into the breakfast room, he placed a soft kiss on the nape of Celia's neck and enjoyed watching a shiver wash over her body.

"Good morning, beautiful."

"Good morning to you, *my lord*."

The naughty girl knew he liked it when she pretended formalities.

"Countess." He let the last letter hiss over her skin earning another shiver. "How did you sleep?"

"Very well? And you?"

"My arms were empty. I dreamed of having you there to fill them."

She turned and he saw the longing in her warm brown eyes. He couldn't wait another second.

"Will you marry me so our arms never need to be empty again?"

She blinked and stuttered. They were forced to pull away when Guthrie entered with a dish.

They stood in silence while the older footman situated it to his liking and left again.

"You know I don't wish to—"

"I know. As you've said, but is that because you fear it would be like your first marriage?" He winked. "Because I assure you, it would not. Particularly in one very pleasurable way."

"I understand that. Which is why that is not my concern."

"Then what is it, Celia? Allow me to put your fears to rest. We would be perfect together. We are friends above all else, which I feel is a better foundation for marriage than most people have when they wed."

"I cannot argue that I see you as one of my dearest friends. If not the dearest. But I can't allow myself to be trapped by a man."

"And that is how you would see a marriage between us? A trap? You think I would chain you up and keep you from doing what you want?" He forced the smile to stay in place even as she turned the knife in his chest. How many ways would this woman destroy him? He shouldn't have asked. It had been too soon. He'd grown impatient.

"If what I want is to experience sexual relations with other men?" she asked.

He glared at the carpet. "That wouldn't be acceptable, but I'd make sure you didn't wish for anyone but me. By now you certainly know how single-minded I am when it comes to your pleasure."

"Yes." Her cheeks flared with a blush proving she was recalling some time in their recent past when he'd pleased her. "But I only know you, Kit. I only know your touch and your taste. Imagine if you came to me in the same way. Wouldn't you wonder what other experiences you could be missing with other women?"

"I can't say for sure since I already had other experiences with women, but I would hope to know the difference between an experience, and a life-altering moment with the woman I wanted to spend my life with."

Even as he pleaded his case, he saw her answer in the set of her mouth. She was about to reject him. Again.

Fortunately, more trays were brought in then so they were forced to silence. They took their seats and waited to be served without looking at one another. They were only alone again a few seconds before Gray came in.

There would be no announcement this morning.

Kit hadn't won her hand. He wasn't her fiancé, however he was still her lover and that was something he would continue to enjoy.

At least until she moved on to someone else. He frowned at his food, no longer very hungry.

CELIA ARRIVED AT the ball alone and waited for Kit to arrive. A few men approached and requested a dance. No one she felt any attraction to.

When Kit didn't arrive by the time the music began, she worried she'd attended the wrong function. She was certain he'd told her he was attending the Sheridan ball. That was the reason she was there. But where was he?

As the night went on, she realized how much she missed having Kit there to laugh with. She'd actually looked to her side to share a smile with him when Lord Fortingham tripped over his wife's elaborate gown. He'd reached out for anything to stop his stumble and his hand landed directly over the woman's bountiful breast.

But the space beside Celia was empty and the moment went by without proper appreciation.

The night seemed to drag on, which was odd. Normally these events went by rather quickly.

Or they had when she'd been with Kit.

She wondered if he was upset about the way their conversation had gone that morning at breakfast. When he'd proposed marriage and she'd refused. He'd come to her room afterward and they'd made love as was becoming their ritual, but then he'd left to meet up with Gray soon after they'd finished.

No. He understood what she wanted. And she understood what he wanted. Something else must have kept him from attending tonight. Regardless of the reason, she was on her own.

Perhaps it was for the best. She could focus on finding her next lover instead of trading comical quips with Kit about Lord Fortingham.

She took in the men standing about. Most in conversation with other women. There were a few who were tempting, but when they looked in her direction, she quickly looked away so not to make eye contact.

She didn't know them. She didn't know what kind of men they were.

She checked the stairs again wishing for the hundredth time that Kit was here. He might know these men. He might even know them well enough to provide an introduction.

Unable to bear another minute of the ball, she left and instead of going home, she headed for Berwick Street.

Letting herself in through the back, she went through the house and found him sitting in his study with the door open. An empty glass sat on the desk beside him as he turned a page in a large ledger.

"You weren't at the Sheridan Ball this evening," she stated, causing him to look up. Unlike most times she addressed him, he didn't offer a smile or look at all happy to see her. He didn't look disappointed to see her either, but definitely not overcome with joy or desire.

"Good evening, countess."

Countess. They were back to that, were they? Without the purr in his voice to make it sound seductive, she felt the coldness of the title.

"Are you ill?" she asked. Her concern for his well-being had grown as she'd ridden to his home. She'd spun horrible scenarios explaining his absence.

"I'm well. How are you?"

How was she? She was… irritated. She'd wanted to see him and he hadn't been there.

The thought caught her up short. She almost backed out of the room and ran away. What was she doing? What was she thinking? She had no right to be irritated with him. He was not hers. He could do as he pleased. Marry whomever he wanted. She'd given up any right to his comings and goings when she'd turned him down.

She was not his wife. And never would be.

"Forgive me for barging in and interrupting your evening. It's just that I thought you would be in attendance and well, Lord Fortingham… never mind it is of no matter."

"What did Lord Fortingham do?" He sounded as if he was ready to grab up his pistols and call the man out.

"Nothing. I'm sorry. I shouldn't have come."

"Wait," he said as she turned to leave. "It is I who should apologize. I did say I would attend, but when the time came, I… couldn't."

She wanted to inquire as to why, but to ask meant he would undoubtably answer and she wasn't certain she could bear to hear the answer.

"I understand you have no wish to marry. It doesn't change the fact that I want a wife and a family. I'm not sure what course we are on."

"I've been selfish." She rubbed her forehead.

Kit laughed, causing her to look up.

"Selfish?" He shook his head. "No. Be assured, there is nothing we've done together that I've regretted. I'm the selfish one. I'm the one who wants more than what you are willing to give."

She stepped closer and he opened his arms. It was the easiest thing to step into his embrace and wrap her arms around his waist. She rested her cheek against his chest, listening to the steady rhythm of his heartbeat.

She wished she could give him what he wanted. She wished she could say yes and happily take his name. But just the thought of belonging to another man, stole her breath and made it difficult to breathe.

"Perhaps it is time we moved on with our original plans," she said stepping back to look at him. "The one where we help each other find what we're looking for. I believe we've become distracted by the pleasure we give each other and lost sight of our goals."

He nodded. "I believe you're correct." Tilting his head to the side he ran a finger across her lips. "Does that mean we would no longer offer each other pleasure while we're looking?"

Heat flickered to life in her stomach and melted throughout her body just like it did the other times he touched her.

"I don't see a reason why we couldn't continue as we've been so long as we don't lose sight of our goals again."

His grin turned wicked as he leaned down and kissed her. His tongue touched hers as his arms coiled around her, drawing her closer.

"I will do my best," he agreed in a whisper by her ear. A shiver of excitement ran down her spine. "Since you're already here…"

He didn't need to say anything else. She spun out of his arms and rushed for the door, pulling him along with her.

CHAPTER EIGHTEEN

THE NEXT EVENING, Celia and Kit attended the Smithton's Ball. This time, instead of amusing themselves by watching the members of the ton around them, they focused on finding the person who might be what the other was looking for.

"I'm sorry I'm not acquainted with more suitable women," she said the following morning at breakfast.

"I'm sorry all the men I know are either already married, disreputable, or your brother." He scrunched up his nose. "Actually, Gray is both disreputable *and* your brother," he corrected causing her to laugh just as Gray entered the breakfast room.

"Ah, it's good to see the two of you laughing together again. I'm glad you got over whatever quarrel had caused you to frown at each other." Gray snapped his napkin into place and dug into his breakfast as Celia bit her lip to hold in her laughter, barely succeeding.

"Who could stay angry at Kit?" Celia said in answer.

"I've never managed it." Gray shrugged.

When she finished her meal, she excused herself and wished them a pleasant ride. As she passed behind Gray she pointed upward, silently telling Kit to join her in her rooms when he could get away.

Not an hour later, Kit slipped into her room.

"I'm glad we're not frowning at one another anymore too,"

he said in between kisses to her neck. "I like to make you do other things so much more. For example, the way your breath comes in quick pants when I kiss you here. Or the way you moan when I touch you here."

His hand brushed over her nipple and she made the very sound he'd mentioned.

"Yes," she said though he hadn't asked a question. She only knew the answer was, yes.

She didn't understand the eagerness she still felt to be with him, when they'd come together almost daily over the last two months. Shouldn't she have become more patient? It seemed the opposite was true. The more she had him in her bed, the more she wanted.

As was common, they dressed as soon as they were able to catch their breath. At his home, they spent time in his bed, just lying next to each other, talking about odd things that amused them.

At her home, however, they didn't take that risk.

"Tonight, I'll introduce you to Lord Morton. He's a bit short, but so are you so you'll not notice."

She barely followed what he was saying for she heard the telltale sound of the squeaking floorboard outside her door. She'd always made sure to step clear of it when she left her room in the middle of the night so not to alert anyone.

Anyone, of course, meaning her nosy brother.

She pressed her index finger to Kit's lips and pointed to the door. "I think someone's outside the door," she whispered against his ear.

His eyes went wide and he spun her around to finish lacing up her gown. While he worked, she quickly wrapped her hair up and pinned it. He finished dressing in mere seconds. It was a testament to how good they'd become at sneaking around that they could dress so quickly and quietly.

"I'll go out first. Just in case. If someone's out there, you'll know because you'll hear me speaking. If you don't hear anything then give it a minute before taking your leave."

"Very good." He stayed on the far side of the door so he'd be hidden when she opened the door.

She pulled it back quickly hoping to startle anyone who'd been eavesdropping but was surprised to find the hall empty.

"Hmm." She must have been hearing things. She continued on down the corridor toward the drawing room. She would call for tea and read. And of course, think of Kit and the way he'd touched her earlier. He had not run out of ways to elicit pleasure from her body in all this time.

A secret smile came to her lips as she settled into her favorite chair by the window. She couldn't help but think how this was exactly what she'd wanted her life to be like.

Kit waited the full minute after Celia had silently left the room. She hadn't spoken to anyone which meant the way was clear. He opened the door and stepped out. He quietly shut the door behind him before turning and running directly into Graham.

"Bugger," Kit cursed and stepped back. When he saw the anger in his best friend's eyes, he took another step away and raised his hands.

"You fucking prick. You touched my sister." Gray didn't yell, which made it all the more unsettling. Instead, his voice was calm and cold as death. Not good.

"Don't be angry, Gray. It's not what you think."

"Then you're not sleeping with CeCe?"

Kit pressed his lips together. He wouldn't lie even if he'd had a lie readily available. Which he didn't. Gray might not have been a scholar, but he wasn't a complete idiot. He'd not accept another reason for Kit to be seen leaving his sister's bedroom.

"Well, yes, I am. But it's different. We've been at it for months."

Gray's brows pulled together and Kit cursed again. That clearly wasn't the right thing to say.

"What I mean is, she's not just a warm body in my bed. Or her bed as the case may be. Sometimes we're not even in a bed at all. Like when we're at a ball." Kit waved his hand. Bollocks, he was making it worse with every word that passed his lips.

"You've compromised my sister at a ball? You're supposed to be looking for a wife."

"Yes. But Celia is looking for a lover and I've volunteered for the duty until I find a wife. Which I feel as though I have, but she won't have me." Damn it. If Celia would just marry him, he'd be happy. And Gray would certainly be happier than he was this instant. Kit would make certain Celia was happy as well. Everything would be the way it was meant to be.

Why wouldn't she just say *yes*? He knew she saw marriage as a loss of freedom, but she had to know him better than that.

"What is going on?" Celia asked as she came closer. "Why, Lord Stormont, it's odd to see you upstairs in the family wing. In the middle of the day." Her eyes widened as she attempted to help save him.

"It's too late. He saw me leave your room."

"Bloody hell," Celia whispered.

"This ends now," Gray said authoritatively while pointing between them. As if it were his choice. For all the years they'd lived together, one would think Gray had just recently met his older sister for as poorly as he knew her. "You'll not see her or talk to her, and you damn well, won't... *touch* her." He winced. "Do you understand?"

"Really, Graham. He's your best friend and it's not for you to say what I do."

"I am the head of this family and this is my house. I say who is welcome here, and he is no longer welcome."

"Fine. I shall move to my own home. I'll see to it this very day and be out of *your* house by the end of the week. Then I'll be free to see, speak to, *and* touch whomever I please."

"What? No! You can't leave. This is your home," Graham argued.

"You just said it wasn't. Besides, I plan to have other lovers, so it's really best that I move anyway."

"Other… *what?*" Gray spluttered and looked a bit green. Perhaps even greener than he looked most mornings.

"I'm not sure why this is such a surprise. You spend a great deal of your time in the beds of merry widows, do you not? Am I not a widow? Why are you shocked to learn I would not invite delightful rogues to my bed?"

Gray let out a string of quiet curses and ran a weary hand through his hair.

Kit had been amused as he watched her set down her brother, but this talk of other lovers and rogues made his stomach flip uncomfortably.

Gray turned to him, poking him harshly in the shoulder. "This is all *your* fault. You've ruined my sister." He lurched toward Kit but stopped in his tracks, his face pulled up in pain.

"What do you think you're about, Graham Percival?" Celia asked with her fingers clamped on Gray's ear.

"Ow! Let go. Damn you, CeCe!"

"I'll let go when you agree to behave yourself and act like a gentleman."

"I'll act like a gentleman all right. I will see you in the park, Stormont. I demand satisfaction."

"Please. The only person demanding satisfaction of Kit will be me. And I can attest to his abilities to deliver it."

"Clever minx," Kit praised her and stepped to her side. A united front.

"I think I'm going to be ill," Gray winced.

Celia let go of his ear and he slumped against the wall.

"Do you plan to marry her?" Gray asked.

Kit opened his mouth to explain how he'd asked—more than once, but Celia answered instead.

"No. That is, he's offered—as any gentleman in this situation would do—but I've not accepted. I want to live my life on my own terms. As a widow, I have the freedom to do so. As a wife, I become property and my choices become limited to what my husband wishes of me. Why would anyone want to be part of such an unfair institution?"

"Perhaps we can speak in your study?" Kit suggested. "If you've given up on trying to kill me."

"That might be best, though I cannot be certain the urge to dispatch you has completely diminished."

Kit nodded, understanding a line had been crossed and their friendship might very well be forfeit.

"Brother?" Celia's tone was brimming with clear warning.

Gray gave his sister a wide berth as he passed.

"If there's so much as a scratch anywhere on his body, know I will see it and you will pay for it. Do you understand?" She raised a brow and tapped her index finger to her thumb in a rather menacing way.

"I'm definitely going to be ill. For the love of all that is holy, please stop insinuating the two of you will be..." He ended the sentence with an unsettling retching sound.

"Thank you for your protection, dear. I can handle it from here," Kit said placing a kiss on her bare knuckles.

"Of course, darling. Enjoy your chat." She reached up to kiss him on the edge of his jaw.

While he knew the gesture was done simply to provoke her brother, he smiled at the casual affection. He would miss her when their time together ended.

Or if Graham killed him.

And if he lived it still might very well end that night if she helped him find a potential bride. Or she found another lover...

In the study, Kit helped himself to the liquor cart and poured them each a brandy before sitting across from Gray.

"How did this come to be?" Gray asked dazedly.

"I'll explain, but I ask that you hear the story as a friend. As a man who has dallied with his fair share of widows. And not as the brother of the woman I am currently dallying with."

"But I *am* a brother, and if you use the word *dallying* again in regard to my sister, I'll happily strangle you and let CeCe take my ear. I have a second one after all."

"And I'll remind you that some of those widows you're fond of *dallying* with are also someone's sister."

Gray took a healthy swig of his drink. "Fine. I'm a friend." He glared at Kit over his glass. "For now."

"Very well, then. Celia and I—"

Gray shuddered and squeezed his eyes closed. He was clearly back to being a brother already. The only way through this was straight in, so Kit pushed on, ignoring the sounds of misery coming from the other man.

"Right. Perhaps if we pretended it was someone else," he muttered to himself before trying again. "*Selene* and I met at Lady Harrington's masquerade." He selected her *nom de plume*.

"*Celia* was the French woman you were trying to find from Lady Harrington's masquerade?"

"Yes."

"What the devil was she doing there?" He stood to pace the room.

"She'd filched your invitation when it was clear you were too sick to attend and went herself." He explained how Celia—make that *Selene*—had taken a private room and how Lady Harrington had selected him to meet with her.

"And you're to tell me you didn't recognize each other, even with masks?"

"My voice hadn't returned fully from being ill. As far as she knew I wasn't planning to attend because I'd said as much the morning we received our invitations. *And* she'd adopted an impressive French accent, lowered her voice, and called herself Selene. I surely wouldn't have expected Celia to be at such a party. Not to mention the dim lighting in the room and the masks we both wore. So yes, I'm telling you we didn't recognize one another." He cleared his throat. "I can't explain that night and I'm sure you'd just groan if I went into it, but as I'd explained to you afterward—before I realized Selene was Celia—my time with Selene was unlike any other. It was a feeling of intimacy I'd never experienced before. More than just the physical. It was…"

"A connection?" Gray whispered and Kit remembered using that word to describe it.

"Yes. That's what it was. And a freedom to just be with her. As if we belonged… together."

"Friends."

"Yes. I wanted to see her again, but Selene only wanted that one night together, so I respected her wishes even though it felt like I was leaving my soul behind in that room when I left her. I was sure I'd never see her again. Never know again what it had felt like."

Kit rubbed his chest at the hollow ache.

"As you know, I wasn't able to wait very long before I set out to find her to no avail. We were truly shocked when we realized a few mornings later at breakfast. But while it was a surprise, it wasn't an unwelcome one. We have been friends for many years. And finding out our true identities didn't change anything between us as far as our friendship, we were simply able to add in that other part. The amazing, wild—"

"Thank you, that's quite enough. My imagination will surely not withstand more information."

Kit nodded vaguely as he remembered how the excitement of finding Selene had mixed together with the concern of realizing it was Celia.

"You must know, I offered marriage immediately as a gentleman would when he found out he'd compromised a lady and a friend. But she wouldn't have me. Again." He threw his hands in the air and stood to pace the opposite side of the room.

"Did you speak of the first time she refused you?" Gray asked, rather quickly.

"No. You told me she felt horrible for having chosen Hamlin over me and I wouldn't do anything to make Celia feel horrible."

Gray nodded. "Very good."

"Anyway…she's determined to live a life as a saucy widow and take lovers. She doesn't yet realize it won't be the same. Or maybe it will. Perhaps it was only me who was so affected. I am the only one of us who knows how empty the act can be when it's not with someone you care for." He rubbed his forehead. "When I couldn't convince her, I offered to be her lover. It was the only thing she wanted from me and I'd give her anything. Just to have her a little longer."

"You're telling me that instead of calling you out, I should be thanking you for keeping my sister from moving on to half the men in London?"

"I would never ask you to thank me. If I made it sound like an odious chore to be her lover, I misrepresented it entirely. I have enjoyed every second, I assure you." Perhaps the grin that took over his face was a bit too roguish.

"I could have gone without knowing that." Gray winced again and rubbed his temples.

Kit hesitated to bring up something else that would surely do his friend in, but it was best to get it over with.

"There is something else you must know and it won't be pleasant." He braced himself and continued. "Selene came to the masquerade as a… That is, though she had been married she had not…" Kit winced. This was more difficult than he'd expected and Gray was doing nothing to keep him from having to keep trying. "She was a virgin."

Gray's eyes narrowed.

"You took my sister's virtue?"

"Yes. Though it is hers to give, is it not? And there is a good reason why she wanted to give it to me."

Gray didn't move so Kit thought it might be safe enough to continue.

"Lord Hamlin, that is the new Lord Hamlin has threatened her settlement, saying the marriage was not legitimate because it wasn't consummated. He's going to bring it before the House of

Lords."

Gray's response was to punch a rather prominent hole in the plaster of the wall. Kit was pleased to have Gray's anger pointed in someone else's direction, but the situation was quite serious.

"Of course, we will have Hale and Julian attend and with the two of us and Hayworth we will surely out vote him. There will be no need for an examination."

"An examination?" he shouted.

"You know such things can be requested by the lords. But it won't come to that. We'll see that it doesn't."

Gray threw back the rest of his drink and poured another before taking a breath that seemed to deflate him completely.

"It seems I will need to thank you after all, though I'm not going to do so right now."

"Understood," Kit said but then decided to push the matter. "Is it so bad to know that I care for Celia and hope to convince her to marry me at some point?" Kit frowned. "It always comes down to money, doesn't it? When I had none, she wouldn't have me. Now I still don't have enough to convince her I don't care about hers. She can keep every farthing of Hamlin's coin for herself. I only want her."

Gray stared at him for a full minute before looking away. "I fear I've made a lot of mistakes in my past."

Kit let out a breath assuming Gray was speaking of all the years they'd spent carousing.

"If I do manage to sway her, would I have your blessing?" Kit asked.

Gray pulled back in surprise. "She's made it clear she doesn't need my blessing for anything she does. She's my sister, but I have no say over her life now that she's of age. I never did."

"True. Still, it matters to me that you would think me good enough to call brother."

Gray blinked and looked away. "I already think of you as a brother." He seemed rather uncomfortable. He cleared his throat and stood straighter. "I can only hope Celia would find such an honorable man as you for her husband. And I'm sorry I wasn't able to do more back then to bring you together."

"She made her choice," Kit said.

Gray looked as if he might argue but said nothing else. Kit was touched by his words. They were close friends, but as it was with close friends, they'd seen almost too much truth. That Gray would find him suitable for Celia was a great honor.

"Thank you, Gray. I still hope to have the chance to win her heart."

"Please," Gray said, looking quite miserable. "Don't thank me."

Kit didn't try to explain for he'd gotten an idea. He'd never point Celia in the direction of a man who was unsuitable. But perhaps if she did explore her desire to have another lover, she would see how unappealing such brief encounters could be.

Or maybe she would embrace that life and he would be alone yet again.

$$\sim\!\!\sim\!\cdot\!\sim\!\!\sim$$

CHAPTER NINETEEN

WHEN CELIA RETURNED to Penbrook House, Kit had left and her brother was waiting.

"Where have you been?" he asked as if he had every right to know. Which he didn't. She was her own woman. She didn't want to be controlled by a husband; she surely wasn't to be controlled by her younger brother.

"Not that I need to account for my whereabouts to you, but I did tell you I planned to go look at properties."

He shook his head. "You don't need to move out. This is your home. In fact, I wouldn't even have a home were it not for your sacrifice years ago. I have no right to dictate what you do here. I'm sorry for the way I reacted. As you can imagine it was quite a shock to be walking past your room and hear Kit's voice coming from inside."

She had heard more than she wished when walking past *his* chamber over the years. Giggles and moans and… she winced.

"Right," he said, apparently seeing how well she understood. "But we are adults now. As you pointed out, you're a widow of your own means. It's not my place to stand in your way. I know what you gave up by marrying Hamlin. What you sacrificed so that I may live in comfort. Hamlin took care of Father's debts and got the estates running again. I don't think I've ever properly thanked you, Celia. At the time I was ashamed that you had to marry to save me. You've always been there to care for me and I should have done more for you. I should have told you…well, it doesn't matter now, does it? If everyone is happy with how things turned out, then we shouldn't need to revisit the past."

She would almost say her brother was babbling, but he didn't do that.

"As you said, it's in the past. Hamlin was not so bad a husband. He was kind. Because of the marriage to him, I'm now free to live the life I want."

"Yes, about that…" Gray cleared his throat.

"Please don't think to lecture me about propriety when you've a vaulted reputation for being a rake."

"No. I wouldn't dare be so hypocritical. But I would ask that you take care, Celia."

"I know of letters and sponges. Don't worry."

"Dear God. If I make it through the day with my stomach contents intact it will be a wonder. But that was not what I meant, and *definitely* more than I needed to know."

Celia couldn't help but laugh at his reaction. She hadn't realized how much fun this could be or she might have told him sooner.

"I meant to take care with your heart. Empty liaisons with faceless lovers won't satisfy you forever. Trust me, I know."

That haunted look that washed over her brother's face when he spoke of such things pinched his eyes for just a second before it was gone. She'd asked many times what had happened that hurt him, but he would never say. She knew he wasn't speaking of her own situation, but his own past.

"They are a good distraction for a while," he went on. "But you'll want more someday. I only hope it won't be too late."

With that he left and closed the door to his study. But not before she'd seen the pain etched on his face, deeper than the glimpses from before. Graham was truly hurting, and from the looks of the devastation she saw during his escape from the room, he'd been hurting for far longer than she'd noticed.

Was he right? Would she one day long for the very thing she passed up?

⇛⇚

KIT PERUSED THE card room looking for anyone good enough for Celia. He'd already explored the far reaches of the ballroom and determined no one out there was qualified.

He was beginning to see a problem with his plans.

Many of the men in the ballroom were there because, like him, they were looking for potential wives. More specifically, the majority were seeking rich wives to help them out of financial straits. Kit felt immensely fortunate that he was no longer in that position. He was free to select a wife of his choosing, though not the one he truly wanted. He frowned at the men around him.

While the ballroom was filled with men looking for wives, the cardroom was filled with men who were either married already or were forced to attend. Or who were avoiding managing mamas and their available daughters because they didn't wish to wed.

These were the men he should focus his search on. However, he knew these men from various evenings in their company, which made them impossible rogues.

"Stormont, take a seat and give me your money."

Kit laughed as he sat next to Lord Mendelton.

"You've known him long enough to know he doesn't give his money away at the tables," Lord Raysworth reminded his friend.

The two men were gamblers, but unlike Kit, had wealth to support such activities. Kit was certain Roger and Andrew had spent many a morning in the same state as he and Gray since they often attended the same hells.

No. These men were not suitable for Celia. For that matter, neither was he.

He stayed until the men finished their game.

"Come with us. We're heading to the theater. The show should be ending by now."

It was common for this group to show up in the back room

after the play to visit the actresses. The women were happy to continue entertaining even after the play had ended. One woman he'd spent time with explained the energy from the crowd and the desire to spend this energy in bed with a vigorous lover.

"No thank you," Kit said. "I have other plans."

"I haven't seen you making the rounds with Graham lately, would those plans be to find a lovely bride and get shackled?" Andrew asked.

Kit smiled. "Perhaps, but let's not speak of it too loudly. I don't wish to alert the mamas."

Roger leaned in and whispered, "Your secret is safe with us."

He found Celia by the refreshment table speaking to a woman he knew to be married to either Lord Westfield or Lord East-something. Older than Kit, and married, the men didn't move in the same circles as his friends so he didn't know them well.

"Lord Stormont, may I introduce you to Lady Eastbrook."

"Ah," he said before reining in his happiness at not having to wonder over that later. "It is a pleasure, my lady." He bowed as he should. They exchanged vague pleasantries before the lady moved along to find her husband.

"I was certain she was Lady *Westbrook*, I'm glad I didn't speak it out loud," Celia admitted.

Kit laughed and felt, once again, that he had already found the person for him. She just didn't know it. He hadn't been able to convince her to marry him years ago and he doubted he would now.

"Any luck?" he asked, hoping maybe she'd found the perfect woman who could overshadow Celia and make him happy.

"I'm afraid not. It would be much easier if you didn't have a restriction."

"I told you I don't want a young miss. All the simpering and giggling would be tedious."

"Not all debutantes simper," she said. "I see you came back to me empty-handed as well."

He let out a breath. How could he tell her he couldn't find a man suitable for a brief tryst? All the unmarried men and half of the married ones would jump at the chance. And while he had made a restriction on her search, she had selected no such criteria. She didn't want to keep the man; she only wanted the experience. Any man with the proper working equipment could give her that.

No. It was he who had set unattainable conditions on her relationship, making it certain he would fail to find someone fit for the task.

"If you wanted to know which women were up for accepting the attentions of a man, I could go around the room and point them out in seconds. But the men…" He shook his head.

"You told me you didn't take many women to your bed."

"I haven't, however every man knows which women are available for such things and those who aren't." He appraised the crowd and offered a few names.

"My, I didn't realize everyone would know."

He blinked at her in surprise. "It is London, Celia. Everyone knows everything among the *ton*. In fact, once you find someone, I imagine you won't have to look for another. Your name will be passed on to the next man and the next."

Her face went pale. "Forgive me, I must go."

He took her arm, worried she might fall. "Are you well?"

Her eyes glistened as she frantically looked for the exit.

"This way."

KIT DIRECTED CELIA toward the balcony and out into the side garden as if he knew she needed air.

She hadn't thought she cared about her reputation. She was a widow, freed to do as she pleased. But it was one thing not to have to worry about being ruined and yet another to have her name bandied about the *ton* as nothing more than a mistress with a title.

"What is it, Celia?"

"Have you told anyone?" she asked, her voice quiet and breathy.

"Told anyone what?"

"About us? About what we've done?"

He stood straighter. "Of course not. I mean, Gray obviously knows but he certainly won't tell anyone else."

She relaxed. She should have known Kit would keep her confidences. But clearly that was not common of the other willing men.

"I've changed my mind," she announced as if he was following along with the thoughts in her head. His perplexed expression proved that wasn't the case. "I don't want to go through with it. I don't want a lover. I don't want a line of men at my door waiting their turn to warm my bed. I wanted freedom. I wanted to select the men myself, not just be the next inn to stay for the night along their journey."

Kit brushed her cheek. "I'm sorry I've upset you. I shouldn't have been so blasé about the matter."

"I've always appreciated that you speak the truth even if it's inappropriate to do so."

"I'm not sure if that was a compliment."

"It was meant as such," she assured him.

He nodded. Then ran a hand through his hair, making a few of the golden strands stick out. She wanted to smooth them down but to touch him right then might lead to other touching. Not that they hadn't done more than touch in a garden before.

"You don't want anyone in town to know," Kit said, coming to stand in front of her again. "Then we leave town."

"Leave? Where would we go?"

"To my home in Scotland. It is large enough that you might find who you're looking for, but far enough from London that you'll not be exposed."

"You actually want to help me with this?" she questioned.

She thought he might wait her out, hoping she would give in

to his request to marry.

Originally, she'd not wanted to consider marriage to Kit because he'd left her when she'd needed him. But it was unfair to judge someone of that age for not wanting to wed. He hadn't been ready, and who knows what would have happened if he'd married her then. He might have grown to resent her. Instead of being great friends as they were now, they could have hated one another.

Still, part of her worried he'd only asked her because he hadn't found anyone else and she was comfortable. For that reason, she'd promised herself not to take him up on his offer. When the time came that he married, he deserved to do so for nothing other than love.

She understood that most marriages of peers were the result of a need and a resolution, be it money or a name. But Kit had shed off his debts and was free to find happiness, not simply an alliance.

She wanted that for him.

Kit glanced away and nodded once. She recognized the look on his face as determination.

"Yes. I'll help you. While I would rather take you to my home to marry you, I understand why that is not an option at this time. But be assured, I don't do this for truly unselfish reasons."

"Then what are your reasons?"

Straightening his shoulders, he looked her in the eye.

"My wish is that after you're permitted your freedom you might decide you're ready to settle down with one man, and I hope to be that man. After all, every rogue gets tired eventually be they man *or* woman." He winked.

"And if my freedom only makes me more determined to keep it? And I don't tire of it?"

"Then I will give up with the knowledge that I helped a friend achieve her dreams."

She hugged him. "You are the very best friend, Christopher."

She felt his lips against her temple in the place she was

marked differently from everyone else and vowed silently to do all that was in her power to return the gift and find the perfect woman for Kit.

As soon as possible.

CHAPTER TWENTY

THEY WERE QUIET as they left London.

It was one of the many things he enjoyed about being with Celia. While some women were taught to fill any bit of silence with chatter, Celia was content to sit in peace and allow the moment to be.

How nice it would be to have a companion who was suited for letting a person to their thoughts?

"I have a new requirement for my wife," he said.

"Oh?"

"She needs to be quiet."

Celia's brows pulled together in a way he'd only seen when she was about to take hold of Gray's ear.

"Pardon?" The single word came across the carriage like a lash.

Kit realized how his words might have been interpreted and shook his head.

"That is to say, I want her to be content with silence. As we are right now. I don't want every moment of my life filled with chatter. I will most definitely want to have conversations and will want her to speak her mind, but in the times when no discussion is necessary, I want to make sure she is suited to just be still."

He winced and shook his head.

"I don't imagine that made any sense. You must understand that after my parents died, I spent a lot of time alone. The servants cared for me when my uncle was at sea which was a large part of the time. And while the servants saw to my needs, they didn't offer much in the way of companionship. As a result, there are times when I need to just sit."

She nodded. "I understand. And probably for a similar reason. My father didn't know what to do with a daughter, nor did he care to invest the time to try. He and Graham fought often so I was content to stay in my rooms and not call attention to myself. Silence doesn't disturb me as it does some others."

He was glad she understood him so well. He found himself leaning closer to kiss her, but then pulled away when he remembered why they were heading to the country in the first place.

"I think it best we move forward strictly as friends," he announced though his chest ached to hear it.

Her eyes widened in surprise and she blinked a few times. "Very well. If that is what you wish."

"It's not actually. I want nothing more than to debauch you right here in this carriage, but I find myself hoping for something that can't be, so I must stop."

She nodded. "I'm sorry if I've hurt you. That wasn't my intention. I hope you know that."

"You've been very clear about what you wanted. I'm not so caught up in my own importance to not see you have different needs. It doesn't mean either one of us is in the wrong."

"I have felt guilty for not being able to offer you more."

"No, Celia. You have nothing to feel guilty about."

"Perhaps neither of us needs to feel guilty about anything. I enjoyed every moment we were together intimately. I have no regrets. I will always look back at this time with fondness."

"As will I," he agreed easily, feeling a weight lift. They'd offered each other comfort and pleasure during this time of transition in their lives. He didn't have any regrets either.

She leaned over and rested her head against his shoulder and he pressed a final kiss to her citrus-scented hair.

After days of travel, they pulled into the drive of Blairgowrie Castle. When they came to a stop, the servants descended to take care of their luggage and arrangements. Celia was whisked away to her suite in the opposite wing as his, per his request.

It was one thing to wish to be friends with her, and quite another matter to have her close by in the nights when his body longed for hers.

Keeping his distance as well as his wits was imperative to his sanity. He couldn't keep falling into her arms while also hoping to find someone else to marry. In the same way it was impossible to see the sun while one held a star.

When it was time for dinner, he dressed and headed for the dining room. Celia arrived shortly after, looking quite lovely. Her sable hair was styled in the same way it had been the night she'd been Selene.

He recalled that night and wished he hadn't. After helping her into her seat, he took his own quickly before she might notice the way the memory had affected him.

This was over. They were friends as they had been before the masquerade. As they hopefully would continue to be.

Once he resolved himself to this decision, it made it easier for him to enjoy his meal with Celia. They shared stories of Graham's mishaps and Kit might have provided more than a little ammunition for her to use against her brother when next they disagreed on something.

He would have to apologize to Gray for that later. But it was just too much fun to watch her laugh. He remembered the times before things became complicated between them, when they would spend their mornings amusing each other with inappropriate comments and jests at Gray's expense.

He'd missed this. While he'd enjoyed every second of having her in his bed—or hers—this was different.

"Would you care for port and a cigar?" he asked.

"No, on the cigar, but I'll take a port," she answered.

"Yes, well, we're in Scotland so rather than port, I have good whiskey."

"Then I shall have that instead."

He led her to his study and poured them each a glass.

She looked about his study and laughed.

"I feel privileged to get to see the elusive activities of what happens when the women are exiled to the drawing room to await the men."

"Prepare to be disappointed, countess. We sit around with port and cigars and discuss new laws coming before the house of lords and who will vote for or oppose it."

"You don't speak of who you've taken to your bed?"

"Occasionally it comes up, but I don't. A woman deserves discretion when it comes to such things. Besides, I generally take port with Gray and talking about you would set him off his digestion so close after dinner."

They laughed again.

"I must admit, it has been entertaining to see how Gray's skin turns green when I speak of taking a lover or an insinuation regarding the two of us together."

"You, my lady, are the devil incarnate."

"Why yes, yes, I am." They laughed together again. But unlike the times recently he didn't feel the twist of pain at knowing she would only ever be his friend and not his wife.

As he'd hoped, it was beginning to feel more natural. He'd accepted it wouldn't be more than this and what they had was a friendship many would envy. He'd spent far too much time dwelling on what he didn't have, he'd nearly neglected the wonderful thing he had.

"I've missed you," he said and felt his cheeks burn when he realized his words would make no sense to her.

But she didn't question him or even seem confused by his odd comment. She simply smiled and nodded. "I've missed you too."

CELIA WOKE ALONE and for a moment she found herself wishing she had gone to his home instead of staying at hers. Then she remembered where she was and what had happened the day before.

She and Kit were resolved to being friends only. While she missed him in a physical sense, she understood this was for the best.

Kit was right. They couldn't continue to carry on the way they'd been and still find other people. Specifically other people who wanted the same things they did.

Ready to start her search, Celia headed for the stables. She'd read many a gothic novel highlighting liaisons between the mistress of the house and a strapping groom from the stables.

However, the head groom was actually a woman named Melanie. The only men in the stables was a stout Highlander who was probably in his sixties, and a spotty boy no more than ten and seven.

"Can I help ye, my lady?" Melanie asked.

"I'd like to go into the village. Would you mind to ready a horse for me?"

"Ach, aye. Right away."

"Going somewhere?" Kit asked as he strode into the stables.

"Yes. I'm going into the village."

"Might I accompany you?"

"That would be lovely. Thank you."

Now that they had agreed on keeping their relationship friendly, Kit hadn't looked at her with that familiar longing.

Except, *they* hadn't actually agreed upon it. Kit had made the decision without consulting her and she was left with no option but to go along with his plan. Not that she could disagree with his concerns.

They had grown accustomed to leaning on one another to satisfy their physical urges, but it was time to move on. And that started with a trip to the village to see what men might be available.

Kit commented along the way, pointing out places he'd played when he was a child living there with his father, and later with his uncle or alone with just the servants watching over him.

He told her of the improvements he'd made recently now that his lands were turning a profit.

"I know it isn't done to speak to women of such things as money, but you're not like other women and I'm rather proud that I've managed to turn my finances around after all these years."

"You should be proud, Kit. Most men would continue to run their properties into the ground without a care until it was too late. Then they would marry a woman with a heavy dowry to fix all their problems."

Or a widow with her own wealth.

Celia shook off the thought. Kit hadn't asked her to marry him for her money. Though her funds, in addition to his, would certainly take care of any lingering issues with his estates.

"I only decided to marry after I was certain I could offer a good life for my bride and any children we conceived. I'd seen how you were used for financial gain and I would never want whomever I married to think they were nothing more than a means to an end. I will marry someone because I respect them, care for them, and want to spend my life with them, but never because I need their coin."

"You didn't mention love?"

Kit shrugged and looked away. "I can't say, I would know if someone loved me."

"I'm sorry," she said. She only knew the love of her brother, which was certainly not the same. She hated that Kit had been passed around between his indifferent parents between England and Scotland. Never feeling secure or loved.

He winked, not in the naughty way she'd come to expect but in his normal fun way. "I wouldn't mind if someone offered."

Her throat burned and her eyes watered. If they hadn't been sitting on horses, she would have gone to him and pulled him into a hug.

"I only know brotherly love. I don't think my father was capable of love."

"You don't remember your mother? Did she not love you?"

"I remember snippets of her. Gray doesn't remember her at all. I tried to tell him, but somewhere along the way I think I turned our mother into something she never was. Almost a deity. Eventually, I didn't know what was truth and what I had made up to fill the hole in our lives."

"Holes," he said, correcting her word to the plural.

"Yes. You're right. In a way we lost our father at the same time my mother died. While he was still there in the physical sense, his soul was gone. And a man without a soul is capable of almost anything."

"I'm glad you and Gray have each other. I know most days you drive each other mad, but deep down you're family, and he clearly loves you even if he's quite an—"

"Arse." They laughed.

"Yes, quite."

"This is nice," she said, taking in the trees and the man next to her. He was attractive and she still felt the pull he had over her body, but he was also fun. She enjoyed spending time with him outside of their beds.

"It is. Mind you, I'll miss the sex, and in a matter of days I'll most likely regret my decision to only be friends, but this is nice."

He'd made her laugh again. She loved the way he just blurted out the truth no matter what light it shed upon him. His confidence was one of the many things she found so alluring about him.

"Your stablemaster is a woman," she said out of nowhere.

"Yes."

"Why?"

"Because she knows the most about the horses." He made it sound like it was an obvious thing. Perhaps it was, and she was the one caught up in convention.

"Hale's wife is a master of horses as well. Did you think horses only responded to humans who had a penis?"

She laughed at his outrageous comment and they continued on.

In the village, she was introduced to a number of people, all of which were happy to see Kit. Many thanked him for some kindness he quickly brushed off. They visited the shops and he bought her a few things.

It wasn't until they had made it back to Blairgowrie that she remembered the reason she'd gone to the village in the first place. She was on the hunt for a man who would move her forward in her plan.

She tried to recall if she'd met anyone that day who would do and couldn't think of anyone who had interested her as much as Kit.

Bother.

✦

CHAPTER TWENTY-ONE

K IT ACCEPTED AN invitation to an assembly being held at Lord Gamby's home. The man and his wife were a pleasant older couple, but more importantly, they had four grown sons who had yet to marry.

"Stay clear of the youngest one. He's my age and was a right bugger when we used to run amok in the summers. The three older ones would suit. I've seen the women titter over them."

"I've never tittered, and don't intend to do so now. Especially not over a man."

"Come now, countess," he purred as he stepped closer. "Surely I could make you titter if I tried."

"Which you won't, because we've come to an understanding."

He laughed at her scolding. He loved to rile her up.

"I have another thing I want in a wife," he mentioned. "She must have a bit of spunk about her. I don't want a woman who will easily do my bidding. I'd rather spar with her to get my way."

She frowned. "But you assume you'll get your way in the end?"

"I assume when we disagree, we'll reunite passionately, which despite what the original argument entailed, will end pleasantly."

"You are ruled by your manhood." She rolled her eyes and he wanted to grab her and carry her off to his bed, but he couldn't because they weren't doing that any longer.

He didn't argue. Though if he had he would have explained that his heart definitely played a major role in his decisions for the time being. This cock was not completely in charge.

He couldn't help but notice Celia was nervous in the carriage as they got closer to the Gamby residence.

"Do stop wringing your hands, it will be impossible to eat the mutton with your hands bent so." He twisted his mouth to the side. "Actually, that might be a good idea. The mutton is quite dry."

She laughed, but it was a strained sound that caused him to reach across the carriage to take her hand and give it a reassuring squeeze.

"No one but us know of your plans. If it doesn't feel right, you have no need to carry it out. We'll simply eat the dry mutton, converse pleasantly, and take our leave."

Celia let out a breath and nodded. "Yes, you're right. Thank you."

"I do like to hear how right I am."

His teasing worked, and soon she had relaxed enough to laugh freely and tease him in return.

Kit was pleased by how he was able to switch from Celia's lover to her friend so easily. He would fulfill his promise to help find her a lover and move on with his own plans.

Except as the dinner progressed and he watched the Gamby men fawn over Celia, Kit became more and more possessive.

He wanted to think it was because Celia was a friend and these men—clearly rakes, all—didn't deserve her.

But even he knew the truth. He wasn't as amenable to this plan as he'd thought. He still wanted Celia for his own. When his pointed looks didn't stop the men from flirting with her, he took to telling stories that made it clear he and Celia had a long history and cared for each other. He, of course, didn't allude to any physical relationship, but it was enough to claim her. Even though he had no right to do so.

It was no surprise when she eventually returned to his side, unsuccessful.

"I must apologize," he said as soon as they got in the carriage to return to Blairgowrie.

"Whatever for? I had an enjoyable evening."

"I said we should be friends and then I was in no way a friend tonight. I was horrid."

She shook her head. "In what way?"

"Did you not see me scowling at the men flirting with you? Did you not hear me tell them about how we are such close acquaintances? Or when James assumed I thought of you as a sister, I corrected him in a snappish way?"

She laughed. "I did not. I guess I was too distracted with four handsome men vying for my attentions. I found it most enjoyable. They didn't even stare at my birthmark."

"Why would they? I've told you many times, you make a bigger thing than it is."

"You can't understand, being perfect as you are, how it feels to be imperfect."

"You're not bloody imperfect. You have a mark on your face that is part of who you are. Like having brown eyes instead of blue, or brown hair instead of blond."

"Are you yelling at me?"

"Don't be ridiculous," he said even louder then frowned. "And also, yes, I am yelling. I'm sorry Celia. I want to be supportive. I want you to find what you need, but perhaps I'm not going to be strong enough to actually help you with this."

"If it is any matter, I don't think any of the Gamby men will suit. They were charming and handsome enough, but not for me."

He nodded. This information brought both relief and disappointment. For while he was glad she was still his, he knew the end was still yet to come.

CELIA HADN'T FELT an attraction to any of the Gamby men. It wouldn't have been disheartening except she hadn't been attracted to Mister Kenwood, or Lord Norscot. Lord Wembley had started off rather charming but soon grew overbearing. She didn't even consider the vicar because he was a vicar and seemed beyond such scandalous things as assignations, despite Kit's assurance it happened all the time.

Lord MacGregor seemed like a fine candidate until he mentioned being betrothed. And Lord Humphry was much too young.

The night before they were to leave for London, Celia felt disappointed and...restless. Not just restless, but frustrated as well. And at the center of her irritation was Kit.

"It's our last night here. Would you care to take a stroll through the gardens this evening before we retire?" he suggested.

"No. I think it best that I retire to my rooms. On the *other side of the house.*" Her voice sounded snappish, especially the last bit. She hadn't even realized being kept on the other side of the house had annoyed her, but it had.

Did the man think to keep her at a distance so she wouldn't attack him while he slept? As if she was incapable of keeping her hands off of him. He should be so lucky to be so admired.

Would he take to carrying around a large stick to fend off her advances?

She rolled her eyes and then let out a breath, unsure what had brought about her anger.

Kit hadn't done anything. Perhaps he'd kept her on the other side of the house so he wouldn't be tempted to break their agreement. Not that it had been an agreement so much as an edict from him.

She knew she should apologize, but the words wouldn't come. She was peevish. As if she had missed luncheon, but they had just had dinner. She wasn't hungry, but some craving lingered and demanded to be fed.

"Is something amiss? You were very quiet during dinner."

"Was I? I guess I had nothing to say." Snappish.

Tilting his head as a bird inspected a juicy worm, he stepped closer. "Something is bothering you. Please, tell me." His hand rested on the back of her arm and she felt the flames of desire spark to life. The fire within built hotter, and words she didn't even know she'd felt came pouring out of her mouth unchecked.

"Had I known the last time we were together would be our last, I feel I would have savored each second and stored it away to remember later."

"Is that so?"

"Yes," she said unashamedly. "But you made a decision that impacted both of us without discussing it with me. I'm not saying I don't agree that we should cease intimacies, I just…" She ran out of breath and anger at the same time and now felt a bit foolish.

"Are you proposing we give into desire this one last time so we can make a few final memories to treasure?" He smiled, that naughty turn of his lush lips that made her blood heat so.

"I would not be opposed to such a suggestion."

"Very well." He leaned closer until she felt his warm breath in her ear. "Let's make some memories, countess."

Immediately, the unrest she'd felt earlier drifted away, in the way the sun burns away the morning haze. Everything was clear again and it was the most natural thing to take his hand and allow him to lead her upstairs to his rooms.

Once there, they didn't fall into their normal routine of stripping off each other's clothing in a mad frenzy. Instead, he kissed her lazily as if they had weeks to enjoy each other's company.

In the far reaches of her mind, she knew it wasn't so. They would return to London soon enough, and she would have to let him go once and for all. This night, however was theirs.

Everything between them felt both comfortable and new as

he teased out each moan and touch from her. He was the same man she'd come to know so well, but it was she who'd changed.

Like their first night, using the cover of masks to enhance the freedom to do whatever they wanted, so did knowing this was their last time together.

She didn't hold anything back. She gave him everything. Their bodies fused into a tangle of limbs and kisses. Their gazes held tight to the other, watching every response. Not wanting to miss a single reaction.

Greedily storing away every memory for a time when they were apart.

"I don't think I'll ever have my fill of you," he whispered as their bodies joined together. The same intensity as all the times before, yet even more acute because it was the last time.

She replied with like words, though she couldn't recall exactly what she'd said.

They moved together slowly, drawing out each sensation. Taking and giving. Growing and expanding until, together, they reached the pinnacle of their desires.

As they lay together in replete exhaustion, random thoughts trickled through her mind. How much she didn't want this to end.

Kit leaned up to look at her, his eyes more serious than she'd ever seen.

"Celia."

"Please don't ask me to marry you. I fear if you do, I'll say yes and it will most likely be wonderful, but I will always miss the freedom I feel right now."

"Then we'll continue as planned and return to London as friends."

"Yes."

"Wife or no, I will always respect your wishes."

She knew that was true. She could trust him. And perhaps it would not feel stifling to be his wife. But still…

"Stay with me tonight, Celia. Tomorrow we'll go back to

what must be, but for tonight let us pretend that this is how it will always be."

There was only one answer. "Yes."

CHAPTER TWENTY-TWO

MORNING CAME TOO soon. Kit watched as the sun kissed Celia's skin, bathing her in pale light. He didn't want this to end, but in reality, it had ended even before they'd begun.

Poets said leaving was sweet sorrow, but Kit felt nothing sweet about it at all. Instead, it felt as if his insides were being ripped from his body. And rather than wait for her to wake and face the awkward words he would use to hide his pain, he got up and dressed.

He'd never considered himself a coward until that moment when he dashed out of the house to the stable and had Melody ready his horse for the trip back to London.

"You'll not be taking the carriage with the lady?"

"No." Celia wished for freedom. He'd allow her every bit of freedom from Scotland to London. He'd not have left her to travel alone for it wasn't safe. But she had her maid with her, and the coachman would see to the ladies.

Melody simply did as he'd asked, bringing Rufus around. In minutes he was off, galloping across a field at top speed.

It was common for Kit to give the stallion his head when they left the house so he could stretch out and settle in for the ride, but that was not what this was.

This was a full-on retreat to save his heart.

Poets also said time healed all wounds. That was yet to be determined.

CELIA WOKE IN an empty bed with an even emptier heart. Even before she left the bed, she knew Kit would be gone. The worst thing was that part of her was grateful he'd left without her.

She couldn't face him after what they'd shared the night before and not waiver in her resolve to keep to her plan to experience all that the life of a widow had to offer.

This freedom was her reward for doing her duty for her family and marrying an elderly stranger. She'd saved her father and brother, as well as the tenants and the estates when she'd married Hamlin.

Now it was time to save herself. To have what she desired without having to give up anything to get it. But not at the expense of Kit's heart. He wanted something different than she, but it was no less important.

With a new determination to do the right thing for both of them, she got dressed and prepared to return to her life.

It seemed a terribly long journey as she sat by the window of the carriage looking out at the endless green.

"Do you wish to talk about it?" Nettie offered after the first hour had passed in irritated silence. "It's sure something is bothering you."

"Yes. Something is bothering me, though I'm not sure why. I have exactly what I wanted. I'm no longer a virgin so Lord Hamlin will not be able to touch my settlement even if he pushes for an examination. I've enjoyed my time with Lord Stormont as my lover. And now I'm free to move on with whomever I chose. Just as I'd wanted."

Nettie nodded and waited expectantly. However, Celia wasn't sure what to say next. That should have been the extent of it. Every goal she'd made had come to fruition. Yet, she was still unsettled.

"The viscount has asked me to marry him."

"You don't seem pleased. He's quite a handsome man, and kind from what I've seen. You wouldn't do much better than him." Nettie leaned closer despite them being alone in the carriage. "Scots are known to be beasts in bed. You'd know better than me, but I wanted you to know you might be disappointed with the dandies in London after that mound of man."

"I allow you to speak too plainly," Celia said with a frown which only made her insolent maid laugh.

"If not for my plain speaking, you wouldn't have even considered the idea of taking a lover."

"You're right. I would have most likely married again, thinking I had no other options."

"Marriage is not that bad if it's with someone you like."

"But I don't want to have a husband. I want a lover."

"A husband is often times also a lover."

And it was that thought that continued to haunt her for days to come as they traveled for home.

The first morning after she returned, she entered the breakfast room to find Gray there already.

"Good morning, brother."

"Good morning. How was your trip? And before you answer, please know that I don't want to hear any of the details and am pretending you were with a female friend visiting her elderly grandmother who had taken ill but is doing much better."

Celia patted him on the shoulder. "Understood. Then I'm happy to inform you that the elderly grandmother has made a full recovery and is quite satisfied with her time in the country. I believe she has a spring to her step from all the wonderful—"

Gray groaned. "That's well enough. Sit and eat your meal."

Laughing, she took her seat and thanked Guthrie for serving her.

"I am glad to have you back, and luckier still that you never moved away. I am sorry for trying to order you about. I know better than to try to boss you around."

"Thank you. To be honest, I never really went to find a new

home. I only wanted you to think I did." She knew well how to handle her brother to get what she wanted.

"I know that because I met with the property managers and made sure to tell them how the last place you'd let had burned to the ground." Perhaps, Gray knew well how to manage her as well.

She smacked him, knowing he was joking. Or hoping he was anyway.

Her smile faded as she looked across the table to the vacant seat that was occupied by Kit most mornings.

"Is everything all right?" Gray asked.

She let out a sigh. "I imagine you would not care to know."

"Perhaps not the details, but I am getting better at pretending if you'd like to talk about it."

"Nothing is *right*, per se. But it is as it should be."

"You would not go wrong to marry him, CeeCee." Gray shrugged, giving an air of indifference to words she knew he meant to his very soul.

"I do know that. But I'm not ready to marry and he is."

"He would wait for you to be ready."

"It's not fair of me to ask him to wait for me to be ready. Especially since I don't know how long it might take." If ever.

"All this romantic business causes more pain than happiness. I have no idea why anyone would want to get tied up in such a scheme."

"I agree. Much better just to take strangers to your bed for mutual gratification."

Gray coughed and dropped his fork, as he pushed his plate away.

"Are you not going to eat your toast," she asked pleasantly as she snatched it from his plate.

"Blast it, CeeCee, you did that on purpose."

"What? Never," she poured on the innocence and batted her eyelashes.

"Keep with this behavior and I might kick you out of

Penbrook House myself," he threatened with an indulgent grin.

After breakfast, she left the house for Berwick Street as she had many times over the last few months. This time however she wasn't there to sneak into Kit's rooms, so she used the front entrance.

The butler opened the door and stared as if he didn't recognize her. He was older, but seemed sound of mind the other times she'd encountered him.

"I'll announce your arrival," he finally said and left awkwardly toward the study. He returned and led her to the room where she'd spent many hours in a state of undress. A shiver of anticipation ran up her spine but she shook it off. She wasn't here for that.

"Lady Hamlin," the butler said and left. Kit rose from behind his desk and waited for her to take her seat before sitting again.

"Good day, countess. How are you?"

"I'm well, and you?" If he wanted to exchange pleasantries as if she were nothing to him, then she could do that. For the time being anyway.

"I'm not well at all actually. I missed seeing you and Gray this morning but I didn't know if I would be welcome after how I'd behaved."

"You're speaking of the way you ran off while I was still abed?"

"Yes." He closed his eyes tightly.

"I remember our plan was to remain friends, but not hours after making that pact it appears to have collapsed into awkwardness."

He smiled. "I believe you've spent too much time in my company. You have become adept at speaking the truth as directly as I do."

"It's a fine quality, I think, to speak one's mind so expectations are set and no one is confused or disappointed."

"Go on."

"I don't wish to marry. At least I don't wish to marry at this time. If I did, you would be the only person I would even consider. But that doesn't do anything for the fact that you do want to marry and soon. I said I would help you find a proper bride and as yet, I've not met that obligation. Likewise, you said you would assist me in finding a man suitable for an affair and have not."

He opened his mouth as if to speak, but she continued.

"Both of us assured each other that regardless of the outcome—whether we found the people we were searching for or not—we would always remain friends, and now here we are in agreement that our friendship is at risk. Might I propose we move forward with the original plan so I shall not lose the best friend I've ever had?"

"I do feel that if I was not standing on this side of the desk my ear might be in peril."

She smiled, happy to have the happy Kit back.

"Quite."

His smile faded. "I cannot go on like we've been, Celia. We can't fall into bed again. It hurts too much to leave." He shook his head and ran his palm over his chin.

"We both agreed we would not make more of this arrangement than what it is," she reminded him.

"I'm well aware of what we agreed to. But I also told you my plans. I want a family. For years you and Gray have been my only family. Is it any wonder why I wished to keep you?"

"I will always be here for you, no matter what."

He took a deep breath and nodded. "I know that. Or I should. I've been alone long enough. But as enjoyable as this time has been with you, it cannot go on."

"And that is why I've come. As I said, we need to move on with the other part of our arrangement. We both agreed to help the other person maneuver the *ton* and find someone suitable for our needs. Are you ready to proceed in earnest?"

"You don't think I was looking for a lover for you in earnest previously?" he asked. Her only answer was to cock her eyebrow and stare at him. "Very well, I wasn't."

"I'm as guilty. It was pleasant to keep you to myself for my needs. But that is not fair to either of us."

She realized during her travels, that part of the reason she enjoyed being with Kit was because he was safe. He was known in a world where most things were unknown. But she longed for the adventure of meeting someone new and the experiences she would have with him.

He stood and came around to lean against his desk. "I can't thank you enough for coming today and setting us back on course. I would be grateful for your assistance." He gave a slight bow.

"Very well. Tonight, I will meet you at the Sterling Ball and we will begin our search anew and not stop until we've both found success."

"I look forward to seeing you. Good day, countess." With a kiss to her cheek, he escorted her out.

Once home, she went to her room and slumped into a chair by the window. Their time together as lovers was over. Tonight, they would begin the search to find other people. She should be pleased to finally get on with her plans.

She was terrified.

AFTER GETTING A nod of approval from his valet, Kit rushed down the stairs and out the door. He was running slightly late in meeting Celia at the Sterling ball.

Partly because he'd been distracted in making a list of potential brides and partly because after having made such a list he didn't want to go to the ball. He was instead suffering from a severe case of dread.

He expected his search for a wife to be an exciting step toward the future he'd always wanted. But the fear of being bound to the wrong person made him sweat.

"None of that." He brushed at his black coat and adjusted his tartan sash and white cravat. Despite his stern discussion with himself, his leg rocked the carriage the entire ride.

Oddly enough the moment he spotted Celia standing outside the townhouse waiting for him, a calm washed over him and he felt as if he could face a whole ballroom of potential brides and the plotting mamas as long as he had her at his back.

She turned and saw him approach, offering one of her bright smiles that warmed the deepest parts of him. He was certain the feeling was love, but since it was unwelcome, and unrequited, he didn't explore the emotion with great earnest.

He could only hope one of the many women inside would evoke the same feeling and he'd know she was the one for him.

"Did you have any more thoughts as to who you may want to consider for marriage?" Celia asked as they were enveloped into the heat and heavy scents of the ballroom.

"Yes. I've even made a list." He pulled it from his coat and handed it over for her inspection, feeling proud of himself.

She frowned. "This list has over a dozen women on it."

"In truth, every woman in this room who isn't otherwise engaged, is a potential wife, though I do still wish to stay clear of the debutantes if possible. I know these women and am not repulsed by them."

"That was the only criterium for choosing the person who will bear your children? That she not repulse you."

"I think it a good start, don't you?"

"Very well. I have an acquaintance with most of the women on this list. I'll make a point of speaking with as many as I can and see if any are suitable."

"And what are *your* criterium?" He was interested to know what she would find important in a partner.

"As you said, not a debutante. You need someone with more maturity. She must be intelligent. You like to carry on deep conversations in a diverse number of topics so you would be bored with a woman who could not speak on such things. She must be modest, otherwise, I'll not be able to visit."

He chuckled at that last requirement. As well as the fact she'd misunderstood when he'd asked after her conditions. But she continued before he could clarify.

"She must be looking to marry for the right reasons. Not necessarily that she is holding out for love, but that she considers mutual respect to be important in a match."

He nodded. "I'm impressed that you are taking such care with the search."

She returned an offended look. "I care about you and your happiness, Christopher. I do not want a poor match to result in a lifetime of misery for you. I would never forgive myself if I matched you with someone who made you unhappy."

He felt that familiar warmth wash over him at her admission that she cared for him. He knew it wasn't the way he needed, but he could revel in it all the same.

"I promise to take the same care in helping you select a companion, even if the relationship will be a temporary one."

"I appreciate that. Let us split up to do reconnaissance and meet two dances before the supper dance to confer."

His lips pulled up at her take charge attitude. She could have been a general in his majesty's army.

Taking her card, he wrote his name in for that dance. "That we might strategize."

With a nod she went on her way to explore his options. He made his rounds of the room, greeting a few friends. He was surprised to see Ernest Dalforth in attendance.

"Whatever are you doing here?" Kit asked the man who looked absolutely miserable as he plucked at his cravat.

"My sister is out this Season and as the head of the family, I must be in attendance to scare off every man who so much as looks at her."

"I see. I didn't realize she had come of age."

"She has, and I don't mind to tell you, I'm hoping she'll make a match that can help my situation." He said the last word quieter than the rest and Kit knew what type of situation he meant. It was no secret Lord Dalforth was in financial straits.

Kit didn't think they were in dire straits. Surely giving his sister a season was proof enough Ernest had at least some funds left.

"Her dowry is not much to speak of, it's good that she's beautiful and pleasant. Someone should be willing to overlook the rest when they see her."

"Take care, Dalforth, she's a sister, not an investment. Her happiness should come first." He thought of Celia and the way she'd been sold to Hamlin for a large purse, her happiness not even considered. It was the way of the *ton*, but it didn't make it right.

"Yes, yes. Of course, it does, but I only hope that her happiness comes along with a substantial sum."

"Let us hope it is an amiable situation for both of you." Kit offered a quick bow to the baron and moved along. He might have considered Ernest for Celia but knowing he was on the hunt for funds was an unsafe prospect for Celia.

He made his rounds of the ballroom and the cardroom and found a few men that would be suitable for Celia. He found his criteria for prospective gentlemen to be stricter than the conditions he'd made for his own bride. Because of that, he found most of the men here were not good enough for her.

When it was time, he headed through the crowd toward the dance floor. When the throng of people parted and he saw her, that familiar feeling of peace returned yet again.

Suddenly, he felt the few men he'd identified as a possibility to be unworthy of her as well.

Bollocks.

CHAPTER TWENTY-THREE

"**I** DON'T KNOW what you were thinking," Celia scolded as she shook her head.

"Did you not find anyone on my list to your liking?" Kit asked.

That was a question she didn't know quite how to answer. She hoped the reason she found each of the women lacking was because they didn't fit her stipulations, but she worried there was an underlying reason she wasn't prepared to discuss with Kit.

She needed to focus on the facts. They'd both agreed to take their searches seriously this time. She had to do her part to help him, because she was relying on him to help her as well.

Still, the list…

"Lady Elderidge laughs at everything, even if it isn't funny in the least. Miss Milton wouldn't deign to speak to me as I'm not as perfect as her."

"She said that?" His head jerked up as he searched the room, his fists tight at his side. He was ready to take up Celia's defense and she was touched. But she couldn't set him off after the snobby witch.

"No. Not exactly." She had said *nearly* as much. "A few of the women on your list seem to have their caps set on men already and are waiting for them to come up to scratch. If you wait you could have your choice of the ones left behind."

His eyes went wide. "Are you suggesting I hang about for the castoffs?"

"If you want someone from this list, that may be your only option."

"Is no one at this function suitable?"

She bit her bottom lip as she pondered. "Well, there is one person that met all my conditions but one."

"Which condition?"

"She's a debutante, but mature for her age. Very intelligent, but not stuffy about it. She wouldn't allow you to lord your knowledge of things over her and would challenge you, I think. And she wishes to find a gentleman based upon his merits not his status or financial circumstances. She's quite charming."

"I can't help but notice you have not mentioned her physical attributes, which can only mean I've not met her already because she's a gorgon. I've heard gorgons are intelligent. Quite well read; all the eyes." He gestured toward his head.

Celia couldn't help but laugh. "I assure you she is far from a gorgon. In fact, she might even be the most enchanting creature here."

"But you called her a creature. That can't be good." Kit winced, though she knew he would not hold physical beauty over a person's heart.

"Are you saying you do not wish to meet her? Even for one dance?"

"Very well. What's the worst that can happen?"

"You could be turned to stone and become a statue in Lady Sterling's ballroom for the rest of eternity?"

"Quite." He glared at her. "Lead the way to my impending doom, countess."

The use of her title didn't feel as cold as it once had. Kit managed to make it sound like a term of endearment. Friends. She led the way through the crowd and stopped when she reached the young woman.

"Miss Bennington, may I make known to you, Viscount Stormont."

The young woman curtsied politely as Kit bowed. When he stood, he tilted his head inspecting her rudely. Celia was about to elbow him in the ribs when he started and said, "Willa?"

"Yes. Are we already acquainted, my lord?" Her bright smile faltered.

"We are. I went to school with your brother, Ernest. At Eton before my father sent me off to Heriot's."

"Oh, I see." Her answer wasn't quite disappointed, but almost.

"I just saw him here tonight for the first time in years," Kit said and Willa's eyes lit again with interest. "I did come to your house once when you were just a girl."

"I am no longer a girl." Lady Willa stood straighter.

"I see that. Do you perhaps have a dance left that I could secure?"

She smiled beautifully and held out her dance card for his inspection.

"I shall see you for the supper dance," he said and bowed. "It was a pleasure to see you again."

"I look forward to it, my lord."

Celia and Kit moved away, but she saw him look over his shoulder at the woman he'd obtained a dance with.

"I can't believe that woman is little Willa. She's magnificent."

Celia worried she might need to pick his jaw up from the floor so he didn't step on it. "Yes. As I said. Not a gorgon. You have not been turned to stone."

"True." He bent his arms as if testing their flexibility.

"Now. On to the matter of who you've selected for me, as you now have a dance reserved with a prospect."

Perhaps focusing on her own possibilities would alleviate the pressure in her chest at seeing Kit's reaction to the woman Celia chose for him. She was pleased for him, and if things went well with the girl, Celia would be glad to see him find happiness.

The fact that his reaction stung ever so slightly was of little importance and accounted for the fact they had only recently shifted their relationship from lovers to friends.

Memories of their last night still caught her off guard and made her blood heat as well as her heart hurt. It was bound to get easier.

"Very well," he said. "At the moment I only saw three men here I would consider for your… *appraisal.*" He pointed them out and introduced her to the gentleman she found most appealing.

Lord Beckstone was tall with dark hair and stunning blue eyes. There was a dimple in his chin that never went away which gave him the look of being pleasant. But she was to find out during their dance he was not very pleasant at all.

"You are Lord Penbrook's sister are you not?" Beckstone asked while staring openly at her birthmark.

Out of habit, she turned her face so he couldn't see it. After the months she'd spent with Kit and his constant praise she'd almost forgotten she was unappealing to some men because of her imperfection.

How silly she was to pick the most attractive of the men Kit presented and think she would lure him to her bed as if she was some great seductress. This knowledge made her feel awkward, and the feeling was made worse when she stumbled and then stuttered an apology without looking the man in the eye.

"I seem to remember your husband as being quite aged, was he not?"

"He was. But he was a kind man." As casual conversation went, Lord Beckstone was moving swiftly into personal topics one didn't speak of with people they'd just been introduced to.

"Yes, I imagine he would have needed to be kind." Again, he glanced at the mark on her face as he said the last word with a sneer. "I've heard the marriage was not legitimate. The case is being brought to the house soon. I can say you seem to be the type of woman who assumes she deserves more than she should."

He looked at her as if the very idea of touching her during the dance repulsed him.

The entire meeting was a disaster and she wanted to flee the ballroom and go home where it was safe. She didn't belong here with all these beautiful people of the *ton*. What had she been thinking?

Why had Kit thought this man would want to be her lover? He was awful. For a brief moment she worried Kit had done this on purpose to keep her from finding a man, but she decided Kit would never expose her to someone he knew was this cruel.

When the dance came to a close, some thirteen hours later— or so it seemed—she headed to the nearest exit. Kit caught up with her on the terrace.

"What has happened?" he asked. Then he gave her a wicked smile. "Are you to meet him in some dark place in the garden?"

She laughed, but the sound held no humor. "No. Definitely not." Her lip quivered and her eyes stung. Neither of which escaped Kit's notice.

"What did he do?" Once again Kit's fingers were balled up and his brow was creased in simmering rage. Celia almost wanted to launch Kit at the horrible man she'd just danced with, but she couldn't allow him to do something that would ruin his chances at finding a suitable wife.

"It wasn't him. It was me. I forgot who I am for a moment."

"What the hell does that mean?"

Without thinking her fingers unknowingly reached for her temple as if to hide the spot from him. It was preposterous. Kit had seen all of her. More than anyone else. She couldn't hide anything from him.

"That blighter," he muttered, and turned to go back inside.

"No. Please don't make a scene. Let us just move on. Lord Beckstone is not to be my lover, and I'm fine with that."

"I'm sorry, Celia. I didn't realize he was a wretched prick."

"Now you know he is." She offered a weak smile to let him know she was unharmed, though inside she was still reeling with the man's rudeness. "Also, he told me Edward's case will be heard by the House of Lords soon."

Kit nodded. "Gray didn't wish for you to worry over nothing.

Besides, even if it doesn't go in our favor, as we expect it will, an examination would only prove your rights to your settlement. It might be uncomfortable, but it would not change anything."

She nodded. He was right. She didn't wish for such an intrusion into her privacy, but there was nothing Edward could do to get his hands on her money now. She'd seen to it.

She wouldn't be ashamed of such deceit, not knowing that Arthur had wanted to make sure she was provided for. He'd known the truth and gave her that settlement anyway. She was only doing what needed to be done to ensure what her husband wanted. She also knew well enough that Arthur would rather give it to her than to see his fortune spent blindly at the gambling hells.

"Come. Let me introduce you to Lord Rathmore," Kit said as if it was the easiest thing.

"I don't think I'm quite ready for this. I thought I was, but I think I need more time."

He shook his head. "Allow me to introduce you to the other men, just introductions. You do not need to jump into bed with anyone tonight. Please don't let that scoundrel ruin your night, Celia." The last sentence was whispered by her ear. "You are stronger than him."

She squared her shoulders and nodded once. Kit was right, she wouldn't allow one man to put her off her plans for happiness. She wanted to experience all the pleasure a man had to offer.

She placed her hand on Kit's arm and smiled. "Please lead the way."

AFTER INTRODUCING CELIA to Lord Rathmore and giving the man a steady look of warning, Kit went to collect his dance partner promptly. Willa was the only woman who had attracted his interest in the least.

She was standing next to her brother when Kit approached and bowed before her.

"I believe this dance belongs to me, my lady."

She curtseyed and offered a dazzling smile. "Yes."

Ernest frowned as Kit led the man's sister to the dance floor. No doubt Ernest recalled Kit's financial situation as being bleak, he wouldn't know Kit had turned his finances around and could now support a wife and family comfortably. Though he was not quite flush enough to get Ernest set to rights as well.

Kit would worry about getting the man's blessing when and if it came to Kit wanting to offer marriage. For now, it would just be a dance and dinner.

Willa smiled up at him. "It seems my brother disapproves of you."

Kit laughed. "And it seems you are pleased by your brother's disapproval."

She laughed as well and he found that while the sound didn't warm his soul as Celia's laugh did, it was not at all unpleasant. Perhaps these things took time to grow on a person. Maybe one day, Willa's laugh would affect him in the same way.

"Please do not misunderstand," she said. "It's not that I don't take his opinion seriously, it's that he only cares about a man's purse."

"I'm aware. Please know that I am capable of making a wife comfortable if not her brother." It was not something discussed with a woman, especially a potential bride, but that custom seemed silly. Shouldn't the woman know of such things to better determine if he would make an adequate partner?

She smiled again. "It seems the perfect situation to me."

"I feel I have missed a great deal of entertainment by never having siblings. My dear friend and his sister are much the same as you and Ernest in that they enjoy tormenting each other. But I would guess if things turned bad, you would give your very life for the other."

"Oh yes. It is a strange relationship indeed. And I have six brothers and sisters. I love and loath them equally at times."

"I hope to have a large family someday." Another thing that wasn't generally discussed with a young miss, but something she should know before considering him.

"As do I."

"My home in Scotland is well suited for a large family," he mentioned.

"I quite enjoy Scotland."

Their gazes met and he felt contentment. Not in the way he felt when he'd held Celia in his arms, but it was something he knew he could live with at least. And maybe someday be happy.

He escorted her to supper and they continued to converse about all manner of things. Celia had been right in that Willa would challenge him with her knowledge of certain topics. She seemed to have everything he wanted—or rather Celia had wanted for him.

He looked up from his dinner companion and found Celia smiling at Lord Rathmore at the other end of the table. Kit knew Rathmore wouldn't mistreat Celia. In fact, he might prove to be too honorable for her plans, but hopefully she would enjoy his company.

While the thought of her with another man still stung, he hoped he was one step closer to moving on.

He smiled at the woman next to him, having missed what she'd said. He would put his energy toward this woman.

The one who wanted the same things as he.

CHAPTER TWENTY-FOUR

CELIA LIKED LORD Rathmore very much. He was quite entertaining. Perhaps not as funny as Kit, but she couldn't expect as much from anyone. So far, she and Rathmore had spent most of their dinner ignoring the other people around them while flirting with each other.

He was attractive, fair like Kit, but without as many different shades of blond. His eyes were dark and kind, and not once had they settled on her mark.

However, his gaze hadn't settled on her décolletage either, so she couldn't be sure he was interested in a physical encounter.

He enjoyed music and visiting the theatre as many men did. He had one older sister and had become a marquess at the age of fifteen after his father died.

"I understand your brother is a marquess as well, though I don't think I've had the pleasure."

She paused to study his features in order to determine if he was bringing up Gray to be snide. She didn't see any evidence he was judging her based on her brother's reputation.

"He is a marquess, though it might be a bit of an overstatement to call it a pleasure to know my brother." She laughed. While she didn't want Lord Rathmore to disparage her brother, she was permitted to do so, having known him all his life. "He doesn't attend any society events. He's quite the rake."

"I see. Well then nothing I do will shock you." His brows

lifted in a knowing way and Celia's skin went hot. He was flirting with her again.

"I would say not," she responded with a coy grin.

Despite their exchange over dinner, he simply kissed her hand and bid her goodnight when it was over.

"I look forward to seeing you again," he added before walking away.

"As do I," she said more to herself.

The initial disappointment slipped away as relief flooded in. As much as she wanted to move on with her plan to take a man to bed, and as much as Lord Rathmore seemed a likely partner, she wasn't quite ready to proceed.

Perhaps it was nerves. This was a big step. True, she was no longer a virgin, but she only knew one man's touch. She couldn't be certain they all liked the same things. What if she and Lord Rathmore did not match up as well as she did with Kit?

When she'd made love with Kit it felt as if they had become one in a way she'd never expected. She didn't need to speak of what she wanted. She only need think it and somehow, he knew as if he'd heard her thoughts.

Of course, there were the times when he'd asked her to tell him specifically what she'd wanted and even encouraged her to use dirty words to describe it.

The memory made her cheeks heat. Surely, she couldn't use such vocabulary with Lord Rathmore. He would most likely be scandalized and toss her from his bed.

Before she made her way out of the house, she was stopped by a man she had never met. He was older than she by probably ten years or so, and offered her a kind smile.

"Lady Hamlin, if I might have a word?"

She returned his smile. "It seems you know who I am, though I'm sure we've not been introduced."

"Yes, pardon my poor manners. I am Lord Seville."

Celia cast about for some recognition and found none. Fortunately, she did not have to wait long for the man to get to the reason he had stopped her.

"I am an acquaintance of Lord Hamlin."

For a moment, Celia thought of Arthur, but then realized this man was referring to Edward. She stood a bit straighter, anticipating a threat.

"Edward owes me quite a bit of blunt. While it's not polite to speak of such things with a lady, he tells me you are the reason he's not yet paid his debts. I've come directly to you on his behalf to see them settled."

The nerve of Edward to make it seem as if she was delinquent in paying his debts.

"I am sorry you have been misinformed, Lord Seville. I am not the reason his debts have not been paid. You see, he is responsible for settling his own debts. I will not see to use my own funds to pay another's debt, just as you would not be expected to pay the debts of one of your distant family members."

"I would if I had obtained funds that rightfully belonged to another."

"Again, I have not obtained funds that rightfully belong to Edward, despite what he might think. If you will excuse me, this conversation grows tedious and my carriage will be arriving."

The man put out his arm to block her path forward and for the first time, she felt a jolt of fear shoot up her spine.

"Listen to me. If you'd rather settle this matter in the House of Lords, so be it, but I will get what I'm owed, one way or another."

"Excuse me, Seville, but it sounded as if you were threatening the lady? Surely, I misheard," Kit said as he came to stand next to her.

Seville glared at Kit for two heartbeats before standing down.

"Of course not. I only meant to inform the lady that a vote on the matter of her settlement will not go in her favor. I've heard many who hold seats have already stated how a widow should not hold so much wealth. It is a disservice to her, you see. She is vulnerable to falling for some ruse that would leave her destitute."

"I'm sure her brother, as well as the Duke of Roxburghe, and the Earl of Melville would not appreciate you thinking them inept in offering the lady their protection. I, myself, take such offense and would ask you to leave at once."

The man blustered about and Celia worried he would continue, but he must have seen something in Kit's eyes that changed his course for he simply muttered something about seeing them soon before hurrying off.

Kit offered his arm as they went out to wait for her carriage to be brought around.

"My, you certainly know how to make the evening interesting."

"Do you think he was telling the truth about having the votes to require an examination?"

"No. Don't worry about him. Your brother and I are handling things. We have a lot more friends than Edward because obviously we are better company."

"I'm not worried about Edward's friends as much as who he owes money to."

Kit frowned. "Leave it to us."

"Very well," she said, because there was little she could do about it anyway.

"Did you enjoy your company at dinner?" he asked with a wry smile. She appreciated him changing the subject.

"Very much." She shrugged. "Though it appears I'm still to go home alone."

"Allow me to escort you home then," he offered when her conveyance arrived. Taking her hand, he assisted her in and took the seat opposite hers. "So, you fancy Rathmore?"

"I do. He's charming, but I can tell there's something more to him underneath."

"I believe that's an apt description of Willa as well. She's quite lovely on the outside, but there's more to her than just physical appeal. She's interesting."

"You are not repulsed?" she teased.

"Certainly not. Thank you for the introduction. This might actually work out. For both of us."

"Is it possible that after a rough start, we've both found our perfect match tonight?" she removed the pins from her hair, happy to let her hair down.

"Perhaps. I will call on Willa tomorrow and offer a ride in Hyde Park as is expected."

Celia studied her feelings at Kit's comment and was pleased to find she didn't feel more than the smallest twinge of jealousy. She was happy Kit had found someone pleasant. Perhaps her own joy made it easier to encourage him, but for whatever the reason, she was most grateful that the two of them had fallen easily back into the friendship they'd shared before their affair. She had worried they would not be able to go back to being the way they'd been.

"Don't forget to take flowers," she said.

"Should I not have them sent?"

"I think it more personable that a man take them to a lady during his visit. Besides, then you can see her response."

He nodded. "I wouldn't be discouraged that Rathmore didn't suggest continuing your evening at your home, he's respectable, but not without his liaisons."

She smiled. "To be honest, I'm not sure I had the courage to proposition him anyway. I did enjoy the flirting, perhaps the pursuit is as gratifying as the reward."

He tilted his head as if considering her comment. "I would say in *most* cases the pursuit is more pleasurable than the actual act."

"Is that so? I didn't feel that way with you." How strange to be able to speak of their situation so freely. No regret.

"Nor I with you, but what we have is quite different than a simple sexual encounter. We have a friendship."

"Yes," she agreed, happy that he felt the same way as she did. It wasn't often they didn't agree on something. Even when he said things to rile her up, it was generally only to tease her. In most things they were aligned.

He helped her down from her carriage when they arrived at her home.

She brushed a hand over her skirts though a wrinkle was of no concern when her hair was down and she was heading in for the night. She hurried inside so no one would see and Kit followed.

In the drawing room, she poured them each a brandy and after kicking off her slippers she tucked her feet under her on the settee. Kit took the chair opposite her.

"I hope both of us can find a similar friendship in the person we choose to spend our time with. I understand friendship is not required for my needs, but it is welcome. Sex is wonderful, but I also enjoy the moments afterward immensely."

"As do I," he answered and then looked around as if surprised to find himself in her drawing room. "I assume Gray is still out."

She nodded. "Carousing, I'm sure."

"I don't miss that." He shook his head.

"Can I get you another brandy?" she asked, looking down at his empty glass.

"I should probably go. I only wanted to see you home safe. Which I have." He gestured toward the door but made no move toward it. "Thank you for tonight, Celia. It was most successful."

"Yes. I believe it was."

His gaze moved down to her lips and for a moment she thought he might kiss her. She felt the familiar anticipation of his touch, but the haze in his green eyes dissipated and he cleared his throat. "Goodnight, countess."

There was a moment of awkwardness as he left the room after kissing her cheek in a friendly way instead of touching her lips.

Perhaps it would take more time to get them on solid footing. It had felt natural to kiss him. She would need to be careful of such things so they didn't fall into old habits.

She retired to her room where Nettie helped her change before crawling into her empty bed.

What would it be like to have Lord Rathmore in her bed? She wondered about his Christian name. Surely, she couldn't be expected to cry out his title in the heat of passion.

As she imagined how it might be between them, she suddenly realized the face in her fantasy had shifted from that of Lord Rathmore to Kit. And the dream itself was not a vision of the future, but a memory from their past.

The last time they'd made love.

She tossed and turned, hoping to change the vision back to the man she had a possible liaison with, but she couldn't grasp on and keep him there.

Eventually she gave up, hoping her faulty imagination was due to her lack of experience with anyone other than Kit. Surely it was normal for her to recall the person she knew rather than the one she did not.

At least she hoped as much.

One thing she was certain of, tomorrow night she would make sure she didn't go to bed alone.

THE NEXT NIGHT, Celia turned in her bed and groaned at the ceiling in her bedchamber. She couldn't sleep. Frustration had taken over her body and made her too stimulated to rest.

She had not gathered up enough courage to invite Rathmore to her bed, despite them spending another evening together flirting and sharing heated looks. It seemed the man wanted to court her when all she wanted was…

She couldn't even think the word without thinking of the act. And thinking of the act brought visions of Kit to her mind, naked visions.

Twice she got out of bed planning to go to Kit and beg him to alleviate the need she felt, but she couldn't set herself up for such rejection. And he would be right to reject her.

It was clear he was getting closer to Willa and seemed happy. He'd complained when Celia had met him at the ball that night that he hadn't been able to take Willa riding because of poor weather. But she saw how much time they'd spent talking. He'd danced with her twice. Both waltzes. Celia couldn't do anything to jeopardize what Kit was building with the young woman.

When morning finally came, she went down to breakfast too early for Gray to be there. Not yet hungry, she retrieved a book from the library just so she would have a distraction.

Kit arrived before Gray and being alone with him made her need worse instead of better.

When the footmen left the room, Kit slanted a questioning look at her. "What's amiss?"

Damn him for being able to read her so easily. Not that she would try to hide her discontent.

"I find myself...uneasy. Do you ever suffer the same affliction?"

He laughed and then settled at her glare. "Uh, no. But only because I take care of my discomfort myself." He frowned at his plate. "I'm courting a debutante, I shall be caring for my own discomfort for some time, I think."

"Yourself?" she questioned.

He held up a hand and wiggled his fingers. She shook her head once, not understanding and then—"Oh. I didn't realize..."

He looked over his shoulder toward the door and leaned in as he whispered. "You've never touched yourself, Celia?"

"No. I was always told I was to remain *untouched* for a husband."

"Clearly there's no reason to hold back now." He sat back in his seat with a smug grin. He was so handsome she felt her blood heat, which didn't help her condition at all.

"You're quite right." She nodded and set her napkin aside. "Excuse me. I must go now. Thank you."

She got up to leave the room and stopped at the sound of his groan.

"What is it?"

"I must go on about my day knowing you are in your bed pleasuring yourself?" He shifted uneasily in his chair.

"Unless you'd care to join me and we can pleasure each other." She said it in jest, but a part of her hoped. That part was set to be disappointed.

He hesitated as if considering for only a few seconds.

"No. I cannot. I am to go riding with Willa in the park since it looks to be a nice day. I must be true to her as she may one day be my wife."

"Of course, I understand." She did understand, but when her body was on fire with need, as it was now, it caused her mind to become muddled. It seemed she could only think of the one thing she craved. "Enjoy your ride."

"Enjoy your…" He motioned toward the door and sighed.

CHAPTER TWENTY-FIVE

K IT LEFT PENBROOK House shortly after Celia quit the room. It was difficult to enjoy his breakfast when temptation beckoned. It would have been an easy thing to go to Celia's room and take her up on her earlier offer of sating each other's needs. But they'd agreed that part of their relationship was over.

Instead, he'd gone home to take care of…matters.

And now he had a wife to woo.

He pushed thoughts of Celia from his mind as he stepped down from his carriage and rushed up the steps to Derforth House. The door opened immediately and Willa stood next to the indulgent butler who held out her pelisse. Kit smiled at her eagerness feeling excited himself.

Willa looked lovely in her walking dress. With the tension eased from his body, he was better able to smile and play the doting companion rather than the scoundrel he normally was in a beautiful woman's presence.

"I'm glad the weather is more agreeable today. I admit to being excited about our outing today, my lord. I do enjoy our conversations."

"As do I," he said truthfully.

He did enjoy talking with her. She was quite good at talking. In fact, her lips hardly stopped moving when he was near her. He much preferred it to being with a woman who was too shy to speak.

Perhaps he could fall in love with Willa. Maybe they could make a happy life together. He hated that the thought of moving on with someone else made him instantly think of Celia and what could have been between them.

Standing straighter, he made a silent promise not to slip into those thoughts again. Celia was not to be his. No matter how he might have wished it.

Before he'd even helped Willa into the conveyance, she was off in conversation, hardly waiting for him to answer the first question before asking the next.

"I'm sorry, my brother often says I'm guilty of unleashing a verbal barrage on innocent bystanders."

"Not at all. Though I find myself unsure which of your questions to answer first."

She laughed at herself and shook her head. "Please feel free to answer any or none. Perhaps you have your own questions."

He paused thinking over her words. Perhaps he was guilty of letting her rule their discussions. Had he not asked anything about her?

He already knew about her family. He knew she liked riding. They'd shared their mutual desire for a large family and how they enjoyed town, but found they preferred the country.

What else could he wish to know?

His thoughts went dark as he considered his other questions. What color were her nipples? Would she squirm as he kissed the inside of her thighs?

He cleared his throat and pushed those inquiries far away. He would not know the answers to those questions today. Or in the very near future. Courting a debutante could take months. And then if they agreed to marry it would be additional months or even a year before they actually wed.

He swallowed down a groan.

"Do you like dogs or cats?" he asked instead. Pets were safe enough.

"Dogs. Though I have both at Dalforth Manor. What about

you?"

"I've never had a pet so I'm not sure." His answer rather ended that thread of conversation.

As he struggled to come up with something else to discuss, he was flagged down by someone who was sure to ruin his day. Stopping the carriage he excused himself, and gestured for his coach to hold the horses while he stepped away to address Lord Hamlin.

"As you can see, I am busy. Whatever you have to say, do it quickly."

"It's come to my attention that you have been spending a lot of time with Lady Hamlin."

Kit looked over his shoulder at Willa who was frowning at the man.

"As you can see, that is not Lady Hamlin."

"I didn't mean at the moment, but I've heard you spend a great deal of time at Penbrook House."

Kit wanted to plant the man a facer and be on with his day, but later today the lords would gather to vote on Edward's claims that Celia didn't deserve her settlement, so Kit stayed to hear what the man had to say.

"It is no secret Lady Hamlin's brother has been my close friend since we were lads," Kit said with an air of boredom.

"You know what I'm getting at, Stormont. If you've dallied with her, I have a proposition for you."

"A proposition?" Curiosity won out, though his fingers clenched into fists.

"If you will say she was a virgin when she came to your bed, and turn your vote for me, I will share the proceeds with you. I know you could use the blunt."

Kit could only stare at the man, as words abandoned him. It was clear the blighter was quite desperate if he held any hope that Kit would betray his best friend for coin.

"You are despicable. Not only would I have nothing to do with such a proposition, but I will tell all who will listen how you were willing to lie to get what you want. What you have no rightful claim to. I will see you in a few hours and when the vote is cast against you, the laughter you hear will be mine."

With that, Kit hurried back to his carriage and apologized to Willa.

"He is most unpleasant," Willa said. "My brother said he cheated him out of a fair amount of money at the tables a few weeks ago."

"I am not surprised. Let's forget about him. You were saying, before we were interrupted..." Kit took the coward's way out of having to carry the conversation.

Fortunately, Willa showed mercy and took over the discussion once again.

He hadn't realized how difficult it was to talk to an innocent young woman. Everything he would have normally said to Celia had to be run through a filter. Most topics were quickly tossed aside as inappropriate.

He would need to get better at this. And soon. But first he had somewhere quite important to be.

He returned Willa and her maid to Derforth House and offered Ernest a ride to the House of Lords for the session that afternoon.

"You do plan to vote in favor of Graham's sister, don't you?" Kit decided to confirm before allowing the carriage to move on.

"Yes. Do you think anyone would dare to cross Lord Penbrook in regard to his only sister? Only someone courting death would be so dimwitted."

Kit nodded and thumped on the roof to carry on.

As they entered Westminster Kit found Gray waiting. Hale had arrived from Scotland. Hayworth was there, as were other men Gray knew from Eton.

"Who does Hamlin have to vote on his side?" Hale asked.

"Only a few men he owes money to. Timmons knows this may be the only way he's to see any of the blunt he's due."

"Beckstone will side with him as well," Kit said, remembering what Celia had told him after she'd danced with him."

"No, he won't." Kit looked up to see Lord Rathmore standing at the edge of their impressive group. "He owed me money and I told him I would waive the amount if he voted with us."

Kit had known the man to be honorable. While he wasn't overjoyed that Celia had her sights on the man to become her next lover, Kit felt he had at least earned such a right here today.

The group entered the chambers and took their assigned places, awaiting the session to begin.

Lord Hamlin looked pale and sweaty. Whether his own guilt was eating at him or he cowered from the many glares sent his direction, Kit wasn't certain.

When the time came for him to take the floor, Kit had to lean in to hear his breathless voice as he stammered over the declaration.

"Speak up," the lead speaker ordered and Hamlin cleared his throat before trying again.

"I declare that my grandfather, the Sixth Earl of Hamlin was tricked into offering a settlement upon his wife, Lady Celia Dorsett Hamlin that is unjust under the accusation that the marriage was not consummated and is rendered therefore illegitimate."

"What proof do you have of this?"

"A chambermaid at Archstone will give witness that the bedclothes were not marked after the wedding night, my lord speaker."

The men at the front of the room muttered to one another.

Hale, being a duke, was the first to rise and speak.

"Lord Speaker, if you would," he looked around. "I don't wish to share such intimate details regarding my own marriage, but my wife has given me leave to do so if it might deter an invasive investigation."

"Go on, your grace," the speaker said.

"Thank you. I can speak in regard to experiencing a similar situation with my wife, whom I assure all here was in fact a virgin, that the age of the bride is a factor in such things. A more mature woman, especially one who is active as with my duchess, as well as Lady Hamlin, may not produce such proof as one might expect. I've a doctor waiting outside who can confirm this if you wish to hear from an expert in such things. Or perhaps we might ask the lords present who are married if they have experienced such things."

There was a murmuring throughout the room, but no one jumped up to offer such testimony.

Gray rose next. Kit saw his hands clenched in fists by his side.

"Might I say something as well as the brother of the woman whose virtue is being called into question?"

The mumbling rose louder and Edward went from pale to a greenish hue.

The speaker smacked the desk with his mallet in an effort to demand quiet.

"Go on."

"The previous Earl of Hamlin, my sister's husband, did not set up the settlement on my sister before the marriage. It was done months later when he'd grown ill. Would a man do such a thing for a wife if he had not consummated the marriage? The same chambermaid that will say the sheets were unmarked will also be able to testify that the couple shared a bed. So who are we to doubt what happened in their marriage bed if the earl clearly saw it to be a real marriage."

Kit stood next and introduced himself.

"Rather than testify, I wish to learn Lord Hamlin's motives by calling his grandfather's marriage into question at this time, years after he's been gone. I daresay, it seems suspect as the man has gone deep into debt with many gaming houses as well as other peers. If he forces an innocent woman to be subjected to an examination, I as well as many others, require his finances be examined."

Edward blustered about until the speaker called for quiet yet again.

"Lord Hamlin, it appears your claim will be met with heavy contest. Are you sure you wish to proceed?"

Edward swallowed and slowly shook his head. Timmons slammed his fist and glared at Lord Hamlin.

"Then this matter is deemed resolved. No further inquiries shall be made regarding Lady Hamlin's virtue."

All the men that had been on their side seemed to take a deep breath. Hale patted Gray on the back.

Celia would be spared any examination or forced to testify.

She remained free to continue on with her plans.

⁂

UPON ARRIVING AT the Clemmons' Ball that evening, Celia visited briefly with Kit before Lord Rathmore came to her side to request a dance.

She thanked them both for standing up in defense of her that day at the House of Lords. Gray had told her all that had happened and assured her the matter was resolved and she was safe.

She hadn't realized how much it had been weighing on her until it was no longer important.

"It is an easy enough thing to defend an innocent woman," Rathmore said.

Kit winked at her, for he knew the truth.

"Shall we?" Rathmore asked when the music began playing. She took his hand and smiled as Kit quietly wished her a pleasant evening.

Perhaps tonight would be the night she would not go home alone.

She spent most of their dance trying to step closer to him, only to have him step back. Keeping the proper distance between them, even when they had moved to the corners.

After their dance she waved her hand and mentioned the

heat. "I believe I need to get some air."

"Allow me to accompany you," he offered, holding out his elbow. Once again, he kept his distance even when she attempted to walk closer to him.

She thought once they got out into the darkness of the gardens, he might make an advance. She would be ready to accept.

While she wasn't exactly eager to have such relations outside where anyone could come upon them, she endeavored to keep an open mind. But there was no advance made.

Lord Rathmore didn't so much as steal a kiss when they were behind the hedges. He simply escorted her through the low maze and back to the house. Perhaps they could find an empty room. A plump settee would be more comfortable than a bench outdoors anyway.

"I hope you're not too chilled now," Lord Rathmore said as she shivered in anticipation.

"Not at all, my lord. I'm still quite heated." She fluttered her eyelashes, or at least hoped she'd accomplished a naughty look. But Rathmore didn't respond in a like manner. He simply smiled.

"I shall get you a refreshment. Stay here and I'll return immediately."

She sighed as he wound his way through the crowd to retrieve a lemonade.

As promised, he came back with a glass and launched into conversation while she drank the sweet drink.

She would need to learn her way around men, and she knew just who to ask.

THE NEXT MORNING, Celia waited for Kit to arrive for breakfast instead of starting without him. Like most mornings, Graham hadn't descended from his rooms yet so they were alone for the time being.

She smiled at him and Kit suddenly felt like an animal being stalked by a predator. He didn't have long to wonder what she could want. As soon as his meal was served, she dismissed the servants before launching into her request for information.

"I need your help," she said as he'd shoveled his first forkful of eggs into his mouth.

"Of course, anything," he managed to say after swallowing.

It wasn't just an empty promise. He knew she could ask him anything and he would help her in any way he could. He was a true friend. Or hoped to be.

"I need you to teach me how to be seductive," she said.

Kit frowned at his plate as he cut his ham. "Has Rathmore not come around yet?" What did the man need? A formal invitation into the woman's bed?

"No. We flirt and he's glanced at my breasts, but only when it appears I'm not looking. I've seen him gaze at my lips, but he hasn't even kissed me. How am I to get him into my bed if he won't even kiss me?"

Kit swallowed, not as comfortable with this conversation as he wished to be. But he'd made an agreement to help her find a lover, and she'd more than exceeded his expectations by introducing him to Willa. Things with his potential wife were going well. He would ask her to marry him soon enough and he was certain she would say yes.

If only he survived this meal.

"What have you tried so far?" he asked, thinking it best to know what hadn't worked.

"I did just what I did with you. I have made myself available to him."

"Yes, but you're a lady, and as such, he probably suspects you want marriage rather than a tup."

"Don't use that word, it makes it sound disreputable." She wrinkled her nose in the most appealing way.

Kit laughed. "Because sleeping with a man only for pleasure can be made to sound respectable?" At her glare he waved his hand. "Never mind. I won't use the word again. Shall we say, *bedding*? What about *fucking*. Can I say that?"

"No." She shook her head as he chuckled. "Do you know you say that word with a Scottish accent?"

"Hmm. Most likely because I learned it from my father." He shook his head, getting them back to the original topic. "You may need to do more than make yourself available. He might want you to take the initiative. You may need to seduce him."

"Yes. Which is why I need your assistance. To tell me how I should do that?"

Kit winced, and looked around the room wondering how he might get out of this. Had he thought himself a good friend? Obviously, he was not as good as he'd thought. Giving up with a heavy sigh, he turned back to her.

"You'll want to be assertive, but not too much. You don't want to be forceful. Perhaps act as if you'll die if you can't have him, but don't seem desperate."

"You do realize you've not said one thing without contradicting it in the following sentence?" she pointed out with her brows up and her hands on her hips.

"It's a subtle action, but also firm. You want him to know you want him without having to say it aloud."

"Again. You are making no sense. You say one thing and then the opposite."

"Exactly. I think you have it now. I must go. Willa will be waiting for me."

He spun on his heel and rushed from the house, leaving her staring after him. It was one thing for them to go their own ways and find other people, but quite another for her to expect him to aid her seduction of another man.

He couldn't do it. If it made him dishonorable to go back on his agreement with her, then so be it. It couldn't be helped. Even the thought of another man touching her made him want to go into a rage.

But he needed to respect her wishes. She wanted excitement

and pleasure not marriage or children. They were not suited.

Except for the way her nearness heated his blood and his constant desire to be with her.

Shaking his head, he went to prepare for another drive with Willa—someone who did want the same things he wanted. If only he could get his heart onboard. It wasn't fair to her and whatever relationship they may have going forward, to harbor an attraction for Celia. He would need to stay away from Celia.

Which meant he couldn't go to Penbrook House for breakfast. He would no longer wait for Celia before entering a ball or soiree. She would have to win Rathmore on her own.

FOLLOWING KIT'S VAGUE and unhelpful instructions, Celia selected her most provocative gown and left for the Raybold ball. She waited outside the house until she heard music inside and determined Kit was not coming.

Once inside she saw she was wrong. Kit was there and was already conversing with Willa and her brother. He looked up and then quickly turned away. Her throat tightened with angry tears she refused to give purchase.

Kit had abandoned her. After she'd seen to her end of their arrangement, he was defaulting on his duties to help her find a lover.

Very well, she didn't need him.

She searched the room for her prey, but it was he who approached her.

"You appear to be looking for someone. Perhaps, I might be of assistance," Lord Rathmore said.

She smiled. "Yes, that would be most helpful as you are a good bit taller than I and can see more of the room."

His smile dropped away slightly until she laughed. "Minx," he muttered close to her ear. "It matters not who you might be searching for, for I have found you and do not intend to let you escape."

"I must be honest and say, I have no plans to escape. In fact," she whispered. "I might run, but I hope you will give chase."

His eyes narrowed in confusion. She felt her cheeks heat. He hadn't understood her jest. Rather than let it go, she tried again.

"That is to say when I leave here tonight, perhaps you will be leaving at the same time."

"I believe we generally depart at the same time; when the event concludes."

"You are correct. But perhaps tonight you won't retire to your home but will instead travel on to another location."

"What location?" he asked, looking more perplexed than seduced.

"Forgive me, I see someone I must speak with," she said and rushed away toward Lady Elderidge. She would appreciate a bit of laughter at the moment.

With the woman's help, Celia managed to escape the ball after the second dance without having to face Rathmore again.

She collapsed into bed, exhausted, with tears streaking down her face. It wasn't her disappointment with Lord Rathmore that had her so upset. It was Kit's abandonment that had broken her spirits.

She wiped the tears away and vowed to do better the next night.

CHAPTER TWENTY-SIX

Aﬀﬁﬄ THREE DAYS of avoiding Celia, Gray showed up at Kit's home late the next morning.

"You and Celia haven't taken breakfast at Penbrook House so, I decided to come here to see you." He frowned as he took in the otherwise empty room. "Please don't tell me she's still in bed. Not because I have issue with the lateness of the morning, but because I don't wish to think of my sister in your bed." He shivered.

Kit thought he might be ill. Celia hadn't been home the last few mornings? That could only mean she was in someone else's bed. Rathmore.

His hands clenched into fists until he focused on releasing them. What did it matter who she took breakfast with? He was going to marry Willa. He had been avoiding Celia anyway. Why should he care if she found what she'd been looking for in Lord Rathmore? Kit was going to marry Willa. Damn. He was repeating himself in his own thoughts.

"You'll be relieved to know she is not in my bed. Nor will she be again," Kit announced right before the footman entered carrying the dishes with their meal.

Gray waited until the man was gone again before glaring at Kit. "What did you do? I warned you what would happen if you hurt my sister."

"What did *I* do? I asked her to marry me. *Again.*"

"

"And?"

"And? And she refused me. *Again.*" Kit frowned and speared a piece of ham he no longer had an appetite for. "She doesn't want to wed. Which left me no choice but to search for a bride elsewhere."

"Perhaps if I spoke to her." Gray tapped his chin with his index finger.

Kit raised his brows and laughed. "Yes, because you are so adept at having your sister follow your suggestions in all else, why shouldn't I have considered employing your powers of persuasion previously? What good fortune I have."

"You could have simply passed on my offer."

"Yes, well, I find I'm still a bit sore over the matter and it brings out the prickly part of my humor."

"I'm sorry."

Kit didn't hide his surprise at this. "Sorry? I thought certainly you'd be overjoyed that I'd no longer be chasing after your dear sister. Isn't this exactly what you wanted?"

"You'd think as much, but now I find I feel the opposite. I can't think of anyone else who I would want to see on a regular basis whenever my sister visits. Or to provide my nieces and nephews."

"I hope you're not pining for your extended family just yet, as your sister has no plans to marry anyone. She still insists on being the merry widow with a line of lovers out her door."

Gray groaned and shook his head. "And what about me? Am I allowed to see you or am I only supposed to show loyalty to my sister?" He threw his hands in the air. "This is exactly why I didn't want you involved with her."

"Yes, because this situation is most inconvenient for *you.* Pay no mind to the fact that I truly wanted to marry her, and now I may spend my life with a woman I feel content with but not in the same way I felt for Celia. Your sister continues to make a mangled mess of my heart, but, yes, Gray, I'm so sorry you are put out."

"I appreciate your concern."

"Bloody arse," Kit muttered under his breath, while Gray took the last slice of bacon.

Kit smiled and steepled his fingers. "If your sister is not in my bed, and is not in her own, it's likely she's found a lover and is with him."

The bacon fell to Gray's plate and he pushed it away with another moan of distress. He deserved it.

"I may have some news soon. I'm courting someone and we are getting along quite well. I think it would be a fine match."

"A fine match? Do you hear yourself? That's all you can say to recommend the person you plan to affix yourself to for the rest of your days? Fine? Fine is what I say when Celia asks if I like the new rug in the parlor. It's not a word to describe something I really care about."

"Thank you, Gray. I'm sure I will come to think of Miss Derforth as more than fine."

"Miss Derforth? As in Ernest's little sister? Willa?"

"Yes."

"Good God, man. Is she even out?"

"Yes. She's a grown woman now. Quite charming and beautiful." He waved his fork. "As well as other things besides merely fine."

"This is how it's to be then? You are getting leg-shackled and my sister is out doing who knows what, and I'm to be alone." He shook his head. "Celia will just have to understand that you and I are friends and will continue to be so."

At the moment, Kit wasn't sure he cared if Gray remained his friend. Fine was a perfectly good word for more than parlor rugs.

"Your sister and I are to remain friends. Therefore, I see no reason why she would be upset by us remaining friends as well."

"You and CeeCee are to remain friends? But neither of you came to breakfast."

"Yes." He shrugged. "I believe the thing is to *offer* friendship, but then avoid each other at all costs. I assure you I didn't come up with the concept myself."

"I see. It's most inconvenient. Better to stay alone, like me."

"Except I've been alone long enough. I want a family, Gray."

"Prepare to feel pain, my friend. For that's what family brings."

Kit acknowledged the fact that a family would not always be a joy, but he couldn't resist the desire to be part of something more than himself. Not to mention the matter of the title.

"What of your title?" he asked the question aloud to Gray.

"Bugger my title to hell. My father was a wretch and I hate that I have to own anything of his. I wouldn't burden another soul with the taint of the Penbrook name."

"You could do more to repair the name so it would be something honorable to pass to your son should you be blessed to have one."

Gray looked at him briefly and glanced away. "Perhaps someday."

Like many times before, Kit detected a small glimpse of pain in Gray's eyes before it hardened over.

Kit knew the man hid a great deal of hurt away from the rest of the world. A pain that kept him from finding happiness with a wife and family. But Kit was willing to face the chance of that fate to end the loneliness that had been a constant pain until Celia.

"Promise me one thing," Gray said. When Kit only waited, the man looked him in the eye intensely before speaking. "Don't settle for just anyone to fill the emptiness in your life. A poor choice would be more disastrous than making no choice at all."

Kit nodded in agreement, hoping he wasn't doing that. Willa was a fine woman. No one would ever be Celia, therefore, no matter who he selected, they would not be the person he truly wanted.

Blast and damn.

THE NEXT DAY, after another night spent tossing and turning, Celia decided to change tactics. She couldn't continue to go out at dawn and walk her frustrations away. It wasn't working and she'd soon need another pair of boots.

She needed help, and not the kind of help Kit provided. Which was no help at all. She met Gray for breakfast. She'd been avoiding the breakfast room the past few days. She didn't want to see Kit's smile and hear his tales of love. Willa was a wonderful girl and Celia was happy Kit found what he wanted. She just didn't want to hear about it over her eggs.

"Where's Kit?" she asked, surprised he wasn't following his normal tradition of attending breakfast at Penbrook House.

"He hasn't been here all week. Not that you've been around to notice. And I'm not asking where you've been, and wouldn't want to hear the answer if I had asked, which I have not."

"Of course." Celia sipped her coffee and kept her eyes on her plate as if she guarded some great secret. The only thing she had to hide was the fact she'd yet to proposition Lord Rathmore and he'd yet to proposition her. They circled about each other like boxers in a ring.

"Perhaps Kit had a late night." Gray raised his brows as if this news would irk her. It didn't, but mostly because she knew it wasn't true.

"Kit is courting a debutante, so I can assure you if he had a late night, it wasn't doing what you're imagining."

"And I assure you, sister, I'm not imagining anything when it comes to Kit." He winced and handed over the butter for her toast. "But if I was—and again I never would—I would wonder why you refused his offer of marriage."

She huffed out a breath. "As I've told you both now many times, I have no interest to marry. I would think you of all people would understand, as you don't hold with the institution at all and have no plans to marry either."

"I know why I don't wish to marry. But I would think a young woman such as yourself would want the security marriage provides. As well as children and a home of your own."

"I have money. And as such I can buy security and a home of my own. And, yes, I have thought about children, but as you said, I'm still young."

"You're not *that* young."

She threw a roll at him, hitting him right in the face. She let out a breath and slumped in her chair.

"The truth is I miss Kit a great deal, and I would have been content to stay with him indefinitely. If he'd not proposed marriage, all would have been quite well."

"For you."

"Yes," she answered quietly, feeling like a petulant child.

"But you knew from the start what Kit wanted."

"Yes. But he also knew what I wanted. Which brings me to why I've come down for breakfast this morning." She folded her hands in her lap and straightened her shoulders. "I wonder if I could employ your help, not as a brother, but as a friend."

His lip pulled up on the one side. "We're friends now, CeCe? Does this mean you will no longer twist my ear if I unnerve you?"

"We shall see. It depends on whether or not you serve useful."

"Very well." He waved a hand. "Please allow me the opportunity to be your friend."

"What do you find appealing in a lover?"

He choked and stared at her with bulging eyes. "Pardon?"

"I asked what it is that attracts you to a woman you take to your bed."

"I'd like to retract my offer of friendship and go back to having my ear twisted, it would be less painful than this conversation." He rubbed his temples.

Ignoring him, she proceeded with her interrogation. "What qualities does she need to exhibit?"

He chuckled. "She needs to be breathing and willing, sister."

It was quite like Gray to say something shocking to unbalance her, but she didn't show her surprise, instead she leaned closer and smiled. If he thought he could scare her away from this topic, he was quite wrong.

"Willing to do what exactly?"

"I think I may be ill," Gray said as he did at many breakfasts, though this time for a different reason.

⁕

CHAPTER TWENTY-SEVEN

AFTER CONCLUDING THE detailed conversation with her brother—of which she feared she'd never succeed to block from her mind—Celia determined she needed a woman's help. Men were either too vague or descriptive to the point of unsettling her stomach. Damn her brother.

Having no married friends, Celia considered the Duchess of Roxburghe for a brief moment as her husband was friends with Celia's brother, but she worried the duchess, having a husband who clearly doted on her, had no need for such mechanics as seduction.

Instead, she found herself knocking on the door of the one woman she knew could assist her.

A strapping footman opened the door. He didn't wear the livery she was accustomed to seeing when visiting other homes in town. He wore a normal waistcoat and cravat, but lacked a shirt.

He seemed to preen under her gaze and she looked away after handing the man her calling card. "One moment, I'll see if my mistress is at home."

As Celia waited in the elaborate foyer decorated with paintings of naked couples in provocative poses, she wondered if this were a terrible mistake. Before she'd had a chance to flee, the footman returned with a smile. "You may enter."

Celia stepped into what she assumed was a drawing room. She hadn't been inside this room when she'd visited previously.

The heavy drapes were pulled shut giving the illusion of night despite it being two in the afternoon.

Lady Harrington smiled and stood to greet Celia. She was wearing a dressing gown and from the low gape in front it didn't appear she had anything on underneath. Her white-blonde hair was loose and disheveled, and her cheeks sported a bit of color as if she'd been out in the cold and just returned indoors.

Celia was late to realize she'd seen the same coloring on her own cheeks after she and Kit had made love. She glanced toward another footman lounging shirtless on a settee.

"Please leave us women to our visit, Marcus," Lady Harrington said. The man immediately stood and bowed to them before leaving. "Should we have tea? I rarely get visits from proper ladies, I'm afraid I'm ill prepared." She held up a glass of amber-colored liquid.

"I would love a glass of whatever you're drinking." Celia hoped it was brandy. She could use something to smooth this conversation.

"It's whiskey," Lady Harrington said.

Celia nodded. "Yes. Thank you."

With a shrug, the woman got up herself and poured a glass. She presented it to Celia and they both sat on the settee that had moments ago supported a large, shirtless, footman.

"Whatever can I do for you, Lady…?"

"It's Lady Hamlin, but please call me Celia. I'm afraid you would only know me as Selene."

The other woman blinked and then smiled. "Ah! I wondered who you really were. I'd tracked you to using Lord Penbrook's invitation, but I was at a loss."

"My brother, Lord Penbrook, was ill the night of your fête so I took the liberty of using his invitation since he could not."

"I see, and I assume you enjoyed yourself at my masquerade?"

"I did indeed."

"I won't have another until late in the fall, but I'll be sure to send you your own invitation for my next gathering."

"Thank you, I look forward to it," Celia said, unsure of what else to say. With the allure of privacy now gone she felt rather exposed. There was no way she could attend.

"And what can I do for you today, Celia?"

"Since attending your party, I've decided I'd like to take a lover."

"The man you were with that night inquired about you. Lord Stormont would be glad to make your acquaintance."

"Yes. Actually, I know Christopher rather well as he and my brother are close friends. We've since realized who we were, and what we did... together... that night." Celia couldn't help but glance toward the door in the direction of that room where her entire life had changed for the better. "We were already friends. And became... closer after our revelation."

Her smile could only be considered cat-like. "I must ask, how is he? I've never had the pleasure, but he seems as though he'd be attentive to his partner's needs."

Celia coughed and nodded without looking the woman in the eyes. "Uh, yes. Quite attentive. Very good." Better than good, but she was afraid if she provided more details, she might catch fire. Did women truly speak of such things when in private?

"No need to be shy in my home. This is a safe place for whatever pleasures you may desire." Was the woman looking at Celia's breasts? "How may I assist?"

"Unfortunately, I have an imperfection." Celia gestured toward her face.

The woman frowned and shook her head. "It is perfection in its own right. It makes you different from every other woman. The ladies of the *ton* wish to look and act the same, but a man searches for the differences and latches on to the woman who stands out from the crowd."

Celia blinked. "I never thought of it like that. You're saying this mark makes me different and that's a good thing?"

"It doesn't detract from your beauty, but enhances your

uniqueness."

"That is comforting to hear as I cannot get rid of it and have only found one way to cover it up and that is with a mask."

Again, the woman smiled like a sated cat. "Anonymity heightens one's desires, does it not?"

"Uh. Yes." She swallowed and decided to push on. "I wish to take a lover, Lady Harrington and you see, Lord Stormont is looking for a wife. Widows such as ourselves have no need to marry. In fact, marriage means a loss of freedom and I want to explore my freedom, not give it up."

The woman's smile fell away and she, herself, seemed to fade. Her pale hair and icy blue eyes held no color of their own. Only the scarlet dressing gown kept her from looking like a ghost.

"You did not have love in your marriage?"

Celia hid her surprise. She didn't expect this woman, who held elaborate parties solely for the pleasure of the flesh, to speak of love.

"No. It was a marriage of convenience and my husband was more than seventy when we wed. In truth, I didn't know a man's touch until I attended your masquerade." She realized too late she shouldn't have shared something so personal. "That is, in the way I did with Lord Stormont." Lady Harrington didn't seem to hear her muddled answer, instead she stared off toward the fireplace.

"You assume I chose this life. That this is some reward for outliving my husband?" She didn't sound accusatory, but Celia again regretted coming here when the woman's voice trembled on her last word. Celia heard the pain radiating out of her. "I'm a merry widow who can now do as she pleases. Such *freedom*."

Her voice cracked on the last word and Celia wanted to sink into the settee and disappear.

"I'd give anything to exchange this freedom for my life with Freddie. I don't take lovers as a freedom, Lady Hamlin. In fact, it's torture to know whoever warms my bed, I'll never love anyone as I once loved my husband. Physical pleasure is all I'll ever have, but it leaves the heart cold and empty. Are you certain it will be enough for you?"

"I was forced into a marriage I didn't choose with a man I had never met, so our views of the institution are vastly different. To me it seems like a prison. Once I take my vows, the man I marry will own everything I have, including myself."

"But if you choose the right man, you may not mind giving yourself to him. Marriage or no. And he will give himself in return. In the right circumstances you receive something far better in exchange for the freedom you speak of."

Celia couldn't help but think of Kit and how giving he was with his pleasure as well as his smiles and his time. He'd told her he didn't need her money, but having been without funds for so long and sold to a man for his fortune, she didn't want to be without a way to support herself.

"I will say, having the freedom to do what I want is a great pleasure, but my bed is so cold and empty each night, I can hardly bear it. I thought if I had a man…" Celia couldn't finish the sentence for she realized it wasn't a man she wanted in her bed. It was one man. Kit.

"Not every man will want to stay the night. In fact, many will only stay for the deed to be done, and then they'll leave to go back to the person they truly love."

"Pardon, but the men here must—" Celia gestured toward the door where the attractive Marcus had left.

"I pay them, Lady Hamlin. While a pleasant distraction, I know they would not spend a moment of their time with me if I did not compensate them for it." She smiled. "If you'd like to take one of them home for the evening, you are welcome to, but know this, while they are quite good at what they do, you will get nothing emotional from them because they don't care about you, or me for that matter."

"I did hope for something a little more substantial."

"If you want to be doted on then I would suggest becoming a mistress. You would be free to select whose attentions you wanted, and they would give you the best of themselves along with trinkets and the illusion of affection. Some may even love you. But it will be temporary."

Celia frowned, not liking the idea of being a mistress. She could only imagine how her brother might react to such a thing. While she was eager to see more of life outside of a marriage, she still had her reputation to think about. Widows were given liberties, but a lady becoming a mistress would not be tolerated by society.

"I don't think that is for me either. I'm afraid I have wasted your time today, Lady Harrington. I should go."

"Think about what I've said. It seems clear to me that you do want love and a marriage, you only need to find the right person this time."

Celia practically ran from the house. In her carriage, she had difficulty catching her breath. Was it true? Was she destined to find more emptiness with her lovers until one day she wanted more?

Would she wish for a husband and children one day? The thought of it did not make her cringe. Not when she saw the tall, green-eyed man next to her as they watched their exuberant, blond children running through the gardens at Blairgowrie.

If she continued this search for freedom and pleasure, would she miss her opportunity to have love? She'd thought the emotion an unattainable thing, but perhaps, as Lady Harrington suggested, it was only a matter of finding the right person.

Chapter Twenty-Eight

After another enjoyable ride in the park with Willa, Kit went to his club for dinner and found the man he was looking for straight away. He took a steadying breath, ready to move on with this most important step.

"Good evening, Ernest," Kit greeted the man who gestured he was welcome to sit.

"Stormont. I'm surprised you're not at home readying yourself for a ball."

"Actually, that is my plan, however I wish to discuss an important matter with you first." Kit smiled. Or hoped he was smiling. He was rather nervous.

The man frowned. "I'm sure I can guess what you wish to discuss. I've seen you chasing after Willy. I do wish she had found someone a little heavier in the pockets, but you do seem to care for her and as we discussed recently, her happiness is my *highest* priority." The man's words could only be described as insincere. He barely managed to hide his disappointment. Kit felt the need to confirm.

"To be clear, you would give your blessing to the match, were I to propose?"

"I would. Her dowry isn't much to speak of."

"I will leave it for her and add to it so she is settled properly." He'd invest it wisely so it would grow to a handsome sum, as husbands had a tendency to leave this world before their wives.

"I would suggest you don't tell her I approve of the match. The last time I encouraged someone's suit she ended the association immediately just to spite me. She doesn't want me *interfering*. In fact, I should probably pretend I *don't* favor you so she'll consider your proposal."

Kit watched as the man threw back his glass of whiskey and rubbed his forehead. Willa had seemed quite pleasant. Was she to be this much trouble with him, or was it merely sibling opposition? The man must have caught Kit pondering, because he cleared his throat and said, "I assure you, her defiance is only with me as an older brother. She'll be a most biddable wife."

Kit laughed. "I don't wish for a biddable wife." Though reasonable wouldn't be too much to ask.

"That's probably for the best," Ernest muttered, before saying louder, "I look forward to welcoming you to the family." He sounded only slightly more enthusiastic than he had originally. Kit wondered how bad off the man was. His question was answered when he perked up and leaned closer. "Say, you might be able to help me."

"In what way?" Kit wanted to be agreeable but he wouldn't be able to offer much in the way of funds without putting his own situation at risk. But he'd help the man if he could. After all, they would be family. Or they would if Willa accepted his proposal.

"My circumstances would be greatly improved if I were to find myself a wife of means. Someone like Lady Hamlin for example. I know men shy away because of the mark on her face, but I'm not bothered by such a thing. She's lovely enough and seems spirited."

"And has no wish to marry," Kit said quickly. He put up his hand to stop the man when it seemed he planned to protest. "At all."

Ernest deflated with a solemn nod. "If you can think of anyone else..."

After securing Ernest's approval, and assuring the man he would keep his eye out for an heiress to save him from himself,

Kit returned home so he could be fitted out for the evening, possibly the most important evening of his entire life.

He was going to propose.

By tomorrow, he could have a fiancée.

He paused as he looked on his reflection in the mirror, noting the sadness lingering in his eyes. He should be happier. Willa was perfect. Beautiful, funny, smart and an engaging conversationalist. He could not find anyone more suited for him.

Except…

He shook his head. Tonight, he would give up on his dream of having Celia as his wife once and for all.

He had hoped he'd already given up on that dream, but there it was, still hanging on like a burr. He must move on. They wanted different things and while he was now certain he loved her, it didn't mean he couldn't find love and happiness with Willa.

"Is everything to your liking, my lord?" Hart asked.

"Of course." He set his valet's mind at ease and left his home. The home he planned to fill with a family.

By the time he exited his carriage at the ball, he found himself to be quite nervous. His hands were damp inside his gloves, and a trickle of sweat slowly made its way down his back.

This was the right thing to do. He needed to get married and produce an heir, but more than that, he wanted a family. He wanted to belong.

It seemed like fate was testing him when the first person he saw as he walked into the ballroom was Celia. She offered a smile and his heart picked up as his body responded. She was as beautiful as ever in an emerald gown that was cut low enough to show off those enticing breasts he'd once enjoyed.

He swallowed and gave a nod to her before turning and heading off in the opposite direction. He needed to stay away from her until his heart gave up on the possibility of her.

He found Willa and Ernest, who were clearly having a spat about something. When Kit arrived, Willa beamed at him and took his arm even before Kit had offered it.

"I'm so very glad to see you this evening, my lord. Perhaps we could take a walk around the ballroom."

"Of course. I'd love nothing more." Except to have a moment alone with her so that he might blurt out his proposal before he melted into a puddle on Lady DePaul's floor. Or worse, changed his mind entirely.

No. That was not an option. He smiled down at the woman who he hoped would be his wife and put everyone else out of his mind.

⇢⇢⟨⟨⟨⟨

CELIA CURSED HERSELF for wearing her green gown as she made her way to the lady's retiring room. It was her lowest cut dress and she'd hoped it would draw Lord Rathmore's attention.

That wasn't entirely true, she'd hoped it would attract Kit's attention, but she didn't want to admit that to herself because then she would need to explore the reason why. Kit wanted to marry and start a family and she wanted…

Well, now she wasn't entirely sure. After speaking with Lady Harrington, she had doubts about spending the rest of her days with different men visiting her bed. She'd thought it exciting and adventurous, but now that the woman had exposed a different perspective, Celia realized it would be lonely and empty as well. But marriage?

Behind a privacy screen, Celia worked her corset up from where it had slid and adjusted the bodice of her gown. As long as she didn't partake in any lively dancing, her bosom should stay where it was.

She paused in her adjustments when she heard someone else enter the room. Peeking through the crack in the screen she saw it was Miss Willa and two other young women. All in the pale dresses of a debutante.

"He's asked for a waltz. Again," Willa said, excitement clear in her voice.

"Lord Stormont does indeed seem smitten with you. He's only danced with you all season," another young woman said.

"That's not true. He also dances with Lady Hamlin," Willa corrected.

"As if that counts. They can only be friends. He wouldn't consider more than friendship with her."

"Why would you think that?" Willa asked. Celia silently thanked the girl for sounding defensive.

"He would never choose a woman with a spot on her face over *you*," Willa's friend stated as fact.

Celia held her breath. This would be the moment she would hear something regretful about herself and her confidence would be shattered. She'd planned to entice Lord Rathmore this evening, but that would take all her courage.

Willa laughed, a beautiful tinkling sound like one would expect from an angel. "That's ridiculous. It's but a small blemish. Lady Hamlin is lovely. And I for one would much rather acquaint myself with someone who wears their flaws—miniscule as they are—in plain sight rather than someone who is cruel and thoroughly rotten on the inside."

It was a clear insult to the other woman, but it went unnoticed as the ruthless girl continued. "All I meant is that it's clear Lord Stormont fancies you over her. I would be surprised if he hasn't already talked to your brother."

Willa sighed. "I am sure you're right for my brother suggested I spend my time with other gentlemen so not to give Lord Stormont the wrong impression of my interest. Can you believe he doesn't find the viscount appropriate for a husband?" Willa seemed genuinely offended on Kit's behalf. Celia liked the girl even more.

"What will you say if he asks tonight? He's very handsome, but so is Lord Marsden and he's shown you equal attention," the other friend said in a quieter voice.

"Marsden is an earl, while Stormont is just a viscount," the harpy said.

Willa responded immediately in an accusatory tone. "I'll remind you my brother is only a baron. I care not for a title. I won't marry for money or titles, despite what my brother may wish. I must at least like the man who is to be my husband."

The group left still chatting, but Celia could no longer hear what they said. With one more tug on her gown, she left the room as well and went to find Kit. She thought he was avoiding her, and as she moved closer and he ducked out to the terrace, it became obvious she'd been correct.

She found him standing at the balustrade looking out into the darkness and moved to stand next to him.

"Lady Willa is a lovely woman," she whispered.

Kit looked over at her briefly before turning back and nodding.

"I saw her true character tonight and am happy to report she is genuinely a wonderful person with just a bit of spirit to make her fun."

"Yes."

"Her friends seem convinced you will ask for her hand tonight."

He looked at her in surprise. "They do?"

"Yes. But don't fear, she's taken with you, despite Lord Marsden's interest."

"Blighter," Kit mumbled into the cool evening air.

He turned to face her fully. "The truth is, I do plan to ask for her hand tonight. I'm just working up the courage to do so. I find myself more nervous than I expected to be while doing something I want to do."

"You're going to marry Lady Willa?" Celia nearly choked.

"Yes. Why do you seem surprised? After all, that is why I asked you to help me find a potential bride."

"But she was the first woman you've met. How do you know she's the one?"

"I guess I just know." He shrugged.

Shrugged. As if he'd just been asked if he wanted lemon or orange tea cakes.

"This is a very important decision, Kit."

"I understand. Thus, the reason for the nervousness I mentioned previously. You're not helping Celia. Perhaps you should go." He turned back to the blackness.

"I'm sorry. I'm just surprised by the timing of it. It seems I haven't seen you in days. Did I imagine you are avoiding me?"

After a long silence he shook his head. "No. I needed time to myself to think."

"I see. I hope now that you're done with that, we can be friends again." She smiled, but he didn't laugh at her joke.

"In time, I'm sure that will be possible." But not now. He didn't say as much, but she heard it nonetheless. He'd wanted distance from her.

"I am very happy for you, Kit. I'm so glad you've found someone and it appears all your dreams will now come true."

"Do you mean that, truly?" he asked.

She didn't know what he expected her to say, but she offered the truth. "You are my very best friend, Christopher. Of course, I want you to find happiness."

"Thank you, Celia." He was looking at her again, and if he wasn't about to go off and propose to another woman, she might have leaned up to kiss him. "How do I look?" he asked and brushed a hand over his coat.

"Dashing as ever," she answered with a grin.

"Can I see you inside?" he asked, holding out his arm to escort her back to the ball. Always the gentleman.

"No need. I'm fine here for the moment. I believe I'll stay and take some air."

"Very well, then. I guess I've delayed long enough. Wish me luck."

"You don't need luck, my friend. You only need to follow your heart."

He winked at her. He was quite handsome, especially when he grinned in that boyish way.

And he was getting married.

Her mind hummed as he walked away from her. She stood frozen as that fact settled in. Of course, this had been the plan all along. To find a suitable wife for Kit.

They'd been successful in that endeavor, making the next step in the plan for him to propose and secure said bride. Willa would obviously accept his offer and they would be wed. A year from now their first child would arrive, but would Celia be told or just hear about it from Gray?

After all, when Kit married, she would lose him. She knew they would never be lovers again—that had been made perfectly clear even before he'd found a bride. But he would no longer take meals with her and Gray, he'd instead dine with his wife. She and Kit would never again sit together and talk late into the night about all sorts of things. Or share their mornings together.

She was certain the stabbing pain in her chest was from her corset rather than grief for a friendship she was about to lose forever. She swallowed and put a smile on her face that was not quite sincere at the moment, but it would be when she saw Kit was happy with the woman who would make his dreams come true.

Stepping inside the ballroom she tried to catch her breath. It felt as if a piece of her heart ripped free when he'd walked away from her. Kit was getting what he'd wanted and she was genuinely happy about that. She only wished it didn't mean she was left alone.

Except... she didn't have to be alone. After all, she'd had her own plans.

She looked across the crowd and spotted Lord Rathmore watching her. She smiled and he offered an enticing grin. It seemed Kit wasn't the only person to get what they wanted tonight.

She sauntered through the crowd to stand before Rathmore.

"Lady Hamlin, you look exquisite this evening. Would you care to dance?"

"Actually, no. I'd prefer it if you would escort me home." She was done playing at this game. She decided to just say it straight out.

Fortunately, this tactic worked. For his smile grew wider.

"I would be honored."

CHAPTER TWENTY-NINE

KIT WATCHED AS Rathmore rested a hand on Celia's back and led her out of the ballroom. He knew this was bound to happen eventually. He'd done what he could to help her find someone suitable. Rathmore was the best person he could aim Celia toward with her plan to take a lover. Still, it didn't feel… right.

Nothing did at the moment.

Hopefully that would change soon enough. Smoothing a hand over his immaculate coat once more, he went to find Willa.

He felt stiff as he approached her and her friends and requested a walk in the garden. The two other ladies with Willa tittered as Willa reached for his hand, placing her slim fingers gently on his arm. Why didn't he feel a zing of arousal from her touch?

Perhaps it would come later after they were intimate with one another. As if to test his theory she stopped at a heavily shadowed corner of the garden. The young maid serving as chaperone stood much too far away to be of any use. Perhaps, propriety was irrelevant at this point. They would be married soon enough and anything that happened tonight would not be suspect.

Willa's hand coiled around his neck, she tugged him down to her lips, taking him by surprise.

The kiss was nice in the way all kisses were. He would wager, it wasn't her first, but she wasn't a master of it either. Her tongue reached out for his and he waited for his body to betray him in a most ungentlemanly way, but it did not.

Perhaps his nerves had cooled his ardor or frozen it as it seemed to be now. Why could he not respond to this woman in the way a husband—or even a man—should?

When she pulled away, she smiled, but not with the brilliance he had seen earlier in the ballroom. Had she, too, realized their kiss held no passion whatsoever? Should he have tried harder? He'd never needed to try with Celia.

Bloody hell. How was he supposed to move on with Willa when he kept comparing every touch to what he'd had with Celia? Celia hadn't wanted him, not back then, not now, not ever.

Swallowing down his anger, he smiled again.

"I wanted to ask your feelings on marriage. As far as what you find most important in a match between two people," he said, clearly stalling. He should have just proposed and had it done with.

She tilted her head to gaze up at him and looked so young. She was only five years younger than him, but at that moment he felt aged well beyond his years.

"Friendship," she answered and he relaxed. It was a splendid answer as were her others. "Respect, and definitely laughter." She took a few steps from him. "And what do you wish for in a marriage?"

"I wish for a wife who is more than just another person in my home. I want a true partner. Someone I look forward to spending my life with. Someone who wants to spend their life with me."

She nodded. "Yes. I want that as well." Her smile faded slightly. Was she disappointed that he'd not asked yet? He should get on with it before she grew weary and left him standing there among the shrubs. Alone again.

He cleared his throat and opened his mouth to speak the words that would unite them forever, but it was her voice he heard rather than his own.

"I'm afraid I can't marry you, Lord Stormont. I know you

haven't asked so this is not a refusal. But if you were to ask, I would have to refuse."

"Oh," he said as he tried to figure out why his first reaction to her news was utter relief. "May I ask why?"

"I'm so sorry. You must think me fickle as things between us have obviously been leading to this point, but it was only just as we were speaking of what we wanted from a marriage that I realized I'm in love with someone else."

"I see." Kit offered a smile that was all the more surprising for its sincerity. "Lord Marsden is a fine man."

"Actually, it isn't Lord Marsden." She shook her head and her eyes lit with something he'd never seen when she'd looked at him before. "You see, I met someone at my first ball, and my brother practically salivated at the idea of marrying me to the man because of his wealth and title." She glared off at the darkness and Kit knew that was for her brother rather than him.

"I didn't want my brother or anyone else to think those were the reasons I'd taken an interest in the man, so I cut things off with him rather abruptly. Even though my heart still flutters when we catch each other's gaze across the ballroom." Her smile was back and her eyes shone with happy tears. "He always smiles back, as if he hears my heart across the distance. When I've had the courage to look at him, it always seems as if he is watching me as well."

"Perhaps he's waiting for you to realize that avoiding what you want will hurt you much longer than it will spite your brother."

"Yes." She smiled even brighter if that were possible. "Yes, perhaps he is."

"Then you should go to him, tell him how you truly feel. Allow me to escort you back to the ball."

As soon as they were back in the ballroom, she began looking for the man of her heart. A small crease pulled on her forehead as she moved her head back and forth.

"I'm afraid I don't see him now. He'd been over by the refreshments earlier."

"Who is it we're looking for? I do have height in my favor and can see farther than you."

She laughed. "Yes, of course. I'm searching for Lord Rathmore."

CELIA WORRIED SHE might be ill as Lord Rathmore assisted her into her carriage and took the seat next to her. His hand rested on his thigh, so close to hers, if she had moved her little finger the slightest bit, they would have touched.

She didn't move her finger.

They were both still wearing gloves, but she still felt the possibility of their touching to be too intimate.

A ridiculous notion since they would soon be touching everywhere, with no gloves or other clothing between them. She glanced up and met his gaze in the dim light of the carriage. Was he thinking of kissing her?

The thought excited her as much as it terrified her. Not that she was inexperienced and feared kissing a man, but that it was a different man than Kit.

Would he feel different? Taste different?

Of course, he would. He was different. He wouldn't yet know the things she liked that Kit knew. Would he ask her to tell him? Would she feel comfortable to do so or would she appreciate the things he did even more than Kit? She couldn't imagine liking anything more than what Kit had made her feel.

She frowned as she realized she'd spent the entire ride to Penbrook House thinking about Kit instead of the man next to her. The man she was about to welcome into her home and her bed.

Lord Rathmore reached up to help her down and Celia felt her body tense. Not because his touch thrilled her, but the opposite. It felt like any touch from a footman or a groom when they assisted her into her coach.

Nothing sparked and sizzled as it had when she and Kit touched.

And why was she back to comparing Lord Rathmore to Kit? Worse, why was she thinking of him as Lord Rathmore rather than his given name? The answer came swiftly when she realized she still didn't know the man's given name.

She was about to share her body with a man she didn't know in the most basic of ways. Not that it would be a first. She'd spent the night with Kit when she'd only known him as Lord Desire. But this was…different.

She'd thought that word was the reason she wanted to experience a variety of men, but now it seemed the worst word every thought.

Surely, she could ask Lord Rathmore his given name now and he would tell her, but she had already thought past the issue of his name and realized she didn't know him at all. His name was irrelevant when she considered she didn't know any more about him than what was shared with anyone during a dance or polite conversation over dinner. It wasn't nearly enough to be intimate. She didn't know if she could go through with this.

She paused inside the foyer and dismissed the butler who waited expectantly for her to take her guest to the drawing room. But how would she get Lord Rathmore from the drawing room to her bedroom without the servants knowing? And what if Graham was about. He was most likely at his club, but she wasn't certain.

Inside the drawing room, she should have offered Lord Rathmore refreshment. Or at least a seat, but instead, she hovered nervously by the door as he waited patiently next to her.

How had a few moments of flirting landed her here with a man in her home who expected sex? *Did* he expect sex? He didn't look like a man ready to move onto intimate relations with a woman. He looked… concerned.

"Are you well?" he asked quietly.

"I'm not sure." In truth, she felt slightly faint and hoped she wouldn't fall at the man's feet and embarrass herself all the more. "I'm afraid I may have gotten ahead of myself. You see, I was looking forward to the idea of having a lover and enjoying our time together, but now that the opportunity is upon us, I fear I'm not as comfortable with the situation as I thought to be. Please forgive me for bringing you here with certain expectations. I regret to say those expectations will go unsatisfied because I cannot go forward with my plans."

"No apology is necessary. In fact, I'm relieved to hear you say you've changed your mind. I, too, am rethinking our situation. Not because I don't find you attractive, I do, but because it seems clear to me now that I gave my heart to someone I met early in the season. And while she doesn't seem to want the useless organ, I can't bear to take it back."

It was one of the most romantic things she'd ever heard and she hugged him, hoping to offer some comfort for his pain. A pain that she would most likely experience herself, as the man she now realized she wanted above all else was at this very moment proposing marriage to another woman.

"Would you care to sit and have a drink?" she offered easily now that they had come to a silent agreement to remain friends. "I may not be able to offer you much, but I can offer my understanding."

He smiled and nodded. "That would be lovely."

He only stayed for the one glass of brandy and he never spoke the name of the woman he loved, except to say it was her first season and he was blown away by her charm on their first dance. He'd spoken to her brother the next day. The man was an acquaintance and had put his full support behind Jonathan—he'd told her his given name at one point—and the match. But at the next ball the lady had refused to dance or speak to him.

"The odd thing is, I still catch her watching me. A few times our gazes have met and she's been slow to look away as if she wants more, but something is just not right. I have asked for her to stand up with me for other dances, but after a number of refusals, I was left with no choice but to respect her clear message of disinterest. Except it isn't so clear anymore. Not with the way she watches me. I'm not sure what I might have done to earn her rejection."

"Perhaps it is nothing more than a misunderstanding. Perhaps she was just as taken with you during that first dance, but worried she hadn't met enough other men to make a sound decision. I know, for me, I thought I wanted experience. To explore intimacies with more than one man. Now, however, I realize only one man will do."

"Lord Stormont," he guessed.

"Yes."

"I suspected he was more than just a friend. Despite him suggesting the two of us would be well met, I detected reluctance on his part."

"He has found someone else he wishes to marry because I told him I had no interest in marriage. And now…"

"You are interested?"

"Yes. Isn't love a strange, silly thing?"

"That it is. Quite unwanted, yet it doesn't seem to matter."

"Perhaps the one you love will find herself in a similar situation. Could you ask her brother if she's said anything about you?"

"I did and he was just as flummoxed as I. I imagine I will wait for her until it's too late. If she marries, I will have no choice but to move on. Until then I will continue to smile across the room when I catch her looking. I'll hold out hope that she will give me another chance."

After wishing him the best of luck with his reluctant true love, Celia went to her room and let Nettie help her out of her gown. It was not the way she'd planned the night to go. Instead of starting an illicit affair, she was going to bed thinking of marriage.

To a man who had offered for her and she'd rejected too

many times to count. And now it was too late to change her mind, even though it was clear her heart belonged to him. Would she and Kit spend the rest of their lives smiling at one another across a ballroom?

No. Because Celia was done attending *ton* events.

The next day, she stayed in her room rather than go down for breakfast. Kit hadn't been coming for the morning meal lately, but that didn't mean he wouldn't be there that morning with a big smile on his face as he announced his joyous news.

Celia wanted Kit to have everything he'd ever wanted. She couldn't very well blame him for finding someone wonderful when she'd told him time and again; she didn't want marriage.

Except now the thought seemed more appealing the longer she considered it. She'd never thought herself fickle—not having the option for such a trait in her earlier years. But she now wanted something she couldn't have.

No, that wasn't correct. She wanted something that had been offered and she'd rejected. And it was too late. Unlike the woman Jonathan loved, Kit was to be married.

CHAPTER THIRTY

KIT LAY IN his bed looking up at the canopy until morning seeped in through the gaps of his drapes.

He couldn't bring himself to regret Willa's happiness. Kit might have been happy with her, but she belonged with the man who had won her heart. The man who had quite possibly spent the night before in Celia's bed.

It was quite the convoluted affair. But if Rathmore cared for Willa as much as she cared for him, the man would no longer play the role of Celia's lover. Kit was sure Rathmore wouldn't play her false. Kit knew him to be an honorable man who would be true to his wife.

That would leave Celia free once again. But she only wanted a lover. And Kit wanted her forever. The more he lay there thinking, the more he came to realize that she was the only one for him.

How could he face her at the next ball when she asked him to help her find another lover? He couldn't.

He'd done a fair job of staying clear of her the last week or so. He'd just have to continue to keep distance between them. He'd had enough of balls for the moment. He would take some time and tend to his wounds in private. Wounds that had never quite healed from her rejection years ago.

He managed to stay home alone the next night, but by the following night he couldn't take his own company any longer and decided to go out.

Instead of attending a ball, he headed to his club where he was sure to meet up with his friends. Sure enough, he found Gray and some of the men sharing a drink with Ernest, who was happily telling the news of his sister's upcoming nuptials to Lord Rathmore.

Kit had been correct that Celia would once again be free, not that it would change his circumstances in the least. Just because she was no longer with Rathmore didn't mean she wanted Kit.

"Sorry for your luck, old chap," Ernest said with a slap to Kit's shoulder. "It's for the best."

Kit couldn't help but think Ernest felt it was for the best because his sister was marrying a rich marquess rather than a viscount who was just turning a profit.

"What was he talking about?" Hayworth asked as Ernest headed to another table to continue his celebration. "Why would you care who his sister was to marry?"

"Because he had been ready to propose to the girl, himself," Gray answered even if the question was directed to Kit.

"Willa? But she's just a girl," Hayworth frowned.

"She's of age and a lovely young woman," Kit explained. "Fortunately for her, she was quite swept away by Lord Rathmore and apparently, he is just as captivated."

"You really are planning to marry then?" Hayworth looked appalled as Kit nodded.

"I've been telling you this for months," Gray said while rolling his eyes.

Hayworth shook his head. "I know. But I thought surely you were playing a jest."

Kit shook his head. "Why is it so hard for you to grasp the reality of such an endeavor for a man of my age?"

"I guess I don't want it to be true for it leaves less of us to fend off the rest of the lot," Hayworth said with a dramatic shiver.

"I'll never give in," Gray said matter of factly, before pouring another drink.

"Never is a long time, my friend."

"Is it? You've been looking for a wife and still haven't one. While we have been quite successful in trying to avoid it." Gray laughed.

Kit shrugged. The man had a point. Perhaps they wouldn't ever find brides—Gray because he didn't want it, and Kit because no one else was Celia.

He shook the thought away, but they didn't allow him a reprieve for very long.

"What about Celia?" Hayworth suggested with a nod to Gray. "She's available." As if that was the only point to recommend her. Kit was angry on her behalf.

"She's lovely and I'd marry her this instant."

"But she won't have him," Gray added with a frown.

"Why not?" Hayworth's brows pulled together.

"She wants the adventure and excitement of a lover, not the mundane life as a wife." Kit signaled for another drink. He'd need a steady supply to get through this conversation.

Gray groaned. "I thought I would be glad when your arrangement came to an end, but I find I'd prefer her to be with you than any other blighter she might invite..." He shivered despite the warm evening. "Anyway, you should ask her again."

"I asked her when I was but eighteen and she chose a shriveled-up old man over me. I asked her again when I realized she and I had—" His sentence was cut off by another loud groan from Gray. "And I asked her recently for no other reason than I wanted to spend my life with her. Each time I've asked, she's said no. She's not interested in marriage or... me."

"That first time..." Gray paused and cleared his throat. "I'm sure it has nothing to do with you. Our father forced her into that match with Hamlin. While he wasn't a rough sort, he wasn't a suitable husband for Celia. She was unhappy and associated that unhappiness with marriage. You just need to show her how good it can be with you."

He nodded as if it was as easy as that.

Kit was becoming more irritated with his friends and found himself wishing he'd stayed home after all. Especially later when he realized they were heading to the back room of the theatre where the singers often conversed with male visitors and invited them to their rooms for the night.

As if Kit would be interested in such a thing. Knowing he wasn't he still followed them inside.

"You need to get back on the horse, old chap," Hayworth suggested while nodding at a bountiful brunette.

"Thank you for that incredibly wise advice." Kit shook his head. He missed Hale and Julian. At least they would offer him sympathy.

Gray slapped Kit on the back before heading into the stuffy room overflowing with cloying perfumes and sweat. "We're always looking out for you."

He should have left. He had no wish to enter into yet another relationship with a woman who would never be his wife. But minutes later a woman took the seat next to him and offered a smile.

Her gown was not up for the challenge of confining her immense bosom and Kit frowned at the creamy flesh overflowing her dress because it reminded him of Celia.

Celia wasn't quite so endowed, but her breasts were soft and full with nipples the color—He closed his eyes and forced the thought of her away. He needed to get over this.

He wanted all of Celia, not just her body and not temporarily, but she didn't want him.

He'd asked for her hand three times already, and it was time for him to let her go once and for all.

ON THE FOURTH morning she hadn't gone down to have breakfast with her brother, he arrived at her room. She was glad to have a visitor, even if it had taken four days for her brother to check on her. What if she'd been ill?

Her need for conversation won out over her need to scold her younger brother for his delay.

"Are you well?" he asked with genuine concern in his eyes and Celia pushed her earlier irritation aside.

She let out a breath. "I'm fine."

"Is there a reason you've taken all your meals in your rooms? Have I done something to upset you? Something so vile as to leave me to eat heaps of bacon on my own?"

She smiled. She wasn't able to stay angry with Graham for very long.

"Surely Kit is able to assist."

Gray shook his head. "He's not been to breakfast either."

Celia forced a brittle smile to her lips. As much as she wanted to be happy—*was* happy for him—it still hurt to hear of Kit's plans to marry. But she must push through. She couldn't hide away in her rooms just to avoid hearing of it.

"Of course, I'm sure he is quite busy making arrangements for his wedding."

"Wedding? Kit's not getting married." He tilted his head. "You didn't hear? Willa Derforth is marrying Lord Rathmore."

Celia couldn't contain her shock. The woman Jonathan loved had been young Willa? A smile came to her lips to think of how happy Rathmore must be to have won the hand of the woman he loved after all.

"But that means, Kit…" He must be heartbroken to have lost the woman he'd hoped to wed.

"Yes. I wanted to speak to you about him."

She looked at the clock to see it was much too early for brandy. Though she was certain she would need it for this conversation.

"What do you wish to say?" she asked politely, her back straight as she prepared for her brother to tug at her wounds.

"Why won't you marry him? He told me he's asked you

more than once, and you turned him down."

Celia frowned. His direct question caught her off guard. Before she could consider her answer, the truth began to pour from her lips. As if she was unable to keep this anger pushed down in her stomach a moment longer.

Gray was her brother so she could confide in him. After all, he'd been there that night. The night her heart was broken.

"I hold Kit in the highest esteem," she started. "He would make a wonderful husband and I enjoy his company, but I find I am just so *angry* at him, Gray."

"You could have fooled me for seeing the two of you together. Knowing how… intimate you were. What did he do to earn your ire?"

She shook her head. "Nothing recently. It was years ago. I've pretended to be over it and move on, but the truth is, he abandoned me during a time when I needed him most, and I can't forgive him. I have tried. I even thought I had, but obviously not, since there it is coming out of my mouth. He hurt me deeply and I'll not allow him to just pretend it didn't happen. Do you know he's never even apologized for leaving me to marry Hamlin when I practically begged him to help me?"

She shook her head as tears pooled in her eyes. "No. I did beg him. And still he refused to help me."

She wiped the moisture away.

Gray's face went pale, but he didn't respond. Celia went on, unable to stop her confession now that the first truth had escaped.

"I understand why he rejected me. I really do. He was so young. He didn't want to settle down with a wife at that age, but I needed him and I thought… I thought he would be there for me. And now the times he's proposed I can't help but think of how he wouldn't marry me back then. I'm sure you think it's spiteful, and maybe it is, but how can I trust him to be there when I need him when he wasn't there when I needed him most? I can't help but be angry at him, Gray. I don't want to be, but I am."

Gray swallowed and paced the room for a moment. He sat on

the edge of his seat and stared at nothing before finally speaking in a low voice. "He didn't know."

"Pardon?" Celia barely heard him.

He moved to sit next to her and took her hands in his. "It is all my fault, Celia."

"What is? I don't understand." She hadn't seen him look this grim since their father had been alive. Whatever was amiss, it was something quite serious.

"I didn't know this still caused you pain. I was happy to brush it aside, even if the guilt has nearly killed me over the years. You and Kit were friends, I assumed you had forgiven him. Even if he was never the one at fault."

"What are you saying?"

"That night you sent me to see Kit. You gave me the letter to take to him."

She nodded. "Yes. In it I promised to be a perfect wife. But he still rejected my offer."

Gray shook his head. "I left your room with the letter and Father stopped me. He..." Gray hung his head in his hands, completely shattered.

Celia knew she wasn't going to be happy with the outcome of this story, but she couldn't stop herself from comforting her brother when he looked so stricken. She was an older sister after all.

"Father knew we were trying to come up with a way to get you out of the marriage to Hamlin. He stopped me. At the time, I didn't think there was anything he could say to sway my plan to go to Kit and ask him to marry you, but..."

"What happened."

"He threatened the woman I loved."

"Who?"

"It doesn't matter. It had been an affair years before, but Father knew I still cared for her deeply. He owed someone a large sum of money and you were his only way to get it. He was desperate, and he threatened to have her killed if I didn't step aside and allow you to marry Hamlin. You must understand, I would have done anything to spare you, but I couldn't… not that. I'm so sorry, Celia. I went to see Kit, but I didn't give him the letter and I didn't ask him to marry you. I told him that Father had arranged a marriage for you."

Celia could only sit there stunned. Kit had never read her letter. He'd never known she had begged for his help.

"CeCe…" He shook his head. "You need to know. It didn't matter that Kit didn't read your letter. Without me mentioning it, he offered for you. He asked me to help sneak you out of the house so he could run away with you to Scotland to be married. As you said, he was very young, but he didn't hesitate to protect you with his name."

Celia gasped in surprise and tears welled up in her eyes. "He wanted me?"

"Of course, he wanted you. He still wants you. He was devastated when I met him later that night and told him you were to marry Hamlin."

"You lied to both of us." Her hands tightened into fists. This was not something a twist of the ear would resolve. Graham deserved a sound thrashing.

"I did. I'm sorry—I am. But you must understand. While I knew the woman would never be mine because she was already married to another; I'd heard she was a mother and I couldn't risk her life. Father assured me you would outlive Hamlin and that he was not a violent or cruel man. I had to make an impossible decision."

Celia wanted to be angry at Graham, but it was her father she truly despised. Since it was a waste of time to rage at a dead man, she took a few deep breaths, allowing the anger to seep away, leaving her lighter than she'd been in years.

Kit had wanted to marry her back then. He had wanted to be her hero and save her from her father's machinations.

And all this time, she thought he didn't want her.

CHAPTER THIRTY-ONE

THAT AFTERNOON, KIT was reviewing his books when his butler came in to announce Graham had arrived. It might have been better, if Gray had waited for a response before barging in, but it wasn't like Kit would turn him away.

Gray was welcome to visit, but if he suggested he and Kit go to the club that evening or out to meet people, Kit would refuse the offer.

While Kit wasn't ready to start attending balls again, he wasn't going to spend his evenings the way they once had. The way that ended with Kit sleeping on the floor in the hall at Penbrook House. Those days were over.

"Can I get you a drink?" Kit offered and stood to get it. When Gray replied with a, "No, thank you," Kit knew something was wrong.

It could only be Celia. She was his only family. The only person Gray cared enough about to be upset and refuse an offered glass of whiskey for.

"What's happened?" Kit asked immediately though he wasn't certain he'd survive hearing the answer.

"I'm afraid I need to tell you something."

"Is Celia all right?" he whispered.

Gray's eyes went wide. "She's fine. But I'm afraid I need to tell you the truth of something that happened years ago."

Kit sat as Gray went on with a story about the night Gray's

234

father planned to marry Celia to Lord Hamlin. The night Kit had first offered to wed Celia. He'd wanted to take her to Scotland and marry her, but she'd chosen money over Kit.

Gray held out a yellowed letter with a brittle wax seal of a bird in flight on the back. It had not been opened and there was no address on the front.

"Go on. Read it. It is to you. I was supposed to give it to you years ago. The night I came to your house and told you what was happening."

Kit opened it and read the words Celia had written to him that fateful night.

Dear Christopher,

I understand this letter may come as a surprise, as I have never corresponded with you before. However, I am facing a dire situation and desperately need your help.

My father plans to marry me to Lord Hamlin. I've never met the gentleman, my father has said he is quite pleasant, though I imagine all my father cares about is that the man is quite rich.

I do not want to marry him, and as such I've come to the point of this letter in which I must beg for your assistance. If you could see your way to marry me, then I would be spared the fate my father has chosen for me.

I understand you are very young and have not experienced all the world has to offer. But I promise to give you whatever freedoms you may have otherwise had without complaint.

If you could please consider my offer, it is all I can ask of you. And if your answer is no, we will always remain friends.

Yours,
Celia

"Christ, Gray. You had this letter all this time and never said anything?" Kit was ready to pummel his one-time friend. Except the man went on to explain the threat his father made to someone he'd once loved if Gray hadn't complied with his father's wishes.

Kit couldn't help but think Gray might still love this mystery woman, though he wouldn't expand on who it was, only to say, "She is now married, so it doesn't matter."

And for now, it didn't matter. The only thing that mattered was what Gray said next.

"Celia admitted to being angry with you, all this time, because you weren't there when she needed you. This is why she's turned down your offers since."

Kit knew well, he had not gotten over her refusal and while he'd come to love the woman, his heart was still raw from that night Gray had told him Celia wouldn't marry him.

"But I didn't refuse her," he pointed out.

"Yes. I've since remedied the misunderstanding so she knows of your offer back then."

"That means…" Kit sat and stared at his hands. "She might consider me now that she has this information?" He couldn't hide the hope in his voice. Perhaps his chance to marry the woman he loved was not yet over.

"I believe she is considering that now."

"I must go to her." Kit jumped up.

"I hope you get the response you hoped for. It would be an honor to have you officially join our family. Small as it is."

Kit was so happy he grabbed his friend and kissed his cheek. "I will flatten you later for what you've done, but for now wish me luck."

"I would expect nothing less. Now go already before she finds another man who has loved her for years and wants to marry her."

Kit couldn't wait for a carriage to be brought around, instead he headed for Penbrook House on foot. He reached up to knock on the door but it was opened before his bare knuckles connected with the cheery, blue wood.

Celia stood before him. "Oh, hello," she said, clearly surprised to see him.

"Good day," he answered as he stared at her, taking in every detail, and realizing she was dressed to go out. "I see I've caught you at a bad time, I should—"

"It's not a bad time. In fact, I was leaving to go see you. But you are here."

"Yes. I'm here."

A moment of awkward silence held in the air between them before she smiled and stepped back. "Won't you please come in?"

"Thank you."

She led him to the drawing room and sat on the settee. He sat next to her, watching her throat move as she swallowed. This was the woman he wanted to spend the rest of his life with. And now there was nothing between them that would force her to reject his offer unless she truly didn't want him.

Now was not the time to be a coward. He cleared his throat and smiled. "Gray says he's explained what happened years ago, the night before you married Hamlin. You know the truth."

She nodded. "I had no idea. I thought…"

"You thought as I thought. That the other person didn't want to marry them."

"Yes. Exactly. And I carried that hurt silently for so long. I thought I had forgiven you, but I hadn't. Not really. I believed you abandoned me when I needed you most."

He knew the pain she must have felt that fateful night. And then to have him propose again when it suited him…

He laughed, but there was no humor in the sound.

"Celia. Please be my wife. Not because you need to marry. I know you don't need my title—you are already a countess. You don't need my money—you have plenty of your own, and yours it will stay. You don't need anything really—you have managed without anyone's assistance."

As he said this, he realized how worthless his offer sounded, but he went on.

"You don't need me at all, but I hope you'll say 'yes' simply because you want me. Because you want to spend your life with me. You don't need anything, but I would still offer my heart and love for all the days we abide together. Celia, will you please be my wife?"

He waited. His breath stuck in his chest as he hoped for that one word that would change his life. He hadn't expected it to be the wrong word.

"No," she said while shaking her head.

His breath left in a rush as sorrow surged in once more.

SEEING THE HOPE in Kit's eyes drain away called her attention to the fact she'd just refused him. Or so he was left to think. She reached out and clasped his hand while shaking her head quickly, only to realize that she was now *emphatically* refusing him.

"No. I didn't mean to say 'no.' I meant to say…" She swallowed and met his waiting gaze. "I think you've asked me to marry you enough."

He blinked and stood. "My apologies for taking up your time."

She was making a mess of this. She would have been better off to have just accepted his proposal, but she'd wanted to be clear.

"Please stay. I'm not done."

"I'm not sure I can take much more, countess."

She frowned.

"I meant to say that you've proposed to me three times already, and it should be my turn to ask you."

His brows rose as he sat back down next to her. She placed her hand on his cheek and stroked her thumb over the corner of his mouth. The side where his smiles began.

He wasn't smiling at the moment. He was simply watching her with a tentative and confused look about him.

"It is only fair that I ask you this time. Will you hear me?"

His lips twitched and he nodded once before saying, "Of course."

"Will you marry me, Christopher? Because I *do* want you. But

I need you as well. I need your smiles to make my days brighter, and I need you by my side to make life more bearable. I need your kisses and touches to add pleasure to my future."

She licked her lips and continued.

"But mostly, I know I need you because that night at Lady Harrington's party she asked me my preferences in a partner and I described you exactly. Not only because I find your physical appearance so divine, but because in a time when I felt unsure of myself, I needed the person who made me feel like the best version of myself, who thought of me as enough. I needed my best friend."

"You make me sound like your favorite chair," he said with a smirk on his lips.

"I was wrong to take insult to that. I realize now that one's favorite chair is always at their back, supporting them when they're weary. And no matter where they go it's the place you long to return to."

This was so much more difficult than he'd made it seem the times he'd done it. How had he managed it?

"Will you be my husband, Christopher, because I need you and want you?"

He kissed her, a slow simple kiss before pulling away and saying, "I will take your request into consideration."

"Kit!" She smacked his arm, but he caught it and kissed her fingers before kissing her again.

"Yes," he said against her lips. "Of course, I'll marry you. I have loved you for so long, Celia." He kissed her again, but she could barely return the kiss because she was smiling so widely.

"Thank you," she said.

"It seems you've succeeded in finding a lover. And I have found a wife. This season has been quite the victory."

"Hmm… And you'll be my lover starting tonight?" she asked, playfully.

"No. Starting right now."

EPILOGUE

I T WAS THE new Lady Rathmore and her husband who insisted on hosting an engagement ball for Kit and Celia. After all, the newly married couple might have had a much different future if they hadn't decided Kit and Celia wouldn't do for their own purposes.

"I've never been so happy to have been rejected," Kit said to Willa as they all stood by the entrance to greet their guests. Kit looked incredibly handsome in his evening clothes with his tartan sash draped across his chest. Celia had chosen a sapphire gown to accompany him and because she thought it a lucky color having worn it at the masquerade that changed everything.

"You must know I hold you in the highest regard." Willa smiled. "I just didn't want to marry you, Lord Stormont."

"And I'm glad for it," Celia said. "It took me quite a while to realize how much I loved him, I'm fortunate to have been given more time to come to that conclusion."

"Your time grows to an end, my lady. If you plan to change your mind and escape this blighter, you must do so soon," Rathmore joked.

Celia felt Kit's hand on her waist tighten slightly as if he planned to hold her there rather than allow her to escape. As if she wanted an escape. How different this betrothal was from her last.

Her earlier fears of marriage were long forgotten as she

looked forward to wedding Kit.

She patted his hand and smiled at her fiancé.

"I have no desire to run. I have exactly who I was supposed to be with all along."

They were distracted then by the arrival of the Duke and Duchess of Roxburghe as they made their entrance. They were followed by the Earl and Countess Melville. Celia knew both couples had come from Scotland to attend their engagement ball and she was touched they'd make such a journey when they had little ones.

It was clear both of Kit's friends from Heriot's had found happiness in their wives, she could tell by all the smiles.

"Celia and I plan to spend time at Blairgowrie after we're wed. We hope to have you come visit," Kit offered.

Roxburghe and Melville looked at one another and laughed before Julian spoke.

"We won't look for an invitation for quite some time. You'll find when you get your new wife alone in the country, you'll have other priorities than hosting guests."

Roxburghe nodded. "Aye. It's still a wonder to me why men see marriage as something to be avoided. I feel like a lucky bastard, indeed."

Gray came in behind the couples and winced as he smiled. No doubt because of the cut lip and swollen black eye.

"What happened to you?" Celia worried.

"I'm fine, and it's nothing I didn't deserve." He glanced toward Kit and held out his hand.

Kit shook it and pulled him in for a hug. Celia was close enough to hear her intended whisper to her brother. "You deserved a lot more, but since you're to be my brother I didn't want you permanently disfigured."

It appeared whatever had happened had been dealt with and was now resolved, though she wouldn't pretend to understand further than that.

Celia's breath caught when she noticed their next guest. She hadn't recognized the woman at first glance, mostly because she was dressed in a modest gown of deep rose.

"Lady Harrington, I am so glad you have come to celebrate with us."

She smiled. "I would not miss the opportunity to extend my wish for your happiness." To Celia she whispered, "Is it not better to have the love of one man?"

Celia nodded. "I thank you for sending him to my room that night. I feel I have you to thank for setting us on this path."

"Destiny is a fickle wench," she said with a smile.

"Lady Harrington, might I ask for your first dance," Graham said with a courtly bow. "I'm afraid I missed my chance during your ball."

The woman smiled, more genuine than Celia had seen before. Her cheeks darkened and Celia wondered what had caused a blush to touch the cheeks of the most scandalous woman in London. It was only a dance, not an assignation.

"Yes. I think I would like that," the woman answered shyly and took Gray's offered hand. "Whatever has happened to your face?"

"Let's just say it was a wrong being righted." She heard Gray's answer as he escorted Lady Harrington to the dance floor.

"Hmm. Perhaps your brother has found someone who understands lost love," Kit said.

It was difficult for Celia to think of her brother's pain. Not just because she didn't want him to live a life unfulfilled but because it made her think of how close she had come to living that same unfulfilled life. If Kit had married before she'd realized she loved him…

She pulled in a shaky breath and shook away the horrid thought. She looked up at Kit and smiled, happy she would never know that pain.

"I am so glad I realized how I felt about you before it was too late."

"Aye. I'm glad we have a match that will bring us many years of happiness."

When he bent to kiss her, his lips seemed to miss her cheek and land in the place below her ear that drove her wild at the same time betraying his thoughts.

"You're thinking of starting that happiness tonight in Lord Rathmore's study, aren't you?" Celia whispered so only Kit could hear.

He winked in that naughty way she loved so much.

"At our earliest opportunity, countess."

About the Author

One very early morning, Allison B. Hanson woke up with a conversation going on in her head. It wasn't so much a dream as being forced awake by her imagination. Unable to go back to sleep, she gave in, went to the computer, and began writing. Years later it still hasn't stopped.

Allison lives near Hershey, Pennsylvania and writes Highlander Historical and Scottish Regencies.

Catch up with Allison on any of her social media platforms here:

Website:
allisonbhanson.wordpress.com

Facebook:
facebook.com/BlueRidgeRomance

Twitter:
@AllisonBHanson

Instagram:
@allisonbhanson

Goodreads:
goodreads.com/author/show/9860589

BookBub:
bookbub.com/authors/allison-b-hanson